Santa Fe
DEAD

BOOKS BY STUART WOODS

FICTION

Beverly Hills Dead

Shoot Him If He Runs[†]

Fresh Disasters[†]

Short Straw[§]

Dark Harbor[†]

Iron Orchid[*]

Two-Dollar Bill[†]

The Prince of Beverly Hills

Reckless Abandon[†]

Capital Crimes[‡]

Dirty Work[†]

Blood Orchid[*]

The Short Forever[†]

Orchid Blues[*]

Cold Paradise[†]

L.A. Dead[†]

The Run[‡]

Worst Fears Realized[†]

Orchid Beach[*]

Swimming to Catalina[†]

Dead in the Water[†]

Dirt[†]

Choke

Imperfect Strangers

Heat

Dead Eyes

L.A. Times

Santa Fe Rules[§]

New York Dead[†]

Palindrome

Grass Roots[‡]

White Cargo

Deep Lie[‡]

Under the Lake

Run Before the Wind[‡]

Chiefs[‡]

TRAVEL

A Romantic's Guide to the Country Inns of Britain and Ireland *(1979)*

MEMOIR

Blue Water, Green Skipper *(1977)*

[*]A Holly Barker Novel   [†]A Stone Barrington Novel
[‡]A Will Lee Novel   [§]An Ed Eagle Novel

Santa Fe
DEAD

STUART WOODS

G. P. Putnam's Sons *New York*

PUTNAM

G. P. PUTNAM'S SONS
Publishers Since 1838
Published by the Penguin Group
Penguin Group (USA) Inc., 375 Hudson Street, New York, New York 10014, USA •
Penguin Group (Canada), 90 Eglinton Avenue East, Suite 700, Toronto,
Ontario M4P 2Y3, Canada (a division of Pearson Canada Inc.) •
Penguin Books Ltd, 80 Strand, London WC2R 0RL, England • Penguin Ireland,
25 St Stephen's Green, Dublin 2, Ireland (a division of Penguin Books Ltd) •
Penguin Group (Australia), 250 Camberwell Road, Camberwell,
Victoria 3124, Australia (a division of Pearson Australia Group Pty Ltd) •
Penguin Books India Pvt Ltd, 11 Community Centre, Panchsheel Park,
New Delhi–110 017, India • Penguin Group (NZ), 67 Apollo Drive, Rosedale,
North Shore 0632, New Zealand (a division of Pearson New Zealand Ltd) •
Penguin Books (South Africa) (Pty) Ltd, 24 Sturdee Avenue,
Rosebank, Johannesburg 2196, South Africa

Penguin Books Ltd, Registered Offices: 80 Strand, London WC2R 0RL, England

Library of Congress Cataloging-in-Publication Data

Woods, Stuart.
Santa Fe dead / Stuart Woods.
p.   cm.
ISBN 978-0-399-15490-4
I. Title.
PS3573.O642S35   2008b   2008006561
813'.54—dc22

Printed in the United States of America
1   3   5   7   9   10   8   6   4   2

BOOK DESIGN BY NICOLE LAROCHE

This is a work of fiction. Names, characters, places, and incidents either are the product of the author's imagination or are used fictitiously, and any resemblance to actual persons, living or dead, businesses, companies, events, or locales is entirely coincidental.

While the author has made every effort to provide accurate telephone numbers and Internet addresses at the time of publication, neither the publisher nor the author assumes any responsibility for errors, or for changes that occur after publication. Further, the publisher does not have any control over and does not assume any responsibility for author or third-party websites or their content.

This book is for Leslie Alexander.

Santa Fe
DEAD

ED EAGLE SAT, all six feet seven inches of him, propped up on many pillows in bed, watching Court TV on the fifty-inch flat-screen television of his suite at the Hotel Bel-Air in Los Angeles. He had decided to watch from bed rather than attend the trial of his former wife, Barbara, since he had already spent three days in the courtroom, giving his testimony against her. Now it was time for the summations.

The prosecutor, a woman apparently in her midthirties named Valerie Simmons, whom Eagle found quite attractive, had done a very good job in the trial, he thought, and since he was one of the half dozen best trial lawyers in the western United States, his opinion counted for something. Now all Ms. Simmons had to do was nail the lid on the thing. Eagle would have preferred nailing *and* screwing the lid on it, but he would settle for nailing—anything to get Barbara into a cell for the next fifty years or so.

Eagle's girlfriend of the last year, the actress Susannah Wilde, came out of the bathroom, her hair wet, her robe hanging open. She crawled across his body, deliberately stroking his face with her breasts as she went, and snuggled up next to him.

"Don't wave those things at me," Eagle said. "I have to watch Barbara go down."

"Wouldn't you rather watch me go down?" Susannah asked, tickling his lower belly.

"On another occasion, yes," he replied. "But right now you're going to have to contain yourself, as difficult as that may be."

Susannah sighed and pulled herself upright next to him, plumping her pillows. "Oh, all right," she said.

Valerie Simmons rose and walked toward the jury. "Ladies and gentlemen," she said to them, "I want to thank you for your attention to what has been a lengthy trial. Now, I want to summarize the evidence against Barbara Eagle, as succinctly as I can, and I would remind you that everything I am about to say has been testified to by witnesses. You have heard from Ms. Eagle's former husband, Ed Eagle, how he first met Ms. Eagle when she was serving a prison sentence in New York for armed robbery and as an accessory to the killing of her first husband during that robbery. You have heard how she was released on parole and moved to Santa Fe, New Mexico, where she renewed her acquaintance with Mr. Eagle, and how they came to be married a year or so later.

"You have heard how Mr. Eagle woke up one morning, having been drugged with the sleeping pill Ambien in his wine the night before, and found his wife gone, and how she had taken more than a million dollars of his money from his bank accounts and attempted to take five million more from his brokerage accounts, something he managed to forestall.

"You have heard how Mr. Eagle hired two private investigators to find his wife in Mexico, where she had fled, and how she shot one of the investigators and pushed the other overboard from a ferry in the Sea of Cortez. Both were lucky to survive. You have heard how she hired two men from Santa Fe to murder Mr. Eagle and how one of them nearly succeeded.

"You have heard how she came back to the United States and

checked into a resort in San Diego, where she had her appearance altered by having her dark hair dyed blond and with cosmetic surgery. You have heard how she then traveled to Los Angeles and contacted a friend, Mr. James Long, and how they had dinner together that evening at the Hotel Bel-Air. You have heard that Mr. Eagle and a friend were also dining there and how he did not recognize Ms. Eagle, because of her altered appearance.

"You have heard how Ms. Eagle, later that night, drugged her companion, Mr. Long, once again with Ambien, left his home, returned to the Hotel Bel-Air and sought out the suite of Mr. Eagle. You have heard how she entered the suite next door, in error, and shot Mr. and Mrs. Thomas Dattila of New York, believing that they were Mr. Eagle and his friend.

"All of this is in evidence, and the weight of it is enough for you to send Ms. Eagle to prison for the rest of her life. I ask you to do just that. Thank you." Valerie Simmons sat down.

The judge turned to the defense table. "Mr. Karp?" he said.

Richard Karp rose and faced the jury. "Good morning," he said. "Ladies and gentlemen, this case is about reasonable doubt. If you believe that there is a reasonable doubt that Barbara Eagle killed Mr. and Mrs. Dattila—and that is all that she is charged with—then you are legally and morally bound to acquit her. Everything you have heard from the prosecution about Ms. Eagle's past and what she may or may not have done in Mexico is window dressing, nothing more, and none of what you have heard is supported by any material evidence, just the testimony of questionable witnesses.

"While you heard Mr. Eagle testify that he was drugged with Ambien, there is no scientific evidence to support that contention. What happened was that Mr. Eagle had too much to drink the evening before and overslept. The funds that Ms. Eagle took with her to Mexico, in a desperate attempt to remove herself from an abusive marriage, were marital funds, and she was legally entitled to take them. I would remind you that one of the two men allegedly hired

3

to kill Mr. Eagle is dead, and the other could not pick Ms. Eagle out of a lineup.

"I would remind you that it is not a crime in the United States to shoot someone in Mexico in self-defense or to push someone off a boat in an attempt to defend herself from a rape, and you have heard that both of her attackers survived. I would remind you that, although Ms. Eagle and Mr. Long dined at the Bel-Air the evening before the murder, you have also heard, from Mr. Long, that she spent the entire night in his bed in his home and did not return to the Bel-Air to shoot Mr. Dattila, who, you have heard, was the son of the Mafia kingpin Carmine Dattila, who also met a violent death. It is far more likely that Thomas Dattila was killed by his own associates or competitors than by Ms. Eagle.

"I would remind you that Mr. James Long underwent no testing for the drug Ambien, and he has testified that Ms. Eagle spent the night with him—indeed, that they made love in the middle of the night. I would remind you that it is not a crime for a woman to have her appearance enhanced by her hairstylist and her cosmetic surgeon." He smiled knowingly.

"In fact, stripped to its relevant essentials, the prosecution's case is nothing more than a lot of hot air, backed only by the testimony of an angry ex-husband and the two private detectives he hired to bully and harass her and to come into this court and lie about her. There is no physical evidence, no murder weapon and no motive for the murders of two people Ms. Eagle had never even met.

"I put it to you that the doubt of guilt in this case is not only reasonable but overwhelming, and I ask you, after a careful examination of the evidence—or, rather, nonevidence—to acquit Barbara Eagle and set her free, so that she may still have a chance to find some happiness in what has, so far, been a life full of abuse and harassment by her ex-husband and others. Find her not guilty." Karp sat down.

"What did you think?" Susannah asked.

"Well, they both said pretty much what I would have said, if I

4

had been prosecuting or defending," Eagle said. "I think the jury will convict her."

"Well, then," Susannah said, "while the jury is deliberating, may I distract you?"

"You may," Eagle said, rolling over and taking her in his arms.

SHE HAD BEEN distracting him for ten minutes or so, when Eagle was redistracted by a sudden intensity in the voice of the Court channel's anchor.

"We're just getting word," the anchor said, "that something has happened outside the courtroom where the trial of Barbara Eagle has just ended. Let's go to our reporter on the scene for the details."

A beautiful young woman in a red suit and with perfect hair came on-screen. "Well," she said, breathlessly, "it seems that Barbara Eagle has disappeared from the conference room where she and her lawyer were awaiting a verdict. Apparently, while Mr. Karp had excused himself to go to the men's room, Ms. Eagle somehow got out of the conference room, in spite of a guard on the door, and maybe even out of the building. A search is being conducted for her now."

"Ed," Susannah said, "you've gone all limp."

2 BARBARA EAGLE SAT at the table in a conference room near the courtroom where she had just been tried, awaiting the jury's verdict. She had had lunch in this room every day during her trial, so she knew that it was on the first floor and overlooked the rear parking lot of the courthouse, reserved for judges. She knew, also, that the windows would open only ten or twelve inches, and only from the top.

She had been keeping her lawyer's water glass full for two hours, and she was waiting for results. Finally, he excused himself and went into the adjoining toilet. Barbara moved quickly. She climbed onto the windowsill, stuffed her shoes, handbag and jacket through the top opening of the window, then grabbed the bottom of the opening on the extreme left and swung her right, stockinged foot up until she could hook a toe over the edge of the window. From this point, it was all muscle, and she had had nearly a year in jail to work out. She lifted herself until she could get a knee over the edge, then continued until all that was left of her inside the room was her head, one leg and her ass. She turned to the left, and got her head out the window. From there she wriggled her ass through the window—the dieting had helped—then all she had to do was bring her leg outside after her.

She dangled from the window and took a quick look around the parking lot: a man got out of a car and went into the building through a rear door, but he wasn't looking up, and the parking lot was screened from the street by a high hedge. Once he was inside she dropped to the ground, a distance of some seven or eight feet, landed on the soft earth of a flower bed, behind some azalea bushes, and toppled over. She got up, brushed herself off, put on her shoes, grabbed her handbag and walked quickly across the parking lot to the row of ficus trees that had begun to grow together.

She pressed between them, then stopped halfway through to get a look at the street. The Toyota was parked where it was supposed to be, and Jimmy Long was at the wheel. There were no police cars or cops in sight, so she stepped out of the hedge, crossed the sidewalk, opened the rear door of the car and got in. "Hey, Jimmy," she said.

"Hey, sweetie, we okay?"

"Yep. Let's roll." Barbara lay low on the backseat, and the car started to move.

"Where to?"

"The nearest place you can get a taxi."

"There's a hotel a few blocks down."

"That's good." Her luggage was sitting on the rear seat and floor, and Barbara rummaged in a bag and came out with an auburn wig and a green jacket. She tucked her hair, which was already pinned up, under the wig, sat up and checked herself out in the rearview mirror, then she got into the green jacket and stuffed her beige one into the bag. "Okay, brief me."

"The car belonged to my housekeeper's sister, who has a last name different from hers. I bought it and registered it in your new name, Eleanor Wright. I went to see the photographer you sent me to in Venice, and he was able to change the hair color on the last photos he took of you and make you the same package of documents he did for you before—passport, driver's license, credit cards, Social Security—all with my address on them. Ms. Wright used to rent my garage apartment, but she left a couple of months ago, if anybody asks. Everything is in a paper bag on the front passenger seat.

"The car registration and insurance card are in the center armrest, along with a nontraceable cell phone, prepaid for a hundred hours of use, no GPS chip, blocked for caller ID. I went to the pawnshop in San Diego where you shopped last year and got the gun and silencer you wanted and a box of ammunition. There's ten thousand dollars in mixed bills in the bag, too."

"You're a dear, do you know that?"

"Sweetheart, this is the most fun I've ever had; I've loved every minute of it. I took the letter you sent me and used it to transfer the money into your Eleanor Wright account, so you've got a little over two hundred and fifty grand in there. You can write me a check for the ten grand, plus eighteen grand for the car, plus the twenty-five grand I paid the documents guy." He handed her a checkbook, and she wrote the check and handed it to him.

"Oh, there's another bag on the seat, too, with the auburn hair dye and the book on spas you wanted. Everything you stored in my garage is in the backseat, but it will probably need pressing."

"Jimmy, you're a dream. Now you've got to get home before the cops show up. They're missing me at the courthouse by now."

"Here's the hotel," he said. "I'll get out and hop a cab. You just drive away." He stopped the car.

She got out, gave him a hug and a kiss and got back into the car.

Jimmy leaned through the window. "The car has twenty-two thousand miles on it, it's just been serviced and the gas tank is full. Good luck, kiddo."

"I'll be in touch when I can," Barbara said. She put the car in gear and drove away, careful to obey all traffic laws. At the first opportunity, she pulled into a fast-food restaurant and ordered lunch from the drive-thru.

When she had eaten, she went through her new ID and put everything into the wallet in her handbag, then restowed her luggage in the trunk. Finally, she took the book on spas and began to read. It took her twenty minutes to find just the right place, called El Rancho, secluded on a mountaintop overlooking Palm Springs. She used her new cell phone to call.

"Good morning. El Rancho," a woman's voice said.

"Good morning. My name is Eleanor Wright, and I've just had a sudden urge to get away from it all. Do you have any accommodation available?"

"Let's see, we have a small suite at twelve hundred dollars per day and a double room at nine hundred. The suite has the better view, and the price includes all meals and drinks. No liquor is served. We offer a full range of spa activities, a beauty salon, tennis and golf half an hour's drive away."

"I'll take the suite, please. Would you schedule me for a two-hour massage at five P.M. and make an appointment with the hairdresser and a colorist for tomorrow morning?"

"Of course. May I have a credit card number to hold your reservation?"

Barbara gave it to her and got driving directions from the interstate. On the way she stopped at a liquor store and bought a bottle of good bourbon whiskey.

As SOON AS she had checked into her suite, Barbara unpacked, then went into the bathroom and used the auburn hair dye, cleaning up after herself carefully. She left her hair wet and combed it back. Tomorrow, she would have a better job done by a professional. She had her massage, then dinner in her room, along with a couple of large scotches, then settled down to watch the TV coverage of her escape. Finally, she fell asleep.

SHE WOKE THE following morning to learn from the TV that she had been acquitted of second-degree murder. "Holy shit!" she said aloud. She hadn't figured on that.

3

ED EAGLE NEARLY choked on his eggs. "Susannah!" he yelled.

She stuck her head around the bathroom door. "Yes?"

"Barbara was acquitted!"

"*What?*"

"I'm not kidding; she got off!"

"What does this mean, Ed?"

"It means that all they've got on her now is escaping from the courthouse. She can't be charged with the two murders again."

"Anything on where she is?"

"Nothing; she's very, very good at disappearing."

"Do we have anything to worry about?"

"Well, given that she's already tried to kill us once, I'd say yes."

"Are we okay here in the hotel?"

"You will recall that here is where she tried to kill us last time. We should get out of here. Are you done in L.A.?"

"I need another day to see my agent. We can go to my apartment; Barbara wouldn't know where that is." Susannah had a pied-à-terre in Century City.

"I hate your apartment," he said. "And your ex-husband knows where it is, doesn't he?"

"Maybe. I'm not sure, but I haven't heard from him for a while."

"That's because you've spent most of your time in Santa Fe."

"We could move to another hotel."

Eagle sighed. "All right, let's go to your apartment." He pointed at her tray. "Have some breakfast, then pack and we'll get out of here." He began packing, himself, and he retrieved the small .45 pistol and holster he traveled with and ran the holster onto his belt. He wasn't taking any chances.

BARBARA WAITED UNTIL after nine o'clock, then phoned her lawyer in Los Angeles.

"Good morning. Karp and Edelman."

"Richard Karp, please; it's Barbara Eagle."

"Oh."

Karp came on the line. "Barbara? Where the hell are you?"

"Richard, you don't really want to know that, do you? Let's just say I'm out of the country."

"Have you heard the news?"

"Yes, and I have to say I'm surprised."

"Why are you surprised? I told you I'd get you off."

"And I believed you, Richard, right up until the moment when I climbed out that window."

"Well, now we've got an escaping-from-custody charge to deal with. I'm going to need a ten-thousand-dollar retainer."

"Richard, after all I've already paid you? How difficult can this be? I'm innocent in the eyes of the law."

Karp was quiet for a moment. "Give me a number where I can reach you."

It was Barbara's turn to think. Jimmy had said there was no GPS chip in her new phone. "All right." She gave him the number.

"I'll try to get back to you inside an hour," Karp said, then hung up.

AFTER A LONG look around the Bel-Air parking lot, Eagle got into the rented Mercedes, and Susannah got into the passenger seat. "Keep your eyes open," he said.

"Yeah, for a blonde."

"I very much doubt that she's still a blonde."

"Okay, what should I look for?"

"A woman with a gun."

"Oh."

He drove to Century City, sticking to the surface streets and being very watchful, then parked in the lot under her building. Susannah found a cart, and they wheeled their luggage into the elevator and upstairs.

The place was spotless and not as cramped as Eagle had remembered it, when it was still full of unpacked boxes.

"God, I have sixteen messages," Susannah said, picking up the phone and pressing the Message button.

Eagle took their luggage into the bedroom, which was nearly as cramped as he remembered it. When he came back she was still listening to messages, and she looked angry.

Susannah hung up the phone. "One call from my agent, who canceled our appointment, and fifteen messages from my ex-husband."

"What's his problem?"

"His problem is, he's still angry about the settlement he had to pay."

"Call your lawyer and let him deal with it."

"Every time I so much as speak to him it costs me five hundred dollars," she said.

"You're not going to get any sympathy from me over your legal fees," Eagle replied.

"You lawyers are all alike."

"No, some of us charge a thousand dollars for a phone call. Does your ex have any sort of legitimate beef?"

"Certainly not. He's just nuts, that's all."

"Then instruct your lawyer to get a temporary restraining order. That will stop him from calling you. Does he have your Santa Fe number?"

"He doesn't even know I bought the Santa Fe house—at least, as far as I know. My publicist kept it out of the press, and my number is unlisted."

"How many people in L.A. know you bought the house?"

"Three or four, I guess. I told them all not to tell anybody."

"How often does that work in L.A.?"

She picked up the phone and called her lawyer.

RICHARD KARP PHONED Judge Henry Allman, who had presided over the Barbara Eagle case, catching him before he went into court.

"Yes, Richard?"

"Judge, I've heard from my client."

"And you'll be surrendering her when?"

"I'm sorry; I don't know where she is. She says she's out of the country."

"Then why are you calling me?"

"Judge, the woman is absolutely panicked; that's why she did what she did. I don't think for a minute it was planned, she just went nuts and bolted."

"Well, get her into my court, and she can explain herself."

"Now she's afraid for her life; she's convinced that Ed Eagle will have her killed."

"That's not my problem, until she's in my court. I can send the police to get her, if you like."

"Judge, it's my hope that you'll drop the escape charge."

"Well, you can hope."

"The woman has spent a year in the L.A. County Jail, and she's officially innocent. No one was hurt in her escape, and the incarceration has to count for something; she's already served more time than she's likely to get on the escape charge. I think, given the jury's verdict, that she should be allowed to go and live her life without fear of arrest. She was in a very fragile state, mentally, and she needs to be able to recover without fear of being incarcerated again."

"Have you talked to the D.A. about this?"

"No." Karp could hear the judge's fingers drumming on his desk. "All right, I'll dismiss the escape charges. Write an order and messenger it over here. The D.A. will scream bloody murder, but she always does. Let's get this thing out of the way."

"Yes, Judge, the order will be on your desk when you break for lunch; I'll have the messenger wait for it." Karp hung up and called Barbara Eagle.

Barbara was in the colorist's chair in the beauty salon when her phone vibrated. "Yes?" she said, warily.

"It's Richard. All right, you're off the hook. I have to write an order and messenger it to the judge for his signature, but you're a free woman."

"Thank God," Barbara said.

"No, thank Richard. And you owe me ten thousand dollars."

**4** EAGLE WENT INTO the bedroom to make some phone calls, then he took a shower, having left the Bel-Air in too much of a hurry for one. He laid his clothes neatly on the bed, along with the small .45 pistol. He was still in the shower when the phone rang once, then stopped.

He stood under the torrent of water for another couple of minutes, then turned it off, grabbed a towel and dried himself before he stepped out of the shower. He walked back into the bedroom, got a fresh pair of boxer shorts out of his bag and was stepping into them when he heard the gunshot. He looked at his holster on the bed; it was empty.

Eagle ran to the living room door and stopped. "Susannah?" he called. "Are you all right?"

"I think so," she said.

"Can I come in there without getting shot?"

"I think so."

Eagle stepped into the living room, and then he could see where the gunshot had gone. It was in the chest of a man who was lying on the floor, just inside the front door. He walked over to Susannah and took the gun from her, then led her to the living room sofa and sat her down. "Just take some deep breaths," he said, stroking her face.

"The doorman called from downstairs," she said. "He said Rod, my ex-husband, had walked right past the desk and taken the elevator up before the doorman could stop him. I went into the bedroom for you, but you were in the shower, so I picked up your gun and went to answer the door. When I opened it, he had a gun in his hand; he raised it, and I shot him."

"Just sit here quietly and compose yourself," Eagle said.

"I'm composed. Is he dead?"

"I'm going to go find out right now." He left her, walked to the door and felt for a pulse in the man's neck. Nothing. There was a bloody hole just left of the center of his chest. "He's dead."

"I thought he might be," she replied.

Eagle went back into the bedroom, got his address book and phoned the chief of police, who was a pretty good friend of his.

"Chief Sams's office," a woman's voice said.

"This is Ed Eagle. I'm a friend of the chief's, and I need to speak to him right now."

"I'm sorry, he's in a meeting. Can I have him call you?"

"Please write a note saying the following: Ed Eagle is on the phone. He says there's been a shooting, and a man is dead, and he needs to speak with you immediately. Have you got that?"

"Please hold, Mr. Eagle."

Eagle sat and waited. And waited.

Finally, she came back on the line. "Mr. Eagle, you're connected with the chief."

"Joe?"

"Hello, Ed. What's this about a shooting?"

"I'm at the home of a friend of mine, Susannah Wilde, an actress."

"I know who she is."

"Her ex-husband has just come to her apartment in Century City, armed, and he was shot. He's dead."

"Did you call nine-one-one?"

"No, you were my first thought."

"Call nine-one-one, and let's get that on the record. They'll refer the call to a detective in the precinct that covers Century City, and I'll speak with the watch commander. Don't touch anything; wait for the detectives."

"Thank you, Joe. I'll call nine-one-one right now." Eagle hung up and called the emergency number.

"Nine-one-one. What is your emergency?"

"A man has been shot in Century City."

"Is he still alive?"

"No."

"Are you certain?"

"He has a hole in his chest, he's not breathing and he doesn't have a pulse."

The dispatcher asked for his name, phone number and address. "Someone will be there shortly."

Eagle hung up. "What's the number for the front desk?"

Susannah gave it to him.

Eagle phoned it and told the doorman that the police were on the way and to send them upstairs without delay, then he hung up and went to check the body again for signs of life. Still nothing. There was a snub-nosed .38 revolver on the floor beside it. That was good. He went into the bedroom, grabbed some clothes and went back into the living room, dressing as he spoke to Susannah.

"Tell me what happened when you opened the door."

"I opened it and stepped back at the same time."

"The gun was in your hand?"

"Yes, but I held it behind me; I didn't want to seem to be threatening him."

"Did you see his gun?"

"Yes."

"Where was it?"

"His hand was in his pocket. He said, 'You filthy bitch,' and he pulled the gun out of his pocket and began to raise it. That's when I shot him."

"All right, when the police get here I want you to answer their questions truthfully."

"All right."

"Are the messages still on your answering machine?"

"Voice mail. I didn't erase them."

"That's good. Did Rod seem angry?"

"Yes, but it seemed like a cold anger; there was no expression on his face. It felt as though he had already made the decision to kill me."

The phone rang, and Susannah picked it up. "Yes? Thank you." She hung up. "The police are on the way up."

Since the door was already open, Eagle didn't have to answer it. Two detectives appeared, their badges displayed. "Are you Ed Eagle?" one of them asked.

"Yes."

The two men briefly examined the body, then turned back to Eagle.

"I'm Detective Lieutenant Rivera. This is Detective Sergeant Riley."

"Thank you for coming. This is Susannah Wilde. I'm acting as her attorney, but she's willing to answer your questions."

"Good. Mr. Eagle, will you go into the bedroom with Sergeant Riley? He will question you there."

"No. I'll have to be present while you question Ms. Wilde, so that I'll know what she says to you."

"As you wish. When we're done questioning her, I'll question you separately. There'll be a crime scene team here shortly, so let's get started." The two detectives took chairs opposite the sofa, and Eagle sat down next to Susannah.

"Mr. Eagle, do you mind if I record this interview?"

"No," Eagle replied.

Rivera placed a small recorder on the coffee table and switched it on. "Ms. Wilde, my name is Lieutenant Rivera, and this is Sergeant Riley." He noted the date and time and read Susannah her rights. "Are you willing to answer our questions?"

"Yes."

"For the record, you are represented by counsel, Mr. Ed Eagle."

"Yes."

"Are you acquainted with the decedent? The dead man?"

"Yes, he is my ex-husband. We were divorced about ten months ago."

"Can you give me his name, age and occupation?"

"His name is Rodney Spearman, he's . . ." She thought for a moment. "He's forty-five, and he's a film producer at Centurion Studios."

The questioning continued for ten minutes, until the crime scene team arrived and were briefed, and then it began again. When the detectives had finished questioning Susannah, Eagle took her into the bedroom and made her lie down.

"I don't need to lie down," she protested.

"Yes, you do, and the detectives want to question me alone."

"Oh, all right." She stretched out on the bed, and Eagle went back into the living room and sat down. The detectives questioned him closely. Shortly, the crime scene investigator walked over.

"Lieutenant, you want my preliminary report?"

"Yes, please."

"Cause of death, gunshot wound to the heart; time of death, approximately half an hour ago. We have the weapon, a .45-caliber, semiautomatic pistol." He held up a plastic bag containing Eagle's gun. "One shot fired, range three to four feet. A .38 revolver was on the floor beside the decedent in a position consistent with it being in his hand when he was shot. I'll need to examine the woman's hands for gunshot residue."

Eagle went into the bedroom and got Susannah, explaining what was to be done. She sat at the dining room table with the investigator. When he was done, she got up and went back into the bedroom.

Rivera held up the gun. "Mr. Eagle, you said this is yours?"

"Yes, it is."

"Do you live in this apartment with Ms. Wilde?"

"No."

"Do you have a license for this weapon in Los Angeles?"

Eagle produced his carry license.

"Where do you reside?"

"In Santa Fe, New Mexico." Eagle gave them the address.

"How did you obtain this license?"

"I filled out an application and sent it to Chief Sams."

"I see you've had it for some years," Rivera said, checking the date on the license, then returning it to Eagle. "It's an interesting gun," he said. "Tell me about it."

"It was made by a gunsmith named Terry Tussey, who lives and works in High City, Nevada. One of his specialties is making small, lightweight .45s."

"Ah, yes. I've seen photographs of his work. How much does it weigh?"

"Twenty-one ounces, empty. I would be grateful if you would return it to me as soon as your investigation will allow; it's an expensive weapon, and I don't want to lose it."

"I'll see that you get it back as soon as it's released." Rivera handed the gun to Riley. "All right, Mr. Eagle. Our preliminary investigative conclusion is that this was a legal shooting, so we won't be arresting Ms. Wilde, unless evidence to the contrary emerges."

"Thank you. I should tell you that Ms. Wilde and I plan to fly to Santa Fe tomorrow, where we both have residences." He handed Rivera his card. "You are welcome to speak with her by telephone, through me. If you require her presence in Los Angeles, I'll bring her back within twenty-four hours of the request. In the meantime, anything you can legally do to keep her name out of the press would be very much appreciated."

"I can't make any promises, but I'll do what I can. Mr. Eagle, do you always travel armed?"

"I always have a weapon in my luggage, and sometimes I wear it. I fly my own airplane, so I don't have to deal with airport security."

"Did you have some particular reason to be wearing it on this trip?"

"Yes, I think my ex-wife wants to kill me."

"I read about the trial," Rivera said. "It seems that, between you and Ms. Wilde, you have an abundance of murderous ex-spouses."

"An overabundance," Eagle said, "until today."

The body was removed, and Eagle saw the two detectives out. The bloodstain on the carpet was the only evidence of what had occurred.

Eagle went into the bedroom to check on Susannah. She was lying on the bed, sound asleep.

5 BARBARA EAGLE/ELEANOR WRIGHT regarded her new auburn-colored, artfully streaked hairdo in the salon mirror and nodded. Even if she was no longer wanted by the police, she thought it a good idea to have a different look. Half the country had watched her trial on Court TV and the evening news, and she had no wish to be recognized. It was time to learn whether she would be.

She left the salon, went into the very chic El Rancho shop and tried on bikinis, selecting two, along with some suntan lotion. Her new, slimmer figure was shown to great advantage by the tiny swimsuits. She went back to her suite, got into a bikini, grabbed a robe and headed for the pool. It was nearly lunchtime, and she was getting hungry.

She selected a chaise at poolside, and a waitress materialized a second or two later. "May I bring you something, Mrs. Wright, or would you prefer to choose from our low-fat buffet?" she asked, indicating the setup at the end of the pool.

"Thank you," Barbara replied. "I'd like a turkey club sandwich on rye toast with real, honest-to-God bacon and mayonnaise and a Bloody Mary."

"Of course, ma'am, but I'm afraid it will be a virgin Mary, since we don't serve alcohol."

"All right, all right," she said, and the young woman vanished.

There were some magazines on the table next to her chaise, and she had begun leafing through a *Vanity Fair* when she saw a man come from the direction of the rooms and drop his robe on a chaise two down from hers. He appeared to be in his late forties, but his hair was almost entirely gray; he was tanned and fit-looking, with a flat belly and well-developed musculature.

Barbara pointed her eyes at the magazine and used her peripheral vision. The man walked past her to the diving board, stretched a little, then performed a perfectly executed dive into the pool. He surfaced and began swimming laps, moving easily and gracefully through the water.

The waitress arrived with her sandwich and began setting up the table beside Barbara.

"Who is the gentleman in the pool?" Barbara asked.

"Oh, that's Mr. Walter Keeler," the young woman replied. "He was widowed recently and has been with us for the last month or so, resting and toning up."

It's working, Barbara said to herself. "What does he do?" she asked.

"I believe he sold his company not long ago—some sort of electronics, I think."

"Thank you, dear," Barbara said, signing the check and adding a crisp twenty from her purse.

"Oh, thank you, ma'am," the young woman said. "May I get you anything else?"

Barbara wanted to say *Yes, get me Mr. Walter Keeler,* but she restrained herself. "No, thank you, dear." She busied herself applying suntan lotion, while surreptitiously following Keeler's progress with his laps. He must have swum fifty, she thought, because she had finished her club sandwich by the time he got out of the pool.

He looked toward her as he passed, smiling and nodding. She rewarded him with a small smile, then went back to her magazine.

He stood, drying himself with a large towel. He toweled his hair dry, then ran his fingers through it. "Beautiful day, isn't it?" he said.

She turned and looked at him, affecting surprise. "Sorry?"

"The weather, it's lovely."

"Oh, I'm sorry. Yes, it is."

"It usually is up here. It's cooler than in Palm Springs, what with the elevation."

"Have you been here long?"

"A month tomorrow," he replied.

"That's a long stay."

"You must have just arrived; I haven't seen you before."

"Yes, just last night. I just felt like getting away for a few days."

"Away from where?" he asked.

"I've been staying in Los Angeles with friends. I came out from New York last month."

"Is New York your home?"

"I've just sold my apartment there," Barbara said, "and I haven't decided where I want to alight."

"You sound free as a bird."

"I suppose I am," she said. "It's not quite as much fun as I thought it would be. I lost my husband a few months ago, and I thought a change of scenery might help."

"I'm sorry for your loss," he said. "I know how you feel, because I lost my wife recently. I suppose I'm footloose, as well; I sold my business after her death, and I haven't decided yet where I want to live."

"Where were you living before?"

"In Palo Alto. I had an aircraft electronics business there."

"A pleasant place?"

"Yes, it is, but I'd like to get away from the Silicon Valley crowd. I've been thinking about San Francisco."

"Such a beautiful city."

"Yes, it is. Oddly enough, I've spent very little time there, even though I've been living close by for more than fifteen years."

"Where else are you considering?"

"Oh, I thought about Seattle, but there's such a lot of rain there. The cool summers in San Francisco appeal to me."

"I know what you mean; I've never liked the heat much."

Keeler put down his towel. "May I join you?" he asked, indicating the empty chaise next to her.

"Please."

He settled onto the chaise. "Lunch?"

"I've just eaten, thanks."

"I hope you don't mind watching me eat."

"Not at all."

He ordered a sandwich and a virgin Mary. "I haven't gotten used to the no-alcohol rule, though I suppose it hasn't hurt me. I've lost nine or ten pounds since I got here."

"You look great," she said, "but a man should have two drinks a day, according to the latest medical studies."

"Doctor's orders? I like that."

She sipped her virgin Mary.

"A friend of mine used to call a virgin Mary a 'bloody awful.'"

She laughed. "Well said."

They chatted on into the afternoon, and Barbara invented her background on the fly.

"I'm sorry," he said, "I haven't introduced myself. I'm Walter Keeler—Walt."

"I'm Eleanor Wright," she said. "Ellie." And you and I, she thought, are going to get to know each other very well.

6 EAGLE AWOKE AT seven, as usual, and checked Susannah. She was still soundly asleep. He showered, shaved and dressed, then sat down on the bed next to her and stroked her cheek. "You ready for some breakfast?" he asked.

Her eyelids fluttered and she moved a bit. "Good morning."

"Breakfast?"

"Toast and coffee, please."

"Don't go back to sleep; we need to get an early start."

"Why?" she asked sleepily.

"I've been out of the office for a week, and things have been piling up."

She struggled into a sitting position. "Okay, I'm awake."

Eagle made coffee and toast and poured juice. Susannah's hair was still wet from the shower when she came to the table.

"How are you feeling?"

"Good," she said. "I slept very soundly."

"Did you dream?"

"Probably, but I don't remember what."

She seemed to have no thought of what had happened the day

before. She had been asleep for a good fifteen hours. He wondered if she had, somehow, blocked the shooting from her mind. "I'll get packed," he said, "and you get dressed."

AN HOUR LATER they took the elevator to the lobby, and Eagle held the door for her while she spoke to the man at the desk.

"Terry, please get the carpet cleaners in and have them do the apartment," she said, "with special attention to the area by the front door."

"Yes, ma'am," the man replied, reaching for the phone.

Susannah returned to the elevator, and Eagle let it continue to the basement garage. Apparently, she hadn't completely forgotten about yesterday.

THEY TOOK OFF from Santa Monica Airport in Eagle's airplane less than an hour later, shepherded by air traffic control to the Palmdale VOR, then cleared direct Grand Canyon, direct Santa Fe. Sped along by a strong tailwind, they got a good look at the spectacular hole in the ground and were in Santa Fe in plenty of time for lunch.

"Your place or mine?" he asked her as they drove away from the airport.

"Mine," she replied. "I've got some stuff to do around the house. I'll pick up some things and come to you by dinnertime."

"Out or in?"

"Make a reservation somewhere," she said.

They drove the twenty minutes to her house, and he pulled into the driveway, got her bags out and took them into the house. Before he left, he sat her down in the study.

"How are you feeling?" he asked.

"I'm very well, Ed, I told you that."

"Listen, you've been through a traumatic experience, and it's going to catch up with you sooner or later." He wrote a name and number on the back of his business card and gave it to her. "This guy is the best psychotherapist in Santa Fe. His name is Daniel Shea, and he lives and works two or three miles from here. I think you should have a talk with him."

"Ed, please believe me, I'm fine."

"You have the number. If you start to feel . . . depressed, please call him."

"If I start to feel depressed," she said. "I'll see you later—six or six thirty, at your house."

"Okay." He kissed her and left the house, then drove to his office.

HIS OFFICES WERE only a year old, atop one of the taller buildings around the Plaza, the heart of the city. Eagle strolled through the outer area, waving at his employees. "All right, everybody," he called to them, "get to work; the boss is back."

His secretary followed him into the office. "There's a stack of phone messages on your desk that weren't important enough to forward to L.A."

"Fine, make a reservation for two at Santa Café at seven thirty, please."

"Will do. There's some correspondence, too, and a couple of briefs that you dictated before you left. Please review them."

"Okay, okay." He began making phone calls, apologizing for his absence. Half the people he spoke to had watched his testimony at Barbara's trial. One of the messages was from Daniel Shea. He called the number.

"Dan? It's Ed."

"Hello, Ed. Congratulations on your performance in L.A."

"A lot of good it did me; she's free as a bird."

"How do you feel about that, Ed?"

"Don't you ask me those shrink questions, Dan," Eagle said, chuckling. "I'll feel just fine as long as Barbara is in another state."

"Is that where she is?"

"I hope I never know."

"Ed, we've never talked much about this, but you should know that Barbara, like her late sister, Julia, is an obsessive."

"And what is her obsession?"

"You."

"Oh, come on, Daniel. She's out; she'll want to stay out. She won't want to mess with me."

"Are you forgetting that Julia tried to set up her husband for a triple murder and then killed my brother? And damn near got away with it? Are you forgetting that Barbara hired two men to kill you? I'm telling you, it runs in the family. I never knew the third sister, but I'd be willing to bet she shared the family trait."

"Well, I was careful in L.A. after I learned that she had escaped the courthouse."

"Now she doesn't have to be careful, you know. She can move right back to Santa Fe, if she wants to, and live on her divorce settlement from you."

That settlement still rankled Eagle, but it had been worth it to get rid of her. "Yes, I suppose she could, but why would she want to?"

"Ed, do you know what an obsession is? It's the opposite of a phobia. A phobia is an irrational fear of something: flying, water, open spaces, almost anything. An obsession is a compulsive fascination with something, either a love or a hatred of the object. You are the object, and she is not going to walk away from you."

"By the way, Dan, I've been seeing a woman named Susannah Wilde, and yesterday, in L.A., she shot and killed her ex-husband, who was threatening her with a gun. She's off the hook legally, but I'm not sure about psychologically. It's weird; she behaves as if the shooting never happened, and I'm not sure how long she can keep that up."

"Tell her to call me; I'll work her in."

"I already have. I just wanted you to know who she is when she calls."

"Maybe you should come and see me, too, Ed."

"Come on, Dan. You know I have no neuroses. I'm the sanest guy you know."

"I'll concede that, but it troubles me that you seem unable to face the Barbara problem."

"Dan, if the Barbara problem arises again, I'll deal with it, but I'm not going to spend my days and nights worrying about it."

"That's a sane approach, Ed, but a potentially dangerous one."

"Let's have dinner soon, okay?"

"Are you free tonight?" Daniel asked.

"Tell you what, meet Susannah and me at Santa Café at seven thirty."

"I'd love to."

"She's going to think I'm setting her up, so don't bring up her problem."

"Of course not. See you at seven thirty."

"We'll look forward to it." Eagle hung up and went back to the work on his desk.

SUSANNAH ARRIVED AT Eagle's house and deposited her things in the master bedroom's second dressing room. Eagle had long ago given Barbara's clothes to the Salvation Army, and the room had been empty until Susannah had begun to leave a few things there.

They got into Eagle's car. "A friend is joining us," he said as he pointed the car down the mountain road.

"Who's that?"

"His name is Daniel Shea."

"The shrink you told me about?"

"Yes, but I'm not setting you up. He called this afternoon and suggested dinner, so I asked him to join us."

"You're just trying to get my head shrunk, aren't you?"

"No, I'm not, I swear. Dan's a good guy, and you'll like him."

"Tell me about him."

"He had a brother, Mark Shea, who was a psychiatrist here; he was murdered by Barbara's sister."

"Oh, yeah, your sister-in-law. I remember."

"She had been dead for a year when Barbara and I married."

"So, Dan replaced Mark in Santa Fe?"

"Pretty much. Dan was Mark's heir. They were twins—not identical, fraternal—and Dan inherited Mark's property in Santa Fe. Dan had had a practice in Denver, but he moved here, wrote a letter to all of Mark's clients, saying that he was taking over the practice, and he retained most of Mark's clients. If anything, he has been more successful than Mark was."

"Are you one of his clients?"

"Me? I'm impervious to analysis; I have no neuroses. Dan knows this, but he keeps kidding me about getting therapy."

"Okay, I'll try to talk to him just like a real person, instead of a shrink."

THEY ARRIVED AT Santa Café, Eagle's favorite local restaurant, which managed to be at once cool and festive. Daniel Shea was waiting for them at the bar. He stood up and approached, his hand out.

"Hello, Ed. And this must be Susannah." He shook her hand warmly. He was not as tall as Eagle but broader, a bear of a man.

"Why do I feel so small in this company?" Susannah asked and got a laugh.

They were seated, ordered drinks, consulted menus and ordered food.

"I must tell you," Shea said, "I'm a fan of your work."

"Why thank you, Dan," Susannah said.

"I don't go to the movies all that much, but I see everything on satellite, and I've watched most of your movies more than once."

"Well, I'm settling into my character period, I think, since I'm pushing forty now. The good news is, I produce most of what I appear in, so I just cast myself in good supporting roles."

"That's very smart," Shea said. "Tell me, how does one learn to produce films? It seems very complicated."

"Well, first of all, I've appeared in a lot of them, and I guess it didn't hurt to be married to a producer for some years, and I got to watch him work. He's very good at it."

There was a silence.

"Oh, that's right. I should have used the past tense," Susannah said. "He *was* very good at it."

"I won't pretend I don't know about that," Shea said.

"Thank God. Ed promised me he hadn't set me up for over-dinner therapy."

"You're a smart woman, I think," Shea said. "You'll call me if you need me. A lot of people wait a lot longer than they should, but I don't think you're one of those."

"That's a pretty good observation," Susannah said. "What else have you divined about me during our brief acquaintance?"

"You mean besides beautiful and intelligent? Let's see: frank to the point of being blunt, disdainful of charade, good judge of character."

"Then why did I marry the schmuck I married?"

"You're in the company of millions; love and sex distort judgment."

"Go on with your observations."

"I think that's as far as I'd like to go on short acquaintance; I don't want to get you mixed up with the characters you've played."

"Well, you're pretty much on target," Susannah said, "especially the beautiful and intelligent part."

Eagle laughed. "I can vouch for your perceptions, Dan."

Susannah sipped her drink. "There's something wrong with this drink," she said. "It tastes funny."

Eagle, who was drinking the same bourbon, tasted his, then tasted hers. "They seem the same to me."

Susannah held up a hand, as if telling him not to speak, then she picked up her napkin, held it in both hands and vomited into it.

A waiter rushed over and relieved her of the napkin and handed her another.

"Excuse me," Susannah said, starting to get up. "I'm feeling a little odd." She got to her feet and fainted into Daniel Shea's waiting arms.

"I think it's caught up with her," Shea said, sweeping her up. "Let's get her home."

Eagle followed behind him and helped get her into the car. "Should we take her to the hospital?"

"I don't think that will be necessary." He handed Eagle his car keys. "There's a medical bag in my trunk; get it for me, will you?"

Eagle retrieved the bag. When he returned Shea was sitting in the backseat with Susannah, her head in his lap. He held his fingers to her throat. "Her vitals are fine; she's just having a bout with post-traumatic stress disorder. My guess is she'll be fine after a good night's sleep, though she may want to come and talk to me."

"I'll encourage it," Eagle said.

"Don't. Let it be her idea."

"I'll drive you home when we've gotten her in bed."

"I'd better stay over, to be there if she needs me. You do have a guest room, don't you?"

"A guesthouse; you're welcome to it."

"She may wake up in the night and move around. Try to settle her down. If she becomes agitated, call me, and I'll give her something to calm her down."

"I'm almost as surprised at her reaction as I was at her lack of reaction after the shooting," Eagle said.

"Some people are just stoics," Shea replied. "It takes them a longer time than most people to externalize what they're feeling inside. It's good that she's finally let it out."

Eagle drove on, hoping that this was the worst effect she would experience from the shooting.

**8** EAGLE AND SHEA were having breakfast when Susannah, looking dazed, wandered into the kitchen. Eagle got her into a chair.

"I'm sorry about last night," Susannah said.

"It's all right," Ed said.

"Had to happen," Dan chimed in. "You can't go through something like that without it having an effect. How do you feel?"

"Rested but a little dopey. Did you give me something?"

"No," Dan said. "I didn't think you needed anything."

"I'll make you some eggs," Eagle said.

She picked up half of his English muffin and spread some marmalade on it. "No, thanks, this will do fine."

Eagle gave her some juice and, when she had downed it, filled her coffee mug.

"That's what I need," she said, sipping the strong liquid.

"Well," Dan said, rising, "I have appointments this morning; I'd better get going."

"Can I come and see you?" Susannah asked.

"Of course." He consulted a pocket diary. "How about two

o'clock? I'm usually reading medical publications at that time, but any excuse not to."

"I'll see you at two."

Shea gave her directions.

Eagle got up. "I'll drop you at your car," he said. He turned to Susannah. "Will you be all right on your own?"

"Of course. Get out of here, both of you."

THEY GOT INTO Eagle's car and drove down the mountain.

"She'll be okay," Dan said. "Last night was a good thing for her, a wake-up call."

"I think you're right," Eagle said. "She's a sturdy person."

EAGLE SETTLED BEHIND his desk and looked at the messages waiting there. He returned a couple of calls and signed some letters, then sat alone in his office and thought for a long moment about what Dan Shea had said to him the day before. Finally, he picked up the phone and dialed a number in Santa Monica.

"Dalton," the voice said.

"Cupie, it's Ed Eagle. How are you?"

"Well, hello there. I'm okay, you?"

"Not bad. I watched your testimony on TV; you did a good job." Cupie Dalton was one of the two private investigators Eagle had hired to follow his ex-wife to Mexico when she had decamped with a lot of his money.

"I watched yours, too, and so did you."

"You heard she was acquitted."

"Yeah. Go figure."

"A friend has convinced me that I need to know where she is."

"A good friend," Cupie said. "I'm surprised you couldn't figure that out on your own. She's a dangerous woman."

"I can't imagine that she'd come back to Santa Fe, but I'd feel better if you could track her down."

"I hear she walked on the escape charge, so I guess she's free as a bird."

"Yes. I'd feel better if she were reporting to a parole officer every week."

"Well, yeah. You got any leads for me?"

"Just one: Jimmy Long."

"He was her alibi for the time of the shooting, right?"

"Right."

"What do you know about him?"

"He's a rich kid who always wanted to make movies, and something of a playboy. Surprisingly, he's produced some pretty good films."

"So he's well-known around town?"

"He is. He lives somewhere in Beverly Hills or Bel-Air, I think."

"It won't be any trouble to find out."

"I'm sure he helped her with the escape; she doesn't have any other friends out there that I know of."

"You think she might be holed up at his house?"

"I doubt it," Eagle said. "She was a fugitive for twenty-four hours or so, and that's the first place the cops would have looked."

"Last time, she laid low at a high-end spa place in La Jolla," Cupie said.

"I doubt if she'd go where anyone knows her."

"Probably not, but I'd be willing to bet she'd go to another place a lot like it."

"Well, Southern California is riddled with those places; it would be hard to know where to start."

"Of course," Cupie said, "but I'll bet she chose one not that far away. She'd want to get off the roads as soon as possible after her escape, and no later than dinnertime."

"That's a good thought. You don't think she'd go back to Mexico?"

Cupie snorted. "Not while there's a chief of police down there whose nephew's dick she and her sister cut off."

"You're right."

"I'll start with Jimmy Long."

"I don't think he's going to want to talk to you," Eagle said.

"Does he have an office outside his home?"

"I don't know."

"Won't take long to find out."

"She's probably using another name," Eagle said.

"Probably, but I know where she got her last set of documents. I'll pay somebody a call."

"Good man."

"It's a thousand a day with a five-thousand minimum, plus expenses."

"Agreed. She will probably have changed her appearance, too, if her last outing is any indication."

"I'll take that into consideration."

"Just remember that she knows what you look like, Cupie, so she'll have the advantage of you. Don't let it get you hurt, like last time."

"Yes, she does have a tendency to shoot first and not bother with questions, doesn't she?"

"She does."

"Well, you can bet I'll be more careful than I was in Mexico," Cupie said. "Listen, are you sure that all you want is to know where she is?"

"That's all, Cupie, nothing else. Let's be clear about that. Once you've found her, though, I may want you to keep tabs on her location."

"When we get to that point, I can hire somebody cheaper just to watch her movements."

"There's something else, Cupie."

"What's that?"

"She's good at using men. The last time you went after her she never had time to get next to anybody, but she's been on the loose for a few days, and I wouldn't be surprised if she has probably already latched onto somebody."

"The poor bastard," Cupie said.

BARBARA/ELEANOR HAD NOW spent two days in the company of Walter Keeler, and she had played her cards very carefully. She had listened rather than talked, and, eventually, he had poured his heart out. As she had suspected, his marriage to his late wife hadn't been all he had wanted it to be, and there was an element of relief as well as guilt in his feelings about being a newly minted widower.

She had talked about herself only when he had asked her questions, and she had always been brief, sticking to a story that would be easy for her to remember. She had never made any allusion to any future after their time together at the spa, not even "Let's have dinner sometime." She would make it her business to make him want to see her again, and often.

She had her chance as they were finishing dinner in the spa's restaurant.

"You know," he said, "I like this place, but there's something unnatural about not having an occasional drink, and I was stupid enough not to bring something with me."

"Well," she said, smiling, "I guess I'm smarter than you are."

His eyebrows went up. "Oh, yeah?"

"If you'd like some very fine bourbon, let's part company now, then meet in my suite in fifteen minutes."

"What a grand idea!" he said.

"And be stealthy; we wouldn't want to give the staff something to talk about."

"I'll do better than that," he said. "I'll be sneaky."

Barbara stood up and offered her hand. "Thank you so much for dinner, Walt. I enjoyed it."

"So did I," he said. He sat down and waved for the check.

BARBARA WENT BACK to her suite, stripped naked and slipped into a cotton shift with a zipper down the back. She freshened her body with a damp facecloth and sprayed her crotch with something both scented and flavored.

When his knock came, she let him in and waved him to the large comfortable sofa. "How would you like it?" she asked.

"What?"

"Your drink," she said, laughing.

"Oh, on the rocks, please."

She poured two generous drinks and set them on the coffee table, then sat down—not too close to him—and faced him, pulling her knees onto the sofa.

Keeler sipped his drink. "That's wonderful! What is it?"

"Knob Creek, a boutique bourbon. I'll never drink anything else; it's my only real legacy from my late husband." Good to plant that thought now.

"This is the best I've felt for a long time," he said.

"Must be the bourbon."

He smiled and shook his head. "No, it's a lot more than that."

"Oh?"

"Come on, you feel this, too."

"I certainly feel something," she said.

"You're sure it's not the bourbon?"

"Fairly sure."

He put his hand on her cheek and kissed her, sweetly, no tongue.

She returned the kiss in the spirit in which it was offered. He sighed. "It's been a long time."

"Yes, it has been for me, too."

"I have a feeling that empty period of my life has come to a close."

"That's what I'd like to feel," she said.

He kissed her again, this time more passionately.

She flicked her tongue in and out of his mouth and ran her fingers through his thick hair.

He took hold of her, turned her around and laid her across his lap, her head on his shoulder.

She put an arm around his neck and played with an ear. She could feel him hardening under the weight of her body.

"Does this suite have a bedroom?" he asked.

"It does."

"Why don't we continue this conversation there, before I explode?"

"I think that's a good idea," she said. "I wouldn't want you to explode—not just yet, anyway."

He scooped her up in his arms and carried her into the bedroom, laying her on the bed.

She turned her back to him. "Zipper, please?"

He complied, and she heard his own zipper working. A moment later they were fully embracing.

"Easy," she said. "Be tender."

He was, and so was she.

Somewhat to her surprise and much to her delight, he did not immediately enter her. Instead, he parted her vulva with his tongue and lingered there until she insisted he mount her.

They both came that way, then rested for a while. Then she began bringing him back, stroking him first with her fingers, then with her tongue. She would not let go, until he had climaxed again.

They lay under the covers, panting, gradually recovering themselves.

"Did I mention that I have my airplane at Palm Springs Airport?"

"I don't remember," she lied.

"Why don't you and I fly to San Francisco tomorrow for a few days?"

"What a sweet thought," she said. "Don't you think it might be a little early in our acquaintance for that sort of trip?"

"I think we just settled that," he replied.

"But what would I do with my car?"

"Ditch it, if you like; I'll buy you a new one."

"Nonsense," she said. "Perhaps I can get someone from the hotel to drive it to Los Angeles, to a friend's house."

"That's good, clear thinking," he said.

"But you don't have a place in San Francisco, do you?"

"Not yet, but I know a good hotel."

"I didn't bring San Francisco clothes, I'm afraid. I don't think I can get by with a couple of cotton dresses and a bikini."

"That's what shops are for. I think I'd enjoy watching you shop."

"I think I'd enjoy watching you watching me shop," she said.

"You're game, then?"

"That's the nice thing about being free again," she said, with more depth of feeling than he knew. "You can do anything you want to."

"That's right," he said. "You can, and so can I."

"I think doing it together will be fun," she said.

"I will make it so," he replied.

BARBARA/ELEANOR DRIFTED OFF to sleep, physically satisfied but very, very curious. She woke up in the middle of the night to the sound of his regular breathing.

She got up, got online and Googled the name Walter Keeler. It took only a moment to find a news report of the sale of his electronics business. She gave a little gasp. His share of the deal had been $2.7 billion!

She was going to have to play this very, very carefully.

10

CUPIE DALTON DROVE over to Venice and, lucky him, found a parking spot. He strolled along the beachfront, taking the sun, his straw porkpie hat keeping the heat off his bald spot. He caught sight of the sign for the photographer's shop a hundred yards away, knowing from his past encounter with Barbara Eagle that the place was a hotbed of counterfeit document sales. Then he was startled to see the owner, the man he wanted to see, walk out of the shop and start down the sidewalk toward him.

Cupie stepped off the sidewalk and found a spot on a bench, his back to the foot traffic. He waited for a few moments, then hazarded a glance to his right. The photographer was walking briskly, a package under his arm. Cupie watched as he stopped at a mailbox, dropped in the package and started back toward his shop.

Cupie waited until he was certain the man had walked behind him, then he caught sight of him turning into his shop. Good.

Cupie got up, walked down the sidewalk toward the shop and had a peek through the window. The owner's pretty teenaged daughter was the only person in view. Cupie walked in, straight past the counter, toward the rear office.

"Hey," the girl shouted, "you can't go back there. It's private!"

But Cupie was already back there. He pushed the curtain aside and stepped into the surprisingly large office, filled with computers and copying machines. The owner sat behind his desk. He looked up, registered Cupie and started to get up.

"Relax, my friend," Cupie said, taking the chair across from him. "This is going to be short and sweet."

The man said nothing, just glared at Cupie. It was obvious that his memory of their last meeting was an unpleasant memory.

"Now, my friend," Cupie said, in his most avuncular voice. "All I want is her new name."

The man stared at him and said nothing.

"Come on, you and I both know that holding out on me is not going to be good for business. Tell you what: I'll sweeten it just a little." He reached into a pocket for a wad of bills, peeled off two hundreds and tossed them onto the desk. "For your trouble."

Finally, the man spoke. "Five hundred."

Cupie sighed and tossed three more C-notes onto the desk. "I know it's not really necessary to mention this," he said, "but if you give me a wrong name, I won't even need to come back. You'll be raided before you can spend the five hundred—LAPD or the Feds, take your pick."

"The name is Eleanor Wright," he said.

Cupie stared at him.

"And I colored her hair auburn, photographically. It was a good job, even if I do say so."

"Did you give her the whole package: passport, driver's license, Social Security, credit cards?"

The man nodded. "And they'll all stand up. Now, that's all you get for your five hundred."

Cupie stood up. "It's so much easier talking to me than working for a living, isn't it?" He gave a little wave and walked out of the office. "Good day, sweetheart," he said to the daughter as he passed.

He walked on down the sidewalk until he found a bookstore. He located the travel section and found a shelf of books on spas, settling on one that covered Southern California. He paid for his purchase, pocketed the receipt and walked back outside. He found another bench, this one overlooking the sandbox where the muscle boys played. They glistened in the sun, stretching, lifting and assuming poses. Half a dozen gay men were happy spectators.

Cupie began leafing through the spa book. "Now, I'm Eleanor Wright, formerly Barbara Eagle," he said aloud to himself. "If I had just decamped from a courthouse while the jury in my trial was still deliberating, where would I choose to go and rehabilitate my image?" He took a highlighter from his coat pocket and began marking likely spots. His criteria were luxury, seclusion, exclusivity and easy access from greater L.A.

When he had highlighted twelve spas, he took out his cell phone and began calling them. Each time the phone was answered he asked for Mrs. Eleanor Wright. Surely Barbara would not pretend to be a single girl but rather a divorcée or widow. On the ninth phone call he hit pay dirt.

"Oh," a woman's voice said, "you've just missed her. She checked out less than half an hour ago."

"I'm so sorry to miss her," Cupie said. "This is her father. Did she say where she was going? Back here, to L.A.?"

"No, but I don't think so, because she hired one of our employees to drive her car there and leave it with a friend."

"Oh, that would be Jimmy Long," he said.

"Why, that's right."

"It's rather odd that she would suddenly send her car back but not come back herself. How was she traveling?"

"Well, she left with Mr. Walter Keeler, and I know that he had flown into Palm Springs in his own airplane. He's from up in Silicon Valley, the electronics entrepreneur."

"I'm afraid I don't know the gentleman," Cupie said. "Do you think she'll be all right in his company? I worry about my girl."

"Oh, Mr. Keeler is a very upstanding citizen," she said. "I know Mrs. Wright would be safe with him."

"Well, I'm relieved to hear that," Cupie said. "I'm sure she'll give me a call when she reaches her destination. Thank you so much for your help." He hung up.

Cupie walked back to his car and drove home. He couldn't wait to get to his computer. Once at his desk he Googled "Walter Keeler." His eyes widened as he read of the sale of Keeler's company. "Two point seven bil!" he said aloud. He then went straight to the Federal Aviation Agency website, to the page for airplane registrations. He entered the name Walter Keeler and found a CitationJet III registered to him. He made a note of the tail number, then he called up a nifty little program called Flight Aware.

Flight Aware could track the progress and destination of any aircraft, airline or private; all you had to do was enter the flight number or, in this case, the tail number. Cupie did so. Seconds later, a little red airplane symbol appeared on the screen, located over the Central Valley, the farming capital of California, headed northwest. Destination: Hayward, California. "What the hell is in Hayward?" Cupie asked himself.

He got out his road atlas and found Hayward. It was a small city on the eastern shore of San Francisco Bay, just south of Oakland. He picked up the phone and dialed.

"The Eagle Practice," a woman's smooth voice said.

"Ed Eagle, please. It's Cupie Dalton calling."

"Just a moment, Mr. Dalton."

"Cupie?"

"Good morning, Ed."

"News?"

"News. Our girl, as soon as she left the courthouse, drove down to a spa called El Rancho Encantado on a mountaintop overlooking Palm Springs, traveling under the name of Eleanor Wright. She checked in and there met a gentleman named Walter Keeler."

"I know that name, I think."

"You ought to; he just sold his electronics conglomerate and pocketed two point seven billion bucks."

"Are they still at the spa?"

"Nope, she shipped her car back to Jimmy Long's house and left Palm Springs Airport on Keeler's CitationJet, bound for Hayward, California, on the eastern shore of San Francisco Bay. What I can't figure out, at least at the moment, is what the hell anybody would do in Hayward."

"There's a general aviation airport there that serves San Francisco. I land there, myself, when I'm going there on business. It's not like a smaller airplane would want to mix it up with the heavy iron landing at San Francisco International. When did they go there?"

Cupie looked at his computer screen. "They'll be landing in about ten minutes," he said. "And it looks like our girl has hooked herself a big one."

II BARBARA/ELEANOR SAT IN the rear of the jet, her feet propped up on the opposite seat, reading *Vanity Fair*. She loved the airplane, so roomy and quiet. Up front, Walter was speaking to an air traffic controller, getting landing instructions. She could hear the conversation over the music on her headset. Maybe she would take up flying; it seemed easy enough.

The airplane touched down gently at Hayward Executive and taxied to an FBO. She knew that meant fixed-base operator, from her experience of flying with Ed Eagle. A black Mercedes drove out onto the ramp and positioned itself near the airplane's door, its trunk open and waiting. Barbara handed Walter her small bag, containing only her makeup and toiletries and a single change of clothes, having sent everything else to L.A. in her Toyota. She would be starting from scratch, at Walter's insistence. She liked it when men insisted.

An hour later she and Walter were enjoying a fine lunch on the terrace of their large suite at the Four Seasons.

"Have you spent much time in San Francisco?" Walter asked.

"No. I've been here only once, just overnight."

"You'll find great shopping around Union Square, which is just up the street from the hotel. I've kept the car for you, and the driver will take you up there and follow you around, to take the packages off your hands."

"Walt, you think of everything."

The doorbell rang, and Walter got up to answer it. He came back with an envelope addressed to her. "And you'll need this," he said, handing it to her.

"My goodness, gifts already?" she asked, tearing open the envelope.

"The gift of gifts," Walter said.

She plucked a black card from the envelope. "Oh, my God," she said.

"It's the American Express Centurion card," Walter said, "made of titanium, just so it will feel richer."

"But we only decided to come here this morning; how did you get it so fast?"

"The Centurion service is very good. It was hand-delivered from the local AMEX office."

She got up from the table and kissed him. "You are the sweetest man!"

"All right," he said, "go shopping. The concierge has made a dinner reservation for us at eight, so that's your deadline. I have some shopping of my own to do."

"I won't argue with you," she said, grabbing her handbag and heading for the door.

Union Square and the streets around it were a treasure trove, waiting to be plundered, and she did not keep the shops waiting. She bought two suits and a coat from Chanel; half a dozen dresses, a raincoat and several blouses and pairs of slacks from Armani; shoes from Prada and Jimmy Choo; and lingerie, hosiery and cosmetics at a department store. She bought two alligator handbags from Lana Marx and a sweet little diamond bracelet and a gold Panthere watch from Cartier. It was exhilarating. Only days before she had been a guest of the City of Los Angeles, sharing a cell with a chubby hooker, and now she felt like the queen of San Francisco! She found a luggage shop and chose a quartet of handmade Italian cases.

She returned to the hotel at five. Walter was still out, so she called the concierge for a hair appointment in the suite. She made all the boxes and wrappings go away, hanging her new wardrobe in her closet, and had a long soak in the giant tub while she waited for the hairdresser to arrive.

Her hair was shampooed, cut, shaped and dried, and the woman also applied her light makeup. When Walter returned, it was a little past seven, and she waited until he was in the shower to dress.

Walter emerged in a well-cut blue suit and a gold necktie. He stopped short and stared at her in her new Armani dress. "Wow!" he said. "I've never seen anything so gorgeous!"

"Aren't you nice," she said, giving him a tiny peck that would not muss her newly applied lipstick. "Where are we having dinner?"

HE TOOK HER to a restaurant called Boulevard. It was large, a little noisy, in the way that wildly successful restaurants always are, and the food was delicious. They drank two bottles of wine, a chardonnay and a cabernet, both from a Napa vineyard, Far Niente. Barbara tried not to get too drunk, but everything was so delicious and the wines so heady that she nearly forgot herself.

CUPIE SAT AT his computer and trolled the Internet, breaking into hotel systems nearly at will. Cupie and computers had been friends from the day they first met. He found Walter Keeler registered in the smaller of the two presidential suites at the Four Seasons, and he tried to image what a small presidential suite must look like. He called Eagle to report in.

"Good work, Cupie. Just keep track of her—that's all I want. If she heads toward Santa Fe I'll start packing heat. It shouldn't be too hard; anybody who flies his own jet isn't going to be separated too far from his airplane."

"Good point," Cupie said. "I'll check Flight Aware daily for his position."

THEY MADE LOVE at bedtime, then Barbara gently woke Walter in the middle of the night and introduced him to new techniques.

"I've never done that before," Walter said when they were done, panting a little.

"Sweetheart," she said, "for as long as you know me, you will never want for any sexual technique at my disposal. For years I had an awful sex life with my late husband, and I'm going to enjoy making up for it with you."

"Ellie," he said sleepily, "will you marry me?"

"Oh, hush, Walter, and go to sleep." It was working.

HE RUSHED HER through breakfast the following morning. "We have an appointment at nine o'clock sharp," he said.

"An appointment for what?"

"You'll see."

The driver deposited them in front of a handsome old apartment building on a hill, and a real estate agent took them to the top floor in the elevator.

They stepped out directly into the foyer of a spacious apartment. A huge bouquet of fresh flowers sat on a table, their scent pervading the air. They moved through beautifully furnished rooms, bedrooms, a magnificent kitchen, a paneled library and a dining room that seated sixteen. Finally, they emerged onto a huge planted terrace, more of a yard, she thought. San Francisco lay at their feet, the bay sparkling, a fog bank nearly enveloping the Golden Gate Bridge, its towers peeking through.

"It's breathtaking," she said. "But what are we doing here?"

Walter turned to the real estate agent. "Will you excuse us for a moment?" The woman disappeared, and he turned back to Ellie. "Do you think you could be happy living here?"

"Why, of course. Who wouldn't be happy living here?"

"Good. But I'm an old-fashioned guy; you'll have to marry me first."

"But Walter, we've known each other for only a few days. You hardly know me."

"Let me ask you something: Do you think you know me?"

"Well . . . yes—unless you have some deep dark secret you're hiding."

"Nope. What you see is what you get. My feeling is that you are the same way. Am I wrong?"

She put her arms around his neck. "No, you're not wrong."

"I love you, Ellie. Will you marry me?"

"Oh, yes," she said, kissing him, not worrying about her lipstick.

"I've arranged for a license; a judge will bring it at noon. A few friends are coming up from Palo Alto. Is there anyone you'd like to ask?"

"I have no friends in California," she said. "Only you."

"Then I will just have to be enough," he said. "The judge will marry us at noon, then we'll have a luncheon on the terrace."

"Will the real estate agent let us do that?"

"Oh, I almost forgot," he said, beckoning to the woman, who was waiting in the living room. She came out onto the terrace, and he produced a cashier's check. "Here you are; you may close with my attorney immediately." He handed her a card.

"The place is yours, Mr. Keeler," she said. "And may I offer my congratulations?" She shook both their hands and left.

"All the furnishings come with it?" Ellie asked.

"It was an estate sale. The owners died in a yachting accident three months ago, and the agents had the place repainted and freshened up. It comes with two servants, too, a very nice couple, who will be here shortly with the caterers." The doorbell rang. "That will be our clothes arriving from the hotel." He went to let them in.

Barbara/Ellie turned and took in the view again. "There is a God," she said aloud to herself.

12 EAGLE SAT, clearing up his desk. Everybody else in the office had left for the day. The phone rang, and he picked it up. "Ed Eagle."

"It's Cupie."

"What's up?"

"They checked out of the Four Seasons this morning, but the airplane is still at Hayward Executive. I haven't been able to find them."

Eagle thought for a moment. Where would they go without the airplane?"

"Not another hotel; I've been checking reservation lists all day. Anyway, why would anybody move out of the presidential suite at the Four Seasons in favor of another hotel?"

"Maybe there was a fly in the soup. Find them."

"Ed, if I have to leave my computer to find them, I'm going to need some help."

"Hire anybody you need."

"I'd like Vittorio." Vittorio was an Apache Indian who lived near Santa Fe. Cupie had worked with him the last time they had to find Barbara, and he had testified at Barbara's trial.

"Great, call him."

"I think Vittorio would like it better if you called him. He can reach me at home; he has the number."

"I'll see if I can reach him," Eagle said. He hung up and found Vittorio's cell phone number.

Voice mail picked up. "You have reached the number you dialed," Vittorio's voice said. "Leave your name and number."

"Vittorio, it's Ed Eagle. I need to speak with you as soon as possible." He left his office, home and cell numbers.

MR. AND MRS. Walter Keeler sat on their new terrace, watching the sunset and sipping martinis. Their guests for the wedding luncheon had only just left.

Eleanor Wright Keeler hadn't much liked the three couples Walter had invited. She had played them carefully, laughing at the men's jokes but paying particular attention to the women. They had all known Walter's late wife, and each of them had made a point of telling her what a wonderful person she had been, by which they meant that Eleanor had better be a wonderful person, too. She concentrated on giving them absolutely no reason to hate her. She'd make friends with them later, if it became absolutely necessary.

Walter, bless his heart, had stressed to his friends how he had swept her off her feet and that she had married him against her better judgment.

Now it was time for some practical conversation. "Walt," she said, "I know you just sold your company, but what sort of company was it?"

"Well, you know those four big screens you saw in the cockpit of the CitationJet?"

"Yes, that was an impressive display."

"I designed and manufactured them. I began twenty-five years ago, right out of Caltech, by designing an aircraft radio. It was smaller and cheaper and just as effective as anything else on the market, and it made me a small fortune in just a few years. Being a private pilot—I owned a little Cessna 182, at the time—I started dreaming up new ideas for the cockpit. I bought a couple of other companies that made other aircraft products, and I took in a couple of partners by trading stock for their companies. A few years later we had a whole suite of avionics for light aircraft, and then I heard about the global positioning system, which is a network of twenty-five satellites circling the earth and which, at that time, could be used only by the military. I saw the possibilities, and I got a license from the government, in my own name, to design a civilian receiver. Both my partners were older than I and wanted to retire, so I borrowed a lot of money and bought them out, giving them a handsome profit, and when the government finally opened GPS to civilian use, I was ready with the first receiver. That was the smartest move I ever made. The second smartest was to incorporate the screens used on laptop computers as cockpit displays and to design systems for corporate aircraft like mine, which sell at a lower price than the competition."

"And you're completely retired now?"

"Yep. I'm going to concentrate on you, now."

"Well, I assume that, since you seem to spend money like a drunken sailor, you must be fairly well off."

"Ellie, my darling," he said, "you will never have to worry about money again."

"Well, I'm glad to hear it. I'm afraid my late former husband died without a will, and a huge fight with his children over the estate ensued. I had no stomach for the courts, so I lost out."

"I've already given my lawyer notes for a new will, and it will be signed in a day or two."

"Thank you, sweetheart," she said, squeezing his hand. "You've no idea what a relief that is to me."

"By the way, you're free to do anything you want with this

apartment. Throw everything away and start from scratch, if you like."

"I like most of it very much," she said. "Maybe a new paint color here and there; it's mostly Wright as it is."

"Spend like a drunken sailor, as you put it; I can afford it if you spend like a drunken navy."

Barbara laughed and squeezed his hand again.

"By the way, I thought I'd take you on a little honeymoon tomorrow."

"That's fine with me," she said. "I would like a little time to think about what to do with the apartment. Where do you want to go? Where will we jet off to this time?"

"It's close enough to drive," Walter said. "Let it be a surprise."

"You may surprise me all you wish," she said, pouring them another martini from the shaker.

EAGLE AND SUSANNAH were finishing dinner at his house when the phone rang. Eagle took it in the study; he didn't want Susannah to worry about this.

"Hello?"

"Ed, it's Vittorio."

"Thanks for returning my call, Vittorio," he said. "Are you available for some work?"

"Yes, but I'm still in Los Angeles. I finished another job yesterday, and I thought I'd take a day or two off."

"It's good you're there. Call Cupie and go see him, will you?"

"Sure. I saw him briefly after we testified. What's the job?"

"Cupie will brief you."

"Come on, Ed, what are you not telling me?"

"It's about Barbara," Eagle said.

"Oh, shit," Vittorio replied.

13 EAGLE WAS FINISHING a sandwich at his desk the following day when his secretary buzzed him. He picked up the phone. "Yes?"

"Mr. Eagle, there's a gentleman on the phone who says he's calling from Rome, Italy, and he says he needs to speak to you urgently. His name is Donald Wells."

"Never heard of him."

"You want me to get rid of him?"

Eagle sighed. "No, I'll speak to him." He pressed the flashing button. "This is Ed Eagle."

"Mr. Eagle," the man said, "my name is Don Wells." His accent was American.

"Yes, Mr. Wells, how can I help you?" He tried to convey that he was very busy and that the man should hurry up and get to the point.

"I'm in Rome, at the Hassler Villa Medici Hotel, and I received a phone call a few minutes ago saying that my wife and son have been kidnapped."

"Mr. Wells, I think you want the FBI, not an attorney."

"Yes, of course, but I'm a rather well-known figure in the film industry, and I don't want to be on record as having called the police, if this should turn out to be a hoax. These things have a way of finding their way into the press, and that would be embarrassing for my wife and me."

"What would you like me to do, Mr. Wells?"

"I have homes in Santa Fe and in Malibu, but neither phone answers. Could you possibly go to my Santa Fe home and take a look around and call me if you find anything that might indicate that something untoward has occurred? And could you arrange to have someone in L.A. check the Malibu house?"

"Mr. Wells, it would be a lot cheaper just to call the police in Santa Fe and Malibu."

"I'm not concerned about your fees, Mr. Eagle. I know your reputation, and I would very much appreciate it if you would handle this for me."

Eagle took a deep breath and let it out. "All right, Mr. Wells. Please give me your Santa Fe address and tell me how to get into the house."

"The address is 180 Tano Norte. Do you know the road?"

The place was out past Susannah's house. "Yes, I know it. If no one answers the bell, how will I get in?"

"There's a rack holding half a cord of firewood to the right of the front door. There's a key under the left end of the rack."

"How about Malibu?"

"The house is in the Malibu Colony. You know it?"

"Yes."

"Your people should just ask for the Wells house at the gate and give the guard the password, which is Featherweight."

"Featherweight, all right."

"And the key is in a window box to the left of the front door."

"And how do I reach you?"

"You can call me at the Hassler, or you can reach me on my international cell phone." He recited the number.

"Mr. Wells, where would you expect your wife and son to be on this date?"

"I haven't spoken to them for a couple of days, but my wife had planned to fly from L.A. to Santa Fe for a few days. She just wasn't sure yet when she could get away."

"And to which address should I send my bill?"

"Please send that to my business manager, whose office is in Century City." He gave Eagle the address.

"One more thing, Mr. Wells: How would your wife and son be traveling from L.A. to Santa Fe?"

"I'm in a fractional jet program call NetJets, and we fly out of Santa Monica."

"Have you called them?"

"Not yet; I'd like to hear your report first."

"Can you give me a physical description of your wife and son?"

"My wife—her name is Donna—is forty-nine years old, five-seven, a hundred and forty pounds, blonde hair; my son is fourteen, about the same height as his mother, dark hair, a hundred and thirty pounds. His name is Eric. He's autistic."

"Is he in school somewhere?"

"No, his mother has home-tutored him, with the help of various teachers, since he was nine."

"How functional is he?"

"He doesn't talk much, but most people wouldn't know he was autistic on meeting him in our home, but he becomes anxious, if he's away from his mother or me, and then he can be difficult to deal with."

"I'll call you back when I know more," Eagle said. "Good-bye."

"Good-bye."

Eagle hung up and called Cupie Dalton's cell number.

"This is Dalton."

"Cupie, this is Ed Eagle. Are you still in L.A.?"

"Vittorio and I are on the way to the airport for a flight to San Francisco."

"I've got a detour for you," Eagle said, then explained what he wanted.

"Okay, we'll get a later flight to San Francisco." Cupie hung up.

Eagle looked at his watch, then got his coat and hat and walked out of his office. "I have to run an errand," he said to his secretary. "I'll be back in an hour or so."

CUPIE CLOSED HIS cell phone and turned to Vittorio, who was driving. "U-turn, pal."

"What's going on?"

"That was Eagle on the phone. He got a call from Rome from some guy named Wells, who says his wife and son may have been kidnapped. We have to go and check out his Malibu house for any evidence of same."

Vittorio shrugged. "Okay." He whipped the car around and gunned it.

"And let's not get arrested on the way."

"Aren't you carrying tin?"

"Yeah, but I don't like to use it with a cop for something as light as a speeding ticket."

Traffic was easy for L.A., and soon they were on the Pacific Coast Highway, heading north.

"You ever been out here?" Cupie asked, as they came to the long string of cheek-by-jowl beach houses that composed most of Malibu.

"No," Vittorio said. "With these houses jammed together like this, how does anybody get to the beach?"

"That's the idea," Cupie replied. "Nobody does, unless he has the keys to a house. Keeps out the riffraff. It's a long walk from the nearest public beach to out here."

"I thought all the beaches in California were public."

"There's public, and there's public."

They passed the turnoff for the little shopping center that passed for Downtown Malibu and soon turned off the highway into a driveway blocked by a guard shack and a bar across the drive. A uniformed guard stepped out of the shack and waited for them to come to a halt. For a moment he eyed the odd pair: a cherubic man in a seersucker suit and an Indian dressed in black. "Can I help you?" he asked.

Cupie flashed his LAPD badge, the slightly smaller version that retired cops toted. "We're here at Mr. Don Wells's request to inspect his property. The password is Featherweight."

The guard went back into the shack, checked something on a clipboard and pressed the button that raised the bar. He waved them on.

Vittorio followed Cupie's directions. "You been out to this place before?"

"A few times. These are some of the most expensive houses in the United States. Over there," he said, pointing at a large house that backed up onto the beach. "See the sign? Wells."

Vittorio pulled into the driveway. Cupie's car was a gray Ford Crown Victoria, chosen because it looked like an unmarked police car, just for occasions like this. Nobody was going to call the cops, if they thought the cops were already there.

Cupie found the key in the window box. He pulled a wad of latex gloves from a coat pocket and handed a pair to Vittorio. "Don't touch anything, even with these, unless you have to. We don't know what we're going to find, and if it's bad, we want to be investigators, not suspects."

Vittorio nodded.

Cupie unlocked the door and tapped the alarm code into the keypad. "Alarm was armed; that's a good sign." He led the way down a long entrance hall, more of a gallery, really, hung with a collection of abstract paintings. "Let's stick together," Cupie said, "and be careful."

"Come on, Cupie, you think I don't know how to deal with a crime scene?"

"Four eyes are better than two." Cupie produced a flashlight about four inches long. They walked into a large living room with glass sliding doors overlooking a porch and the beach at one end. The room was a good forty feet long, Cupie reckoned. "Great for entertaining a hundred and fifty of your closest friends, huh?"

"I could get my closest friends into a jail cell," Vittorio remarked. "This place looks like a platoon of maids just left."

Cupie used his flashlight to illuminate corners of the spotless room. He looked under sofas and chairs, too. Nothing in the living room. They moved into the next room, a library, with a spacious home office off one end. Nothing.

They retraced their footsteps and crossed the hall into a large dining room, then through a swinging door into a kitchen, appropriate for a large restaurant. The block holding all the kitchen knives was full—no empty spaces—and everything was perfectly neat.

"Upstairs," Cupie said. "Stay close to the wall, behind me, and don't touch the banister." There was a huge master suite upstairs that included two dressing rooms and two baths. Vittorio looked in the closets. They crossed the hall and walked into another bedroom.

"The kid's room," Cupie said, "but weird. No rock posters, no sports-team pennants. I've never seen a kid's room this neat."

Vittorio checked the closets, too. "This place is untouched by human hands," he said.

Cupie led him back downstairs and to the kitchen. "Guesthouse at the other end of the pool," he said. He opened a sliding glass door and walked the length of the fifty-foot pool. The front-door key worked in the guesthouse door, too. They found two bedrooms and a sitting room, and the place smelled a little musty, as if unused for a while. "Let's walk the perimeter of the property," Cupie said.

They did so, finding no footprints outside ground-level windows, no sign of forced entry. They reentered the house through the kitchen sliding door. Cupie called Ed Eagle's office.

"He's out for an hour or so," the secretary said.

Cupie thanked her, hung up and called Eagle's cell phone.

"Eagle," he said.

"We're in Malibu," Cupie said. "The house is clean as a whistle. Any criminals operating here had a lot of house-cleaning experience."

"Lock up and wait in your car to hear from me," Eagle said. "I'm almost to the Tano Norte house."

EAGLE PULLED INTO the driveway and stopped in front of the house. It was a typical Santa Fe home for an affluent family, he thought. Looked to be seven or eight thousand square feet, richly landscaped with native plants, guesthouse fifty yards down a flagstone path. He walked around the house and found nothing more surprising than a four-car garage, then he went back to the front door and found the house key under the firewood rack.

He rang the bell a couple of times and, getting no response, tried the front door, which turned out to be unlocked. The alarm system was not armed, either. "Hello!" he shouted, but got no answer. He turned right and came to the kitchen, a big room, with all the usual top-end appliances: SubZero fridge, Viking range, two Miele dishwashers. Not very different from his own kitchen, he thought.

He checked the dining room next door, then walked into the living room, which seemed to be in perfect order. He walked across a hallway to a large study, with many books on the shelves, then left it through another door and came to what seemed to be a wing of bedrooms.

Directly ahead of him was a set of large double doors. He opened one of the doors and stepped into the master suite. Immediately, he detected a familiar odor, but he couldn't place it. He stopped and thought about it, then it came to him.

It smelled like a butcher shop.

 EAGLE TRIED NOT to move his feet. He leaned over and looked into the bedroom. He could see the corner of the bed and a pair of feet, a woman's, with one shoe missing. He took a deep breath and walked into the room, keeping near the wall.

He stared at the bed for a long moment, until he was sure he had seen enough, then he retraced his steps and stood in the hall, taking deep breaths. When he had calmed himself, he went to his cell phone's address book and called the district attorney's direct office line.

"Bob Martínez."

"Bob, it's Ed Eagle. Write this down: I'm at 180 Tano Norte, that's the old County Road 85, renamed a few years ago, runs off Tano Road."

"I know it. What's up?"

"I had a phone call an hour or so ago from a man named Donald Wells, calling from Rome. He said he had had a phone call saying that his wife and son had been kidnapped, and he asked me to check it out."

"Did you call the police?"

"No, he didn't want that, unless something was confirmed."

"And . . . ?"

"And I'm at the house, and his wife and son are dead in the master suite. There's a lot of blood."

Martínez was not fazed. "Okay, call nine-one-one right now, and let's get this on the record. I'll be there soon." He hung up.

Eagle called 911 and answered the operator's list of questions, then he went outside and sat in a rocking chair on the front porch to wait for the police. His cell phone vibrated.

"Ed Eagle."

"Mr. Eagle, it's Don Wells. Your office gave me your cell phone number. I wanted you to know that I went downstairs and spoke with the manager, who spoke with the hotel telephone operator on duty. The call I got about the kidnapping came from my Santa Fe house."

"Tell me about the call."

"The phone rang, and I picked it up. There was a kind of click and I heard some sort of computer-generated voice, a recording, I guess. It said something like, 'We have your wife and son. Start raising five million dollars, and we will contact you about arranging payment. If you tell anyone about this, your wife and son will be killed.' Then there was another click, and the line went dead."

"Mr. Wells, are you sitting down?"

"Yes, I'm at the desk in my sitting room."

"I'm at your house now, and I'm sorry to tell you that your wife and son are dead."

There was a long silence, and when Wells spoke again his voice was unsteady and his breathing audibly shallow. "Are you sure about this?"

"I'm sorry, I am sure. I've called the police and the district attorney, and I'm waiting for them to arrive." Eagle heard the sound of a police whooper from somewhere up the road. "I can hear them coming."

"But why?" Wells said. "Why didn't they wait for the money? I would have given it to them."

Eagle thought he knew why, but he said, "I don't know at this point. It's important that you stay right where you are; the police will want to speak to you. Please don't leave your suite until you hear from me or the police, but you might ask the concierge to arrange travel for you to Santa Fe as soon as possible. I'll speak to you later to get your arrival time."

"All right," Wells said, sounding dejected but in control of himself. "Mr. Eagle, I want to retain you to represent me in all this."

"You have already done so, Mr. Wells. I'm very, very sorry for your loss. When you feel up to it, you might give some thought to any arrangements you want to make. My office will assist you."

"Thank you," Wells said softly, then hung up.

Eagle looked up to see two police cars and a van pull into the drive. He stood up to greet them. Before he could speak to the first officer, the district attorney's car drove in behind the other vehicles, and Bob Martínez got out.

EAGLE TOOK THEM through the house, following his original path, then he went back to the front porch and sat down again. A few minutes passed, then Martínez and a Detective Reese joined him, pulling up chairs.

"Take us through it from the first phone call," the detective said.

Eagle explained himself. "Right after I spoke to you, Bob, Wells called me on my cell phone. He checked with the hotel operator and learned that the kidnap threat call had come from this house. He said the voice was electronically altered and he was told to raise five million dollars. He was also told that if he called anybody, his wife and son would be killed. It occurs to me that, somehow, the perpetrators may have known that he made the call to me, and that's why the murders took place. I didn't mention this to him. I told him to stay in his suite and that the Santa Fe police would be in touch with him. I also told him to have his hotel make travel arrangements for him to come to Santa Fe."

"Please call him back, Mr. Eagle, and find out when he's due here, then let me speak to him," Detective Reese said.

"We'd better call from inside the house, so we can each be on an extension," Eagle said. "He's retained me to represent him, and I have to be present for any questioning."

"There are two phones in the study," Martínez said, "and we've already processed them and the one in the living room."

"Then let me speak to him first, and I'll tell you when he's ready to talk to you."

"All right," the detective said. "We'll wait in the living room."

Eagle went into the study, sat down at Wells's desk and got connected with Wells. "Mr. Wells, have you made travel arrangements?"

"Yes, I'll fly to New York tomorrow morning, change for Dallas, then for Albuquerque. My plane gets in at seven tomorrow evening." He gave Eagle the flight number.

"I'll have you met and brought to a hotel in Santa Fe."

"Can't I stay in my own home?"

"I'll try, but I doubt it. The police have a lot of work to do here, and the master suite is not habitable at the moment."

"Is that where they were killed?"

"Yes. The police want to speak with you now, but before I put them on the phone, I want you to think carefully: Is there anything you've failed to tell me that I might need to know?"

Wells seemed to reflect. "No, I don't think so."

"Mr. Wells, I must tell you that you will be the first suspect, until the police have been able to eliminate you as such."

"But how could I have anything to do with this? I'm in Rome!"

"Of course you are, but they will suspect you anyway; it's how they work, and you shouldn't be upset by it. Now, tell me, what was the state of your marriage?"

"We've been married for eight years," Wells said. "We are . . . were both very content with things, I think."

"You say 'content,' instead of 'happy.'"

"We were settled in for the long haul," Wells said.

"You said your son was fourteen."

"That's right."

"Then I take it, he was your stepson."

"Yes, but I loved the boy; it was no different than being his real father."

"I should contact the boy's biological father. Can you give me his name and number?"

"He's dead. He was killed in a street robbery in New York."

"How long ago?"

"About a year and a half before Donna and I were married, so between nine and ten years ago."

"Was the perpetrator caught?"

"No, I don't think so. The police said it was an ordinary mugging, gone wrong."

"Anything else you can tell me?"

"I can't think of anything."

"All right, I'm going to put a Detective Reese on the line. The district attorney will be listening on an extension, and so will I. If I interrupt you, shut up immediately, is that clear?"

"Yes, I understand."

"Confine your answers strictly to the questions asked; don't volunteer anything or any theories until you and I have discussed them privately first. I'll call the detective now." Eagle shouted for Reese to come in, then he listened on the extension while the detective questioned his client thoroughly. He did not find it necessary to interrupt.

When the phone call was over, Martínez came into the room. "Okay," he said, "we're done, I think."

"When can Mr. Wells have his house back?"

Reese spoke up. "We'll seal the master suite, and he can stay in another bedroom, if he wants."

"I'll ask him."

Reese left the room, and Martínez and Eagle were alone.

"You know who she was, don't you?" Martínez asked.

"Mrs. Wells?"

"She was Donna Worth. Worth Pharmaceuticals?"

"Ah," Eagle said.

"Five or six years ago, her father, the founder died, and she was his only heir."

"How much?

"Billions," Martínez said.

"I see."

"Do you?"

"Speak plainly, Bob."

"The boy was her only child. That means Wells is going to get the bulk of her estate. I mean, I'm sure there are charitable trusts and bequests, but Mr. Wells is going to be a very rich man."

"That's plain enough, Bob," Eagle said.

Reese came back into the room. "We found an open wall safe in Mr. Wells's dressing room, empty. I'd like to know what was in it when you speak to your client."

"I'll let you know," Eagle said.

 **16** Cupie Dalton and Vittorio arrived at the Four Seasons Hotel in San Francisco, having already checked into a less expensive hotel nearby. Cupie gave the doorman a peek at his badge. "Hi, there. I'm looking for a fellow named Walter Keeler, who checked in here yesterday."

"That an L.A. badge?" the doorman asked.

"Yep."

"Keeler checked out this morning."

"Bound for where?"

"I don't know. He and his lady friend left here in a car-service Mercedes this morning, and a couple of hours later he called and asked that their luggage be sent somewhere else. We loaded it into a van."

"And what would be that address? Another hotel?"

"Let me check with our dispatcher," the doorman said. He picked up a phone at the bell stand and spoke into it for a minute or so, then wrote something down in a notebook. He returned to Cupie, tore the page out of the pad and handed it to him. "That's it, and it's not a hotel."

Cupie glanced at the paper, then tucked it into a pocket and handed the doorman a twenty. "Thanks for your help," he said. The doorman put them into a cab, and ten minutes later they pulled up to the imposing entrance of a large, limestone-faced apartment building.

"There you are," the driver said.

Cupie and Vittorio got out of the cab and stood under the building's awning, since a light rain had begun to fall. A doorman approached.

"May I help you?" he asked, eyeing them suspiciously.

Cupie flashed his tin. "A Mr. Walter Keeler had his luggage sent to this building this morning. Is this an apartment hotel?"

"No," the doorman said, "it's an apartment house, and all the tenants own their apartments."

"Does Mr. Keeler own an apartment here?"

"I think you'd better speak to the super," the man replied. He went inside and made a phone call.

A moment later, a man in shirtsleeves came outside, wiping his mouth with a napkin. "Yes?"

"Sorry to interrupt your dinner," Cupie said, showing his badge. "Does a Mr. Walter Keeler own an apartment here?"

"Is this official business?"

"Let's say it's for the benefit of Mr. Keeler."

"This is a very prestigious building," the super said. "The management frowns on calls from the police. I'd like to cooperate, but . . ."

"We have no intention of disturbing the peace of your building," Cupie said. "I just need to know if Mr. Keeler owns an apartment here."

"Unofficially, yes," the super replied.

"Long time?"

"Since this morning. He and a woman arrived here and met a real estate agent at nine this morning. By noon, they had bought the apartment—the penthouse—moved in and were married by a judge."

Cupie blinked. "All in the space of three hours?"

"That's what I'm told."

"Told by who?"

"Various staffers. The apartment had been on the market for, maybe, forty-eight hours. It was sold furnished by the late owner's estate. Did you want to speak with Mr. Keeler?"

"Not at this time," Cupie said.

"That's good, because he left late this afternoon in a rented car that was delivered here."

"Bound for where?"

The super shrugged. "Who knows? He didn't share his travel plans with me, but he and Mrs. Keeler took luggage."

"Okay, thanks," Cupie said.

The super handed Cupie a card. "This is the management company's number. Any further information you'll have to get from them, and you and I never talked, okay?"

"Not only that, we never met," Cupie replied. The super returned to his dinner.

"Can I get you a cab?" the doorman asked.

"One more question: Do you know which rental car company delivered the car?"

"Hertz," the doorman replied. "I saw the contract folder when the guy handed it to Mr. Keeler." He blew his whistle and waved down a cab. "It was a Mercedes," he said, opening the cab's door.

Cupie gave him a twenty, and he and Vittorio got in. Cupie gave the driver the address of their hotel. "So," Cupie said to Vittorio, "these two people met after a few days, they flew from Palm Springs to Hayward and bought an expensive apartment, and got married the next day. That about it so far?"

"No," Vittorio said, speaking for the first time in an hour. "They went on a honeymoon, too, and not so far away that they'd need to fly. Where around San Francisco would they go on a honeymoon?"

Cupie thought. "Yosemite?"

"Not romantic enough. How about . . . what's the name of that town down the coast, with the crashing waves?"

"Carmel? Nah, that's a three- or four-hour drive; they'd have flown into Monterey."

"Where could they have gone that they could drive to by dinnertime?"

"The wine country," Cupie said. "Napa, maybe."

"Isn't there an airport at Napa?"

"Yeah, but why didn't Keeler land there?"

"Because he had to buy an apartment and marry Barbara. What are the most expensive hotels in Napa?"

"We'll have to get a guidebook," Cupie said. "There's a bookstore next to the hotel."

"I want a steak," Vittorio said.

"Me, too, but let's get a guide to Napa first."

EAGLE AND SUSANNAH had just finished dinner when his cell phone vibrated. "Eagle."

"It's Cupie. You sitting down?"

"Yes."

"Your ex-wife has remarried."

"What?"

"I kid you not; the girl is a fast worker. They arrived at the Four Seasons last night, and this morning Keeler bought a penthouse apartment in a top building. They were married by noon and drove away in a rented car late in the afternoon. My best guess is that they're honeymooning in the wine country to the north. You want me to track them down there or wait for them to return here? I don't think she's going to bother you for a few days, at least."

"No, Cupie, go home and find a way to keep tabs on Keeler from there—the FBO where he parks his airplane, somebody in the apartment building, whatever works. If they fly away from Hayward, I want to know."

"Right. We'll stay the night here, since we've already checked into a hotel, and fly home tomorrow."

"Tell him I'm coming home," Vittorio said.

"And Vittorio's coming back to Santa Fe."

"Send me a bill, Cupie. Good night." He hung up and turned to Susannah. "You're not going to believe this," he said.

BARBARA/ELLIE and Walter Keeler sat in the sunshine in the walled courtyard of Tre Vigne, a lovely Italian restaurant in the Napa Valley, and lunched on fruit, bread and cheese. Barbara felt two things: one, that her recovery from prison had been complete and spectacular, and two, that she had gotten more than lucky in meeting Walter Keeler. The man was an amazing list of all the things every woman wanted in a man: handsome, rich, sensitive, funny, warm and sexy. She wondered why she didn't love him.

She had felt the same way about Ed Eagle at first: that she *ought* to love him. She wondered, not for the first time, if there was something missing in her psychological makeup. She dismissed the idea, because she really had loved one man, her second husband. Of course, he had killed her first husband during the robbery of his diamond business and had sent her to prison with his testimony in the case. And him, she had loved!

Barbara knew she didn't have a conscience; they had told her that during psychological counseling in prison. But that didn't trouble her in the least. It allowed her to think only of herself and not feel bad about it. She knew that when Walter had outlived his usefulness she would dump him without a second thought, and that if he gave her a hard time about it, she would find a way to make him permanently sorry.

But for right now, Walter would do very nicely. He would feed, clothe and shelter her handsomely, introduce her to people and buy her anything she wanted. He was like a walking credit card with social entree and no charge limit. She smiled warmly at him.

"What are you thinking about?" Walter asked.

"Just about how improbably happy you've made me," she replied.

"That's my new job," he said, grinning. "What would you like to do this afternoon?"

"I'd like to visit some wineries," she said. "I've always thought that the making of wine was fascinating."

"Of course. Tell me, do you play golf?"

"I tried it once; I was hopeless at it."

"Everybody's hopeless at it in the beginning. I'd like you to try again, with a really good instructor. I'm a lover of the game, and it would please me greatly if we could play together."

"All right, I will." Anything to keep him happy for a while—at least until he signed his new will.

"I love you, my darling," he said.

"Not as much as I love you," she replied, squeezing his crotch under the table.

ED EAGLE STOOD on the first tee of one of the two golf courses at Las Campanas, a large real estate development outside Santa Fe, and read the list of his partners. The tournament was for the entertainment of the Santa Clara County, California, Bar Association, and a lawyer friend with whom he had done some business there had asked him to play. Eagle's playing partners had been chosen by lot, and now he was looking for them on the first tee. A man approached him.

"Ed Eagle?"

"Yes?"

"I'm Joe Wilen, one of your partners for the tournament." He extended a hand.

Eagle shook it. "Good to meet you, Joe. I was looking for you."

"The others are over here. We're fourth to tee off, I believe." Wilen lead him to where two other men were seated on a bench, waiting, and made the introductions.

The foursome waited their turn, then teed off. They passed the next four and a half hours playing the game they all loved and then settled into the bar at the clubhouse and ordered drinks.

"I've heard about you over the years," Joe Wilen said to Eagle. "You've had some impressive wins in California; I'm glad my company wasn't among your opponents."

"Company? Are you not in a firm, Joe?"

"Until recently I was general counsel for an electronics company. You're a pilot, I expect you've heard of it: Keeler Avionics?"

Eagle's heart skipped a beat. "Indeed, I have a panel full of your equipment in my airplane."

"What do you fly?"

"A JetProp—that's a Malibu that's had the piston engine ripped off and replaced with a turbine."

"Oh, yeah, I've seen a couple of them at my airport. I fly a King Air."

"Fine airplane. Tell me, how did you get involved with the Keeler outfit?"

"Oh, I met Walter Keeler right out of college—on a golf course, as it happened. When he formed the company he asked me to do the legal work, and after the business grew a bit, he invited me to become general counsel. I got in almost on the ground floor, and by the time Walter sold out, I was the second largest stockholder."

"Good for you. I read about the sale; that was a very nice payday."

"Indeed it was."

"I suppose you and Keeler are close."

"Very. I'm still his personal attorney, and I was just at his wedding."

"I heard something about that," Eagle said.

"You did?" Wilen asked, sounding surprised. "I didn't think anybody knew about it yet."

"Oh, word gets around."

"How long have you been in Santa Fe, Ed?"

"A little over twenty-five years."

"I'm very impressed with the place, and I was thinking about looking at some property."

"I'd be glad to introduce you to a good real estate agent, and if you decide to buy something I'd be pleased to handle the closing as a courtesy."

"That's very kind of you."

"Las Campanas is a good choice to buy or build," Eagle said, "especially if you want to play a lot of golf."

"I really like this course," Wilen said.

"It's one of two, and they're the best golf around here. There's a nice public course, and a nine-holer at another development."

"I like the idea of being out in the country, and the views are fantastic."

"Well, when your convention is over, why don't you stay on for a day or two, and I'll get an agent to set up some showings."

"Wonderful!"

"Buy or build?"

"Buy, I think. I'm too impatient to build."

"I'll work on it," Eagle said. I'll work on something else, too, he thought.

 EAGLE SAT BEFORE the fire in the lobby of the Inn of the Anasazi, a luxurious small hotel just off the Plaza, across the street from the old territorial governor's mansion, and waited for Donald Wells to arrive from Albuquerque Airport in the car Eagle had sent for him.

At the stroke of nine, a man walked into the lobby, followed by a bellman and his luggage. He was a little over six feet tall, slender and well dressed in a casual way.

"Don Wells?" Eagle asked.

"Yes," Wells said, offering his hand.

"I'm Ed Eagle. Have you had dinner yet?"

"No, and I'm starved."

"Why don't you check in and get freshened up, then meet me in the dining room. We can talk for a bit."

"Thank you, I'd like that. Will you order something for me? I eat anything."

"Of course. Would you like a drink?"

"Chivas on the rocks, please."

———

WELLS APPEARED, looking refreshed, a few minutes later, and Eagle signaled the waiter to bring their drinks.

"I expect you're tired," Eagle said. "I won't keep you long."

"Not too tired," Wells replied. "I had last night in New York, and I got some sleep."

"Our food will be along shortly. I want to bring you up to date on events since we last talked."

"Please do," Wells said, sipping his scotch.

"The medical examiner has issued his report. It's pretty simple: both your wife and son were killed by two .380-caliber, hollow-point gunshots to the head. They didn't suffer."

"Thank God for small favors," Wells said.

"They had probably been dead for one to two hours when I arrived."

"That means they were probably killed shortly after I received the phone call in Rome."

"Correct. Your hotel was right; the phone call you received in Rome was from the phone in your home, probably the one in the study, since that extension had been wiped clean of any fingerprints."

"Any sign of how they got in?"

"When I arrived, the front door was unlocked, and the alarm system was not armed."

"That's the way my wife would have kept the front door and alarm system during the day; she would have locked the doors and set the alarm at bedtime."

Their food arrived.

"Something the police want to know, and so do I: A safe in your dressing room was open and empty. Had there been anything in it?"

"That's odd," Wells said. "How could they have known the combination?"

"Why do you say, 'they'?"

"Just a general pronoun. I suppose there might only have been one man . . . person."

"What was in the safe?"

"Twenty-five thousand dollars in cash and an equal amount in Krugerrands."

"Why?"

"Call it mad money, in case of some catastrophe: nuclear bomb, terrorist attack, whatever. There's an equal amount in my safe in Malibu. I guess I'm a little paranoid."

"Back to the combination of the safe: How would they have opened it?"

Wells looked baffled. "I don't know. Safecracker, maybe? The safe cost less than a thousand dollars; it was meant to be fireproof and burglarproof, but I don't suppose it would stand up to a professional safecracker."

"What is the combination?"

"It's an electronic keypad; the combination was DWELLS."

"Not very smart," Eagle said.

Wells looked sheepish. "It was the first six letters I thought of, I guess."

"Then they could have just guessed and got lucky."

"I suppose."

"Did your wife know the combination?"

"Yes."

"More likely they pointed a gun at your son and demanded the combination from your wife."

"She would certainly have given it to them, in those circumstances."

"Mr. Wells . . ."

"Don, please."

"Don, did your wife have a will?"

"Yes. Both her will and mine are in my safe in Malibu."

"Have you read it?"

"No; both wills are in sealed envelopes."

"Are you familiar with the terms of her will?"

"Only what she told me: that she had made a large bequest to her family's charitable foundation and some other, smaller bequests to distant relatives, servants, that sort of thing. Then there would have been a large bequest to a trust for our son, to ensure that he had a home and proper care. I think I told you, he's . . . was autistic."

"Is there a bequest to you in the will?"

"Yes, but I don't know of what size."

"Your wife, I understand, was a very wealthy woman."

"Yes, she was; her great-grandfather established a pharmaceutical company in the late nineteenth century. It was a private company, until after her father's death some years ago; it was taken public, then she gradually liquidated her holdings."

"What was she worth?"

"I don't really know, but I think, probably, some hundreds of million dollars."

"I have to ask you some other questions now, and please don't take offense; this is absolutely necessary, and the district attorney is going to want them answered, too."

"Go ahead. I'll tell you whatever you want to know."

"What is your own net worth, Don, separate from your wife's?"

"Well, we owned the two houses together, so half of the value of those, I guess. Maybe twenty million dollars. Then I have some investments, probably another three million, plus other possessions. Maybe a total of twenty-five million dollars? I can have my business manager put together a financial statement, if you like."

"Please do so tomorrow and have it faxed to my office. Now, who paid for the two houses?"

"My wife did; she insisted. While I'm very well off and could have afforded to buy the Santa Fe house, I could not have afforded the Malibu Colony house. She chose them both and bought them."

"But they were put in both your names."

"Yes, that's how she wanted it."

"What sort of income do you earn from your film business? An average for the last five years, or so?"

"Let's see: probably an average of two and a half, three million dollars. I have prospects for a lot more in the future."

"Will your wife's death affect your income?"

"No. She had no interest in my business. She loaned me the money to get it started, and I repaid her."

"I assume you can substantiate that."

"Of course. My business manager has copies of all the documents."

"I'll want to see those, too," Eagle said. "One more question, then I'll let you get to bed, and I need a perfectly honest answer. Remember, this is a privileged conversation."

"Shoot."

"Are you now having or have you ever had an affair outside your marriage?"

"I've slept with a few women, mostly minor actresses or crew on my pictures. Nothing serious, ever."

"Define *serious*."

"Serious enough to make me think of leaving my wife."

"I warn you, Don, if you are being less than frank with me, it will come back and bite you on the ass."

"I'm being perfectly frank with you," Wells said.

Eagle thought he believed the man.

"Good. We have an appointment at nine tomorrow morning in my office with the district attorney, Roberto Martínez, and a Detective Reese. You'll give a formal statement along the lines of our previous conversations on the phone and tonight. I'll pick you up out front at eight forty-five."

"Fine."

**19** IT WAS NEARLY Eagle's bedtime when he got home, and Susannah was already asleep in his bed, but there was something on his mind, and he had to deal with it.

He went to his study and switched on the computer, then opened his word-processing program and began to write.

To Walter Keeler:

Dear Mr. Keeler,

> *You and I are not acquainted, but I am in possession of some informa-*
> *tion which I feel you should have. I met Joe Wilen on the golf course today*
> *in Santa Fe, and during our conversation later at the clubhouse, he told me*
> *that you and he had been business associates and that he is your personal*
> *attorney. I thought it would be better if I asked him to deliver this letter than*
> *if I simply sent it to you. I have not, however, discussed its contents with*
> *him. I have told him only that it concerns the woman you recently married.*
> *The following is everything that I know of her.*

She was born Hannah Schlemmer, in Cleveland, Ohio, one of three daughters, to a Jewish pawnbroker. As an adult she moved to New York City and worked in a restaurant there. At some point she married a diamond wholesaler named Murray Rifkind, and she worked for some time at running his office.

She subsequently met a man named James Grafton and fell in love with him, apparently her first time. Grafton had a criminal background, and he convinced her that the only way they could be together was for him to rob Rifkind's business premises. She went to the office and used her knowledge of its security systems to admit him for the robbery. Grafton then shot and killed her husband. She was shocked, she said, but he forced her to come with him to Miami, where he liquidated the diamonds he had stolen.

Shortly after that, they were both arrested. Hannah then agreed to cooperate with the prosecution and testified against Grafton. She pled to involuntary manslaughter and received a sentence of five to eight years in a women's prison near Poughkeepsie, New York. During this time, I visited her in connection with a double murder in a client's home in Santa Fe, involving her older sister, Miriam, who had changed her name to Julia. Hannah would ordinarily have been considered for parole after three years served, but as a result of a lawsuit against the State of New York alleging prison overcrowding, she was released early and unconditionally. While in prison, she legally changed her name to Barbara Kennerly.

Shortly after her release, Barbara came to Santa Fe and contacted me. I helped her find employment, and we began to see each other socially. A romance developed, and we were married a year later.

We had been married for a year when I awoke one morning to find that I had been drugged the night before and that Barbara had left Santa Fe after emptying my bank accounts of an amount exceeding a million dollars and wire-transferred the funds to a Cayman Islands bank and thence to one in Mexico City. She also attempted to empty my brokerage accounts, but I was able to prevent that minutes before the broker would have wired the proceeds.

I hired a former IRS agent, specializing in forensic financial work, who was able to recover all but $300,000 of the funds. I also hired two private investigators to go to Mexico and try to persuade Barbara to sign divorce papers and a settlement agreement giving her the $300,000. She shot one of the investigators and pushed the other off a ferry in the Gulf of Cortez. Both recovered. My investigators learned during this period that Barbara and her sister, Julia, by then deceased, were being sought by the Mexican police on a charge of having cut off the penis of a man they said was trying to rape them.

Barbara eluded my investigators and crossed the border into California, where she hid in a well-known spa in La Jolla and had her appearance altered. She came to Los Angeles and saw me in the dining room of the Hotel Bel-Air. Because of the changes in her appearance, I did not recognize her.

Later that night, she drugged the man she was staying with, returned to the hotel and went to the suite where she and I had stayed a number of times while we were married. Unfortunately, the suite was occupied by another couple, and she shot both of them in their sleep, then returned to her friend's house. The following morning, he did not realize that she had left the house.

She was later arrested and tried for the two murders. While waiting for the verdict and fearing conviction, she escaped from a courthouse conference room and, with the help of a friend, made her way to the El Rancho Encantado Spa. She had, by this time, bought a forged driver's license and passport in the name of Eleanor Wright. Ironically, she was acquitted at trial, due to the testimony of her friend, who placed her in his home at the time of the murders. It was at this point you made her acquaintance.

I know that all this will come as a shock to you, because Barbara is a very convincing liar. It will seem strange to you, as it does to me, that, having been released from prison and being comfortably married, she would then decamp with my funds and be willing to kill, both to avoid being detained and to take some sort of revenge against me. A psychiatrist friend of mine who knew her says that she is certainly a sociopath and may be a paranoid schizophrenic, a dangerous one. Perhaps it runs in her family, because her older sister murdered three people, one of them her youngest sister.

I tell you these things simply as a matter of conscience, because I believe that you may well be at considerable personal risk. I have no other motive.

My address and phone number are on my letterhead, should you wish to contact me. In the meantime, I hope you will take steps to protect yourself and your property.

Sincerely,

Ed Eagle

Eagle signed the letter, put it into an envelope and sealed it, then he went to bed and slept well.

THE FOLLOWING MORNING, Eagle picked up Donald Wells at his hotel and drove him the short distance to his law office. They parked in the underground garage and took the elevator to Eagle's seventh-floor penthouse offices.

He took Wells into his private office, sat him down and gave him coffee. "Don," he said, "I want you to answer the questions of Martínez and Reese fully, but don't overdo it; that would make you appear nervous and not credible. Answer only the questions they ask; don't volunteer anything. If they fail to ask some question I deem important to your status, I will ask the question. They will record your answers, and they may well videotape you, as well. Do you have any objections to that?"

"No, none at all," Wells replied. He seemed perfectly relaxed.

Eagle's secretary came into the office with a courier package, and he opened it. "Ah, here are the documents concerned with your business setup and your financial statement." He handed the statement to Wells. "Does this seem correct to you?"

Wells looked it over while Eagle reviewed the business documents.

"Yes, it does."

"Then sign it at the bottom." Eagle had his secretary come in and notarize it. "Mr. Martínez and Mr. Reese are here," she said, "and they have some sort of technician with them."

"Please send them in," Eagle said. He stood and greeted the men and offered them coffee while the technician set up a video camera and fitted everyone with microphones.

"Are we ready?" Martínez asked.

"Perfectly," Eagle replied.

Martínez nodded to the technician to start the camera, which was pointed at Wells. Martínez noted the date and time, then began. "This is the recorded statement of Donald Wells as to the facts surrounding the death of his wife and son. Present are Mr. Wells, his attorney, Ed Eagle, Detective Alex Reese and myself, Roberto Martínez, district attorney of Santa Fe County. Mr. Wells, are you aware that your voice and image are being recorded?"

"Yes, I am."

"Do we have your permission to record this interview?"

"Yes."

Martínez read Wells his rights and produced a Bible and swore him in. "Now, Mr. Wells, please give us an account of your actions from the time you first heard of the kidnapping of your wife and son."

Wells went through his story in a lucid fashion, interrupted only occasionally by questions from Martínez and Reese.

"What did you do after you received the phone call saying your wife and son had been kidnapped?"

"I called the house and got no answer, then I called Mr. Eagle and asked him to go to the house and check it out. I gave him directions on where to find a key, and I also gave him the alarm code."

"For the record," Eagle said, "when I arrived at the house, the front door was unlocked and the alarm had not been armed."

"My wife would normally only lock the door and arm the alarm if she was going out or before retiring at night."

Martínez questioned Wells about the contents of his safe, which had been found open, and he replied fully.

"Our theory," Eagle said, "is that the perpetrators threatened the boy, in order to get the combination from Mrs. Wells."

Martínez nodded. "It strikes me as a very good way to give a hired killer an instant payoff," he said.

"That is a conclusion not supported by the facts," Eagle said.

"I had nothing whatever to do with the death of my wife and son," Wells said.

"Then perhaps you can tell me why a kidnapper, facing the prospect of a five-million-dollar profit, would immediately murder his hostages for a fifty-thousand-dollar payoff?"

Wells shrugged. "Maybe he got cold feet, and when he found the contents of the safe, decided to settle for that."

"I should point out, Bob," Eagle said, "that the collection of a ransom is a very high-risk activity for the perpetrator, offering multiple opportunities to be caught, whereas the taking of the cash and gold coins held the promise of a higher level of safety."

"But then why would he kill the woman and the boy?"

"Kidnappers," Eagle said, "historically decide early in their planning whether to kill the hostages or free them after the ransom has been collected. This particular perpetrator obviously traded their lives for his own safety."

"Did your wife have a will, Mr. Wells?"

"Yes, she did."

"Are you aware of its provisions?"

"Only in a general sense, from what she told me. Both our wills were executed on the same day, placed in envelopes that were sealed by the attorneys, then placed in my safe in Malibu."

"And what was your understanding of the benefits of the will with regard to yourself?"

"She mentioned nothing in that regard."

"Was it your assumption that she would leave you a large bequest?"

"We never discussed it; her money was not a factor in our marriage."

"A national magazine has ranked your wife as the fifth wealthiest woman in the United States," Martínez said, "with a net worth in the billions."

"She laughed at that when she heard," Wells said.

Eagle spoke up. "Mrs. Wells did loan Mr. Wells the money to set up what has become a successful film company, and he repaid the loan. Here are copies of the relevant documents and a notarized copy of Mr. Wells's personal financial statement, as prepared by his business manager. As you will see, he has a net worth of some twenty-five million dollars, which does not include Mrs. Wells's share of their two homes, which would normally accrue to him upon her death. He earns a multimillion-dollar income from his film company, as well, so he would have no financial motive against his wife."

"I think we'll decide that after seeing Mrs. Wells's will."

"We will be happy for Mr. Wells to authorize his attorneys to give you a copy of the will, even though we do not know its contents."

"How soon?" Martínez asked.

"I'll call them today," Wells replied.

"What else can we do for you, Bob?" Eagle asked.

Martínez looked at Reese, who shook his head.

"Have his attorneys fax me the will," Martínez said, handing Eagle his card. "That will be all for the present."

"Bob," Eagle said, "is Mr. Wells a suspect in this case?"

"Let's just say that he remains a person of interest," Martínez replied.

"I would prefer it if you would couch that in more positive terms when you speak to the press," Eagle said.

"I'll just say that Mr. Wells has not been charged. Will he be available in Santa Fe if we have further questions?"

Eagle looked at his client. "Don?"

"My wife expressed a wish to be cremated and have her ashes scattered on our property in Santa Fe," Wells said. "I can stay for a few more days, until that is accomplished, but then I must return to Los Angeles for business reasons. I have just finished shooting a film in Rome, and I must begin the postproduction process, if I am to make our release date."

"When will the bodies be released?" Eagle asked.

"Today, I should think. All right, Mr. Wells, you may return to Los Angeles, but I would be grateful if you would be available by telephone."

"Of course," Wells said, handing Martínez his card. "And I want to say how grateful I am for your and Detective Reese's efforts in the solution of this crime."

Everyone shook hands cordially, and the visitors left.

"What do you think?" Wells asked when they were gone.

"You did well," Eagle said.

"They didn't ask whether I was having an affair, as you did."

"Don't worry, they'll ask everybody else you know."

"Do you think I'm a suspect?"

"Right now, you're the *only* suspect."

21 EAGLE SPENT THE remainder of the morning working on briefs and meeting with clients. Just before lunch he had a phone call from Joe Wilen.

"Good morning, Joe."

"Morning, Ed. I've decided to take you up on your offer to introduce me to a real estate agent."

"I'd be delighted to. What is your cell phone number?"

Wilen gave it to him.

"You'll hear from an agent with French and French, named Ashley Margetson. She has an outstanding knowledge of the market, and I'm sure she can show you properties that will interest you."

"I'll wait for her call," Wilen said.

BARBARA/ELLIE WIPED Walter Keeler's genitals with a hot face-cloth, eliciting a happy groan, then pulled the sheet up to his chin. She walked outside, sat down and used her cell phone to call Jimmy Long.

"Hello?"

"It's Barbara."

"Eleanor! How are you? Your car arrived a few days ago. What was that all about?"

"I flew off to San Francisco with a gentleman," she said.

"That was fast work."

"You heard I was acquitted, that I'm a free woman?"

"I did."

"I'm sticking with the Eleanor Wright identity, though. Will you go see our friend in Venice and tell him I need a certified copy of my birth certificate? I want to get a real passport and driver's license."

"Sure, babe."

"I'll reimburse you, of course."

"Don't worry about it. I just turned my new film over to the studio and got a very nice check. What do you want me to do with your stuff?"

"Get rid of it all. Sell the car and keep the money. That will make us more than even. Give the clothes to the Salvation Army or something; I already have a new wardrobe."

"You never cease to amaze me."

"Are you sitting down? Stand by to be further amazed: I was married in San Francisco the day before yesterday."

"Holy shit! Are you kidding me?"

"I kid you not. I am, at the moment, on my honeymoon at a beautiful hotel in the Napa Valley."

"Who's the lucky guy?"

"His name is Walter Keeler."

"Hang on. I know that name, don't I? From the *Wall Street Journal*, maybe?"

"You have a good memory, my dear. He sold his company—Keeler Avionics—a while back?"

"God, yes, I remember. He walked away with a bundle of money, didn't he?"

"He walked away with a busload of money."

"Man, you are something else!"

"We have a new apartment in San Francisco; got a pencil?" She gave him the address and phone number. "I'll let you know when I get a new cell phone."

"Well, baby, I hope this doesn't mean we can't fuck each other from time to time."

"From time to time," she said, laughing. "I won't forget you."

"I'll send you the pink slip for the car to sign, so I can sell it."

"You can mail me the birth certificate, too, and as soon as possible, please. I have to run now, sweetie, but I'll be in touch."

"I'll send you the birth certificate pronto. Take care!"

She hung up and sighed. Soon she would be legally documented again, and there would be no stopping her.

A DAY AFTER Joe Wilen's call, Eagle received another.

"Hello, Joe."

"Ed, I found a place, and it's just perfect. I talked it over with my wife, and she's all for it, so I want to proceed to closing. The house is empty, and it's all cash, so I guess all I need is a title search."

"Give me the details, and I'll get that taken care of immediately. When do you want to close?"

"Do you think we can do it tomorrow? I want to get it done before my wife has second thoughts."

"Tell Ashley to set it up at my office late tomorrow afternoon, and you'll be home in that King Air by bedtime."

"Will do."

Eagle noted the details of the property, gave Wilen his account number for wiring closing funds and said good-bye. He called the title company and got the search started; they would do it quickly for him.

THE FOLLOWING DAY, Ellie and Walter were having lunch at Galiano Vineyards with the owner, Emilio Galiano, an old friend of Walter's. He made some of the best wines in Napa, wines that people lined up to buy well in advance of their general release.

"I must say, Walt," Emilio said, "you have outstanding taste in wives."

"You bet your ass I do," Walter replied.

"You're sweet, Emilio," Barbara said. "Walt, what would you think of buying a little vineyard in Napa? Wouldn't that be fun?"

"Fun?" Galiano asked. "It's bloody hard work, is what it is."

"I've been trying for years to get Emilio to sell to me," Walter said, "but he enjoys teasing me too much about how willing he is to sell."

"I'm not playing with you," Emilio said. "I might just sell. You know, I've been training my winemaker for eight vintages now, and he's very, very good."

Walter sniffed his glass and tasted the wine. "I cannot but agree. Your kids aren't really interested in running the place, are they, Emilio?"

"Well, the girls are busy raising my grandchildren, and I have no sons, so . . ."

"Name a figure," Walter said. To his surprise, Emilio named a figure.

Walter made a sucking sound through his teeth. "Woooo . . . you really think it's worth that much, Emilio?"

"I've been thinking about it, and I do, Walt. Of course, that includes the acreage and the house. Besides which, I wouldn't sell it for less. That price is only for you, because I know you won't kick me out of my winery until you've sucked me dry of knowledge about how to run the place."

"What do you think, Ellie?" Walter asked.

"You and Emilio know best," she said. "I have no inkling of what the place is worth."

Walter reached into a pocket of his jacket, which was hanging on his chair, and produced a checkbook. He wrote a check, handed it to Emilio and held out his hand.

Emilio feigned a coronary. "You mean it?"

"I'll need a day to move enough money into my checking account before you cash the check. The lawyers can close later."

Emilio looked at the check again, then reached across the table and shook Walter's hand. "Done," he said. He took Ellie's hand and kissed it. "The new mistress of Galiano Vineyards," he said.

"Of Galiano-Keeler Vineyards," Walter corrected.

"As you wish," Emilio said, smiling.

No, Barbara thought, as *I* wish. This said to her that Walter would do anything she asked of him as long as she kept him happy. And now she was in the wine business.

 EAGLE PUT A stack of documents on his conference table and began handing them, one at a time, to Joe Wilen for his signature. When that was finished, the seller signed everything, and Eagle presented him with a cashier's check for the selling price, less the real estate agent's commission, a check for which he handed to Ashley Margetson.

"Congratulations, Joe," Eagle said. "I admire your approach to buying property."

"I would have been a lot more reticent if Ashley hadn't shown me the perfect house," Wilen said.

"Joe, may I speak to you privately for a moment?"

"Of course."

The two men said good-bye to the seller and the agent, then sat down on Eagle's sofa. "Joe, I would be grateful if you would deliver a confidential letter to Walter Keeler."

"A letter from whom?"

"From me."

"On what subject?"

"I'll tell you only that it concerns his wife and that he should read it before he makes a new will."

"I'll need to know more than that, Ed."

Eagle shook his head. "I've told Keeler in the letter that you are not privy to its contents. If he wants you to read it, that's fine with me."

Wilen shrugged. "All right, I'll deliver your letter."

Eagle took the envelope from his jacket pocket and handed it to Wilen. "I'm grateful to you, and I believe Keeler will be, too."

"Walt has already given me notes for a new will; I have an associate drawing it in my absence, and Walt is supposed to sign it as soon as I get home."

"Then I'm in time," Eagle said. He stood up and offered his hand to Wilen. "I'll look forward to seeing you and your wife when you move into your new house," he said. "You must come for dinner."

Wilen shook his hand. "Thank you, Ed, and thank you again for handling this closing with such dispatch."

"It was my pleasure." Eagle watched Wilen leave his offices and hoped to God that he would keep his word and deliver the letter.

THE FOLLOWING DAY, having returned to San Francisco with his new wife, Walter Keeler drove down to Palo Alto for the day to see his lawyer and to pack up some of his belongings there to move to the new apartment, so Eleanor had a day to herself. She used her new birth certificate and marriage certificate to obtain a driver's license in the name of Eleanor Keeler, then had photos taken and hired an expediting service to obtain a passport for her.

She spent the rest of her day doing some serious shopping for her new wardrobe, taking pleasure in buying the best of everything with her new American Express card.

WALTER KEELER STOOD in his old home and pointed at things for the movers to take to the San Francisco apartment. Except for his clothes, papers, books and pictures, he would sell the house furnished. When the movers had left, he took one last look around the place, then left and drove to his lawyer's office.

Joe Wilen greeted him warmly. "Just got back from Santa Fe last night," he said, "and I bought a house there."

"That's great; it's a beautiful place," Keeler replied. "You know, Joe, you should sell the King Air and make the jump to a jet. I'm moving up to something with transatlantic range; why don't you buy my CitationJet? It's actually easier to fly than your King Air."

"Walt, that's a damned good idea," Wilen said. Keeler named a very low price, and Wilen agreed. "I'll need to get signed up for the training right away," he said.

"Why wait? The airplane is at Hayward, but I'll have it flown over to San Jose for you tomorrow. You can have my hangar rental, too; I'm building something bigger."

Wilen buzzed his secretary and asked her to cut a check for the airplane and to download the FAA registration forms from the Internet. "We'll wrap it up now," he said to Keeler.

"Good for you, Joe! It's a beautiful airplane; you'll enjoy it."

"The house is not far from the first tee at a development called Las Campanas. Maybe I'll whittle down my handicap, who knows?"

"Oh, I almost forgot," Keeler said. "I've bought Emilio Galiano's vineyard and winery in Napa."

"Wow! I thought he would never sell."

"That's what I thought, too, but I guess I caught him at a weak moment. I asked him to name his price, and he did. I gave him a personal check, so will you move the funds from my investment account and close the deal for me? You have my power of attorney." He jotted down the figure and handed Wilen the paper.

"Sure, I'll move the money right now. Any preference on what to sell?"

"You figure it out, Joe; you know I hate to deal with that stuff."

"Okay, there's enough in your tax-free municipals fund." He buzzed his secretary and gave her instructions for wiring the funds to Keeler's checking account, and when she brought in the form, he signed it and told her to fax it immediately.

Wilen opened an envelope on his desk and set a sheaf of papers before him. "Here's your new will. Are you ready to sign it?"

"Yes, I am."

Wilen handed him the will. "Please read it first."

Keeler read through the new will. "Joe, do you think I should make Eleanor my executor? I mean, I know you'll do a fine job, but shouldn't she have that power?"

"Do you think she has the knowledge and organizational ability to deal with a complex estate like yours?"

"You have a point, Joe. I don't know."

"Then perhaps it would be best to leave things as they are. I'll certainly do everything possible to look out for her interests."

"Of course you will, Joe, and I trust you implicitly. Shouldn't you get some witnesses in here, before I sign this thing?"

"I have one other duty to you first," Joe said. "Have you heard of a Santa Fe lawyer called Ed Eagle?"

"Yes, I believe I have. Didn't he win that big judgment against one of my competitors a while back?"

"That's the fellow. I met him when I was in Santa Fe. We were partners in a golf tournament, and he was kind enough, when I expressed an interest in buying a house there, to introduce me to an agent. He also handled the closing. I liked him very much, and he's certainly a fine lawyer."

"I'm sure he is, but what does he have to do with your duty to me?"

Wilen took a sealed envelope from a desk drawer and pushed it across the desk to Keeler. "He asked me to personally deliver this letter to you."

Keeler looked at the envelope but didn't pick it up. "What is this, some business deal?"

"No, it's not that. He declined to tell me anything about what's in his letter, except that it concerns your wife."

"Ellie? Does he know her?"

"I don't know, but he said it was important that you read it before signing a new will."

"How did he know I would be signing a new will?"

"He knew that you had remarried, so I assume he thought that you would, in the normal course of things, make a new will."

"I'm not sure I like the idea of a lawyer I don't know writing me letters about my wife," Keeler said.

"My impression was that he believed he was acting in your interests."

"You said he didn't tell you what was in the letter; how do you know he's acting in my interests?"

"That was just my impression of his intent. He said that he didn't mind if you told me what was in the letter, but he wouldn't tell me himself."

"Joe, my interests and those of my wife are one and the same," Keeler said. He picked up Eagle's unopened envelope, walked across the room and fed it into Wilen's shredder, then he came back and sat down. "Now," he said, "let's get those witnesses in here."

Wilen called in his secretary and two associates and watched as Keeler signed the will and the three witnesses added their signatures.

"That's it," Wilen said. "Do you want the original or a copy? I can keep the original in my safe, if you like."

"Do that, Joe, and give me a copy for Ellie."

Wilen sent the will to be copied. Shortly, his secretary returned with the copy of the will and the FAA documents and check for the

CitationJet. Wilen signed the check, and Keeler signed the transfer of the registration.

Keeler stood up. "Joe, will you deposit the check for the airplane in my account here for me?"

"Of course. I'll send my secretary to the bank now."

Keeler stuck out his hand. "Thank you, Joe. You're a good lawyer and a good friend."

Wilen shook his hand and watched his friend leave. He wondered what the hell had been in Ed Eagle's letter.

 WALTER KEELER GOT into his rented Mercedes and tossed the envelope containing the copy of his will onto the passenger seat. He pulled out of the building's garage, switched on the radio to a local classical music station and started north on Highway 101, Mozart caressing his ears. He had just passed through Fair Oaks when a report came over the radio of an accident on the San Mateo–Hayward Bridge that was backing up traffic for miles, south of San Mateo. He saw Woodside Road coming up and knew that it would take him to I-280, so he made a left, congratulating himself on saving a lot of time.

Once on I-280, driving north in fairly heavy traffic, he took his cell phone from its holster, called the management company that took care of his airplane at San Jose Airport and asked for the manager.

"Hello, Ralph, it's Walter Keeler. How are you?"

"Just fine, Mr. Keeler. What can I do for you?"

"I've just sold my airplane to my friend Joe Wilen. You know him, don't you?"

"Of course. We take care of his King Air."

"Well, he's going to be selling it, because I've just sold him my CitationJet."

"Congratulations to you both. I hope I'm not losing a customer."

"No, I'm moving up to a larger airplane, so I'll still be around. The CitationJet is over at Hayward right now. Can you send a pilot over there to fly it back to San Jose?"

"Sure. I'll have somebody over there first thing tomorrow morning."

"I think Joe is going to want my hangar, but you can talk with him about that."

"Be glad to. Anything else I can do for you?"

"That's it, Ralph. See you soon." As Keeler closed the cell phone it vibrated in his hand. He looked down at the screen to see who was calling. It was Ellie. He flipped it open again. "Hi, there," he said.

"And hi to you. Where are you?"

"I'm on the way back to San Francisco. I had to leave 101 because of an accident on the San Mateo Bridge, so I'm on I-280 now, and the traffic's okay, so I should be home in an hour or so."

"That's good. I'll have a drink waiting for you."

"I'll see you . . ." Keeler looked up and saw something he couldn't believe: a tanker truck had jackknifed in the oncoming lane and had crossed the median, traveling sideways. "Oh, shit!" he yelled, a second before he and the car next to him struck the tanker.

Ellie listened in disbelief as the noise of the explosion came over the cell phone, a split second before it went dead. She stood on the terrace, the phone in her hand, wondering what to do. She went into Walter's study, found his address book, called Joe Wilen's office and asked to be put through to him.

"Hello, Ellie?"

"Joe, I've just been on the phone with Walt, and I think he's been in an accident."

"Where is he?"

"On I-280, somewhere south of San Francisco."

"That makes sense, I guess. Why do you think he's been in an accident?"

She told him about their interrupted conversation.

"Are you at home?"

"Yes."

"Let me make a call, and I'll get right back to you."

"All right."

Wilen hung up, went to his computer address book and dialed the direct number of the commander of the California State Highway Patrol in Sacramento. The man answered immediately.

"Colonel, it's Joe Wilen."

"Hello, Joe."

"I believe Walter Keeler may have been in an accident on I-280 North, south of San Francisco. Do you know anything about that?"

"Hang on a minute," he replied, then put Wilen on hold.

Joe sat, tapping his foot, hoping that this was all some mistake.

The colonel came back on the line. "Joe, switch on your TV."

Wilen switched on the flat-screen television in his office and tuned to a local channel. He found himself watching a helicopter shot of an enormous fire on the interstate. "Jesus Christ!" he said.

"That's on I-280," the colonel said. "I'll call our nearest station personally and find out if Walter's mixed up in that."

"Thank you, Colonel." He gave the man his office and cell numbers, then he called Ellie. "I've spoken with the highway patrol commander in Sacramento, and there's a huge fire on I-280. Turn on your TV set." He waited for her to come back.

"I see it, Joe. Don't tell me Walter is involved in *that*."

"I don't know, but Walter is a big contributor to the governor's campaigns, and the colonel knows it. We'll find out as soon as possible. I'll call you back."

ELLIE SAT AND watched the fire on the TV. "I hope to God Walter signed that will," she said.

AN HOUR PASSED before the phone rang again in Joe Wilen's office. "Hello?"

"It's Colonel Thompson. Do you know what kind of car Mr. Keeler was driving?"

"It was a rental," Wilen said. "He was moving from Palo Alto to San Francisco today, and he drove down from San Francisco. I expect it was a Mercedes, because when he rented, that's what he always asked for. I don't know the color."

"The color isn't important anymore," the colonel replied. "There was a Mercedes smack in the middle of that conflagration. The fire's out, now, and they're removing bodies. We're going to need Mr. Keeler's dental records."

"I'll have them faxed to you," Wilen said, jotting down the number. "Walter and I go to the same dentist." He hung up, made the call to the dentist and waited.

It was nearly dark when the colonel called back. "Thanks for the dental records, but it looks like we won't need them. We found a fragment of a driver's license on one of the bodies, which was badly burned. It belongs to Walter Keeler."

"You're sure there's no mistake?"

"I'm sure. The car was consumed, but Mr. Keeler apparently got out of the car before the fire got to him." The colonel gave Wilen the number of the morgue where the bodies had been taken. Wilen thanked him and hung up.

He picked up the phone to call Ellie Keeler; then he put it down again and called another number instead.

"Ed Eagle," the voice said.

"Ed, it's Joe Wilen."

"Hello, Joe. Are you back in Palo Alto?"

"Yes. Ed, I'm going to need you to fax me a copy of the letter you wrote to Walter Keeler."

EAGLE WAS QUIET for a moment. "Joe, I'm afraid I can't do that without Keeler's permission."

"Ed, Walter Keeler died in an automobile accident south of San Francisco a couple of hours ago."

"I'm sorry; I didn't know. Did Keeler sign a new will?"

"I can't go into that right now, Ed, but I need a copy of your letter."

"All right. It's on my home computer. I'm leaving the office now; I'll fax it to you in half an hour."

Wilen gave him the fax number. "Thank you, Ed. I'll wait here for it."

Wilen hung up and walked to the window. Lights were coming on in Palo Alto.

His secretary came to the door. "Mr. Wilen, I think I'm done for the day. Is there anything else you need?"

"No, Sally," he said. "I'll be here for a while; I'm waiting for a fax."

"Eleanor Keeler called when you were on the phone a few minutes ago."

"I'll call her," Wilen said. He said good night to his secretary, went back to his desk and dialed the number.

"Hello?"

"Eleanor, it's Joe Wilen."

"What have you learned?"

"I've had a call from the state highway patrol. Walter was killed in the crash. They identified his body from a fragment of his driver's license."

"Are they sure?"

"I believe so, but I've had his dental records sent there for a positive identification. I think it will be a day or so before that can be done."

Eleanor sounded as if she were crying. "This can't be," she sobbed. "We've only been married a week. What am I going to do?"

"Eleanor, do you have any family or friends you can call?"

She seemed to get control of herself. "No, nobody in San Francisco. Nobody at all, really."

"I think the best thing for you to do tonight is just to have some dinner and try to get some rest. I'll call you tomorrow and tell you what I've learned."

"Joe, what am I going to do? I don't even know if I have any money."

"You and Walter have a joint bank account, don't you?"

"Yes, he opened one at the San Francisco branch of his bank last week."

"You can draw on that for anything you may need," Wilen said.

"Joe, I know this is an awful thing to ask, but did Walter sign his new will?"

"Yes, he did, and you are very well taken care of, Eleanor. I'll come up there in a couple of days and go through everything with you, but please be sure that you have no cause for concern."

"Thank you, Joe. That makes me feel better."

"Good night, Eleanor. Try and get some rest."

"I will, Joe. Good night." She hung up.

As Wilen hung up the phone, he heard the fax machine in his secretary's office ring. He walked into her office and switched on the lights. The machine was cranking out two sheets of paper. He took them back to his office.

He sat down, switched on his desk light and began to read. As he did so, his eyes widened. He had been expecting unfavorable information, but what Eagle had to say was astonishing. The woman was not only a fraud, she was very likely a murderer. He read the letter twice, doing his best to commit it to memory.

If Eagle had only told him about this in Santa Fe, he could have prevented Walter from signing the will. He would have done anything to make him read the letter. Now Walter had willed this awful woman more than a billion dollars in liquid assets!

Wilen could not shake the feeling that, somehow, this was his fault. He had failed to protect his friend and client, the man who had made him rich beyond his dreams. He had to find a way to fix this.

ELEANOR WRIGHT KEELER ordered in dinner from an impossibly expensive fancy grocer down the street. She sat on her terrace, drinking from a well-chilled bottle of Veuve Cliquot Grande Dame champagne and eating beluga caviar with a spoon from a half-kilo can. When she had eaten all she could stand, she called Jimmy Long.

"Hello?"

"Jimmy, it's Barbara."

"Hey Babs."

"My husband was killed in a car crash this afternoon."

"Oh, God, Babs, I'm so sorry!"

"Don't be, baby; I'm a fucking billionaire!"

"What?"

"I'm not kidding. He signed a new will today that leaves me everything—well, almost everything. He said there would be some bequests to his alma mater and some charities, but damned near everything!"

"You take my breath away, kid. What are you going to do with yourself?"

"Any fucking thing I want!" she crowed. "I'm going to buy a jet airplane and fly around the world, stopping everywhere! You want to go?"

"You bet I do."

"Wait a minute, I already have a jet airplane. It's not big enough, though. I'm going to buy one of those . . . what do you call them, the ones that can fly from here to Tokyo nonstop?"

"A Gulfstream Five?"

"Yes, that's the one."

"They cost forty or fifty million dollars."

"What the fuck do I care? I've got a billion!" she exulted. "I can buy anything! Go anywhere!"

"That's unbelievable!"

"I know, I know. I just had to tell you, baby."

"I'm glad you did."

"Listen, it's going to take a few days to sort everything out. I guess there'll have to be a funeral or a memorial service or something. Then, when all that's over and the estate is settled, I'm coming to L.A. and buying something nice in Bel-Air."

"Great idea!"

"Something big, for entertaining, something with an Olympic-sized pool—one of those old movie star mansions, maybe!"

"You deserve it, kiddo, after all you've been through."

"You're damned right I do! I'll call you, Jimmy!"

She hung up and did a little dance around the apartment, making exultant noises. She could have anything!

BACK IN HIS OFFICES, Joe Wilen sat at his secretary's desk, reading Walter Keeler's will on her computer. Two pages needed fixing. He began fixing them.

DETECTIVE ALEX REESE of the Santa Fe Police Department read through the last of a stack of financial documents he had gathered from various sources, including Donald Wells's business manager in Los Angeles, then he got up and went over to the D.A.'s office. The secretary told him to go right in.

"Morning, Alex," Martínez said. "What's up?"

"My background check on Donald Wells didn't turn up much. He was born in a little town in Georgia called Delano, and he got his job at Centurion Studios through the chairman there, who is from the same town. He got arrested for domestic violence against a live-in girlfriend fifteen years ago, but the charges were dropped. He had a lot of parking tickets and a few speeding tickets when he was younger, but he seems to have calmed down the past ten years or so."

"Have we got motive?"

"I've combed through all of Wells's financials, and, in my opinion, there's more than enough there for motive to kill his wife."

"Tell me."

"In short, Wells would have nothing, if he hadn't married Donna. When they met, he was working for Centurion Studios as an associate producer, which is one notch up from gofer in that business. He meets Donna, then a couple of months after that her husband is dead, and a year or so later, they're married. She loans him three million dollars to set up his own shop. He rents office space from the studio, pays himself half a million dollars a year, probably six times what he had been making, and starts acquiring books and magazine articles and having screenplays written from them. Out of the first half dozen things he produced, one was a big hit—a horror thing aimed at teenagers called *Strangle.* Within three years he had made enough back to repay his wife's loan.

"The two houses he co-owned with his wife were bought entirely by her, but the deeds were recorded in both their names. This real estate co-ownership adds twenty million dollars to his net worth, as expressed on his financial statement. Apart from the houses, his net worth is under five million, and three million of that is expressed as accounts receivable from Centurion or his film distributors, and he has to perform to receive those funds, delivering scripts, mostly. Set those receivables aside and he's worth less than two million bucks, not much for a supposedly successful film producer. His first benefit from his wife's will is that her half of the real estate goes to him, nearly doubling his net worth. He does have a high income, though, from his company: an average of two and a half or three million a year.

"His wife's will also leaves him five million dollars—more than enough for motive right there—but the fact that his wife and son died simultaneously leaves him in a much more favorable position, since her son was her principal heir. It's only a guess right now— we'll need to subpoena her financial records—but it looks like his inheritance could be in the region of half a billion dollars."

"Wow," Martínez said. "I'd certainly call that motive."

"His alibi holds. I spoke to the manager of the Hassler Hotel in

Rome, and he supports both Wells's contention that he was in Rome when his wife died and that he received the phone call from his Santa Fe house when he said he did."

"So, he would have had to hire somebody. Any candidates?"

"My best guess is somebody he worked with in the movies, either in L.A. or Santa Fe. He's shot a couple of movies here. I've compiled a list of people who worked for him from the credits of his pictures. On the theory that anyone he knew well enough to ask to kill his wife would have worked for him more than once, I've come up with a list of thirty-one names of people who worked on two or more of his movies, and I'm running them through the New Mexico, California and federal databases for criminal records. I should have something by tomorrow that will give me the basis for interviews."

"That's good work, Alex. What if none of them pans out?"

"I'll cross that bridge when I come to it."

"Okay, let me know who in that list of thirty-one people looks good."

"I'm likely to have to go to L.A. to question some of these people, so I'll send you a travel authorization."

"How long will you need there?"

"Probably no more than a week, but Wells isn't going to be a flight risk. He's going to sit tight and let the legal process work to get his wife's will probated, which could take months."

"Right. There's something else I'd like you to look into, Alex."

"What's that?"

"Wells told us in his deposition that Mrs. Wells's first husband was killed in a mugging in New York."

"That's right, he did."

"I'd like to know if there's any chance Wells had a hand in that. Call the NYPD and see if you can track down the detectives who investigated the killings and see if you can figure out where Wells was when it happened."

"That's a good idea, Bob; I'll get on it."

"Don't talk to Wells about it just yet. If he was involved, I want him to think he skated on that one."

"I won't talk to Wells again until I've come to you first."

"Good. I don't want Ed Eagle to know how interested we are in his client, either."

"Yeah, it's interesting that when Wells got the kidnapping threat, he didn't call the police but called a lawyer, instead."

"Yeah, I find that very, very interesting."

JOE WILEN, after a night of little sleep, arrived at his office and found a message from his contact at the state police. He returned the call.

"Good morning, Mr. Wilen," the colonel said.

"Good morning, Colonel. Do you have any news for me?"

"Yes, the dental records you sent us match the teeth of the corpse carrying Walter Keeler's driver's license."

"Would you send me the coroner's report and a death certificate?"

"Of course, I'll do it right away. My condolences on the loss of your friend. We'll be releasing the names of the deceased today."

"By the way, Colonel, did anything in the car survive the fire? Any papers or other contents of Walter's pockets?"

"No, the fire consumed the car and its contents entirely. The only reason the driver's license fragment survived was that Mr. Keeler was thrown clear of the car."

"Thank you, Colonel, and thank you very much for your assistance in this matter. I wonder if I could ask your help on another matter?"

"Anything I can do, Mr. Wilen."

"I'm going to fax you a letter concerning Mrs. Keeler. I'd be grateful if you could ascertain or refute the assertions made in the letter."

"I'll do what I can."

"This must be held in the strictest confidence, Colonel, as you will see, and I'd like you to destroy the letter afterward."

"As you wish."

Wilen thanked him, faxed the letter, then called his secretary. "Margie, please get Lee Hight and the two of you come into my office."

"Yes, sir."

Lee Hight was the associate who had drafted Walter Keeler's will, and Margie had proofed it on her computer. The two women knocked and entered Wilen's office.

"Please sit down," Wilen said. "Lee, Margie, I have some bad news: Walter Keeler was killed in an automobile accident on the way to San Francisco after our meeting here yesterday."

The two women looked shocked.

"I'm very sorry, Joe," Lee said.

"So am I, Mr. Wilen," Margie echoed.

"I've asked you in here, because I have to make an important decision, and before I do, I want to get your opinion. First, I want to read you a letter from a Santa Fe attorney named Ed Eagle. Mr. Eagle gave me the letter a few days ago, when I was in Santa Fe, and asked me to deliver it to Walter. He did not tell me the contents of the letter, only that it concerned the woman Walter married last week. I assumed that the contents were unfavorable to her, because Eagle asked me to deliver the letter to Walter before he signed his will.

"I gave Walter the letter, but he declined to read it. He walked over to my shredder and fed the unopened letter into it. At that point I called the two of you and Helen Brock in here to witness the will. I haven't asked Helen to join us. Lee, when you were drafting the document, did Helen see any of it?"

"No, Joe, she didn't."

"So only the three of us know the contents of the will."

The two women nodded.

"Here is the letter from Ed Eagle." Wilen read the entire letter to the two women.

The two women sat in stunned silence for a moment. "That's appalling," Lee said finally.

"Now, here's my question to both of you. You were both well acquainted with Walter Keeler. Do you think that, if he had been in possession of this information about his wife, he would have signed his will in its present form?"

"No," Margie said. "Of course not."

"Not unless he was out of his mind," Lee said.

"I knew him better than either of you, and I entirely agree. If I had known the contents of the letter from Eagle, I would have insisted that Walter read it before signing, but I didn't. Eagle faxed me the letter yesterday, after I told him of Walter's death."

"Joe," Lee said, "I want to remind you that Walter's will, after all his other bequests, leaves his wife more than a billion dollars in liquid assets."

"Thank you, Lee, but I don't need reminding. Now, the three of us have to make a decision together, and it has to be a unanimous decision. I warn you now that what I am talking about here is nothing less than a criminal conspiracy, a felony punishable by years in prison. I am considering altering the terms of Walter's will by replacing two pages of it with new pages which will accomplish two things: one, I will set up a trust that will pay Mrs. Keeler fifty thousand dollars a month for life, contingent on her noncriminal behavior, and give her possession for life, but not ownership, of the San Francisco apartment, which Walter paid seven million dollars for. Two, it will reduce to one dollar the inheritance of any beneficiary, including Mrs. Keeler, who contests the terms of the will or who complains about it to the press.

"Walter's copy of the will was destroyed in a fire that accompanied the accident, so the original on my desk is the only copy. I am proposing to forge Walter's initials on these two pages with my pen—the same pen that Walter signed with—and substitute the two new pages for the old pages leaving Mrs. Keeler that huge inheritance. I believe that she will accept the will, especially when she learns what I know about her past. Do you both understand what I want to do?"

"Yes," both women said simultaneously.

"If I do this, you will substitute a new computer file on both your computers, so that everything matches. Lee, do you still have my notes for drafting the will?"

"No, after you approved my draft, I shredded them."

"Now, I have to ask each of you what your wishes are in this matter. Please remember that I am suggesting that you become part of a conspiracy to deny Mrs. Keeler the fortune she is legally entitled to and that her husband wanted her to have. If you agree to join me in this conspiracy, you can never tell another soul what I've done, and if you are ever deposed, or if you testify in court about this matter, you will have to perjure yourselves to protect yourselves. Do you understand what I am asking of you?"

"Yes," both women said.

"If either of you feels, for any reason, that you should not do this, I will shred the new pages of the will and have it probated as it stands, and we can all forget that this conversation ever took place. Do you understand?"

"Yes," both women said.

"What do you wish to do? Margie?"

"Put the new pages in the will."

"Lee? This is a particularly important decision for you, because should the conspiracy ever become known, you would lose your law license and your livelihood."

"I have two questions, Joe," Lee said.

"Go ahead."

"First, if this money does not go to Mrs. Keeler, to whom will it go?"

"Under the terms in my redraft, it will be put into a charitable trust already mandated in the will."

"And two, will Mrs. Keeler have any part in managing the estate?"

"No, she will not. I will remain the executor of the will and Walter's trustee, and after the estate is probated, I will have as little contact as possible with Mrs. Keeler. This law firm will manage the charitable trust, and a large part of our work here will have to do with that."

"Then I am happy to take part in denying the bitch the money," Lee said. "Where do I sign?"

"You don't have to sign," Wilen said. "You can both leave now, and I will personally alter the will. Last chance to change your minds."

Both women shook their heads.

Wilen handed them each a computer disk. "Please copy this onto your computers, replacing the old file, and erase the backup files."

The two women accepted the disks and left Wilen's office.

Wilen carefully initialed the two pages and inserted them into the will. He shredded the old pages, then went to his secretary and handed her the will.

"Margie, will you make a copy of Walter Keeler's will for Mrs. Keeler and file the original in the office vault?"

"Of course, Mr. Wilen. I'll have the copy for you in just a moment." She walked to the copying machine, placed the document on top and pressed a button. A moment later, she handed Wilen the copy.

"Thank you, Margie."

Wilen took the copy into his office and sat down. He held a hand out in front of him. It was perfectly steady. He had never done anything like this in his life, but he would have done anything to protect Walter Keeler's interests, in death as well as in life.

DETECTIVE ALEX REESE checked into his Los Angeles hotel, then drove his rented car to Centurion Studios. The guard at the main gate confirmed his appointment, then put a studio pass on the dashboard of his car and gave him directions to the security office.

Reese parked in a visitor's spot, walked into the building and presented himself to the secretary of the head of security. "I'm Detective Alex Reese of the Santa Fe Police Department; I have an appointment with your head of security."

"Of course," she replied, then pressed the intercom button. "Mr. Bender, Detective Reese is here." She hung up the phone. "Please go in, Detective." She pointed at the door.

The door opened, and a man in his shirtsleeves waved him in and stuck out his hand. "I'm Jeff Bender, Detective; please come in and have a seat."

Reese took a seat on a leather sofa, and Bender sat down in a facing chair. "What can I do for the Santa Fe P.D.?"

"Mr. Bender . . ."

"Jeff, please."

"And I'm Alex. Jeff, I'm investigating the murder in Santa Fe of Mrs. Donald Wells and her son, Eric."

"Yes, I know about that; it's been big in the L.A. papers. I assume that, since you're here, Don Wells is a suspect?"

"We have no evidence against him, but he is, of course, a person of interest."

"Yeah, I understand that she was very, very rich. Always a good motive for the husband. I was a homicide cop on the Beverly Hills force; I know how it goes."

"May I speak to you in confidence about this?"

"Of course."

"My working theory of the case is that, since Mr. Wells was in Rome at the time, he could have hired someone to kill his wife, and that, if he did so, he might have hired someone who worked for him in the movie business."

"Reasonable assumption," Bender said. "Have you found anything to back it up?"

"That's why I'm here. Another assumption is that such a person would be someone who Wells knows well and trusts, so he or she would probably be someone who has worked for him on several pictures."

"Wells has produced only eight or ten pictures," Bender said, "so it wouldn't be hard to narrow the list."

"I've already done that," Reese said. "From a list of thirty-one people who've worked as crew on more than one of Wells's pictures, I've found six who have arrest records, and I'd like to discuss them with you."

"Who are they?"

Reese ripped out a page of his notebook and handed it to Bender.

"Five men, one woman," he said, reading the names.

"Do you know them?"

"Only one of them: Jack Cato, a stuntman. I think one of the other guys, Grif Edwards, is a stuntman, too. I know him when I see him. What kind of records do they have?"

Reese consulted a sheet of paper. "Cato has had a number of arrests for disorderly conduct or assault over the past seven years. He seems to have a tendency to get into bar fights."

"Yeah, I've had to bail him out a couple of times, once in L.A., once on location in Arizona."

"And Edwards stole a couple of cars when he was in his early twenties, got probation, which he served without incident, then he took a baseball bat to his brother-in-law after the man beat up his sister. That was two years ago."

"What about the records of the others?"

"The three other men had arrests for domestic abuse, either with a girlfriend or a wife. The woman apparently ran with a Hispanic gang for a couple of years and had a shoplifting conviction. Nothing for the last four years, so maybe she straightened out her life."

Bender went to his desk and began typing on his computer. "Four years is how long she's had her job. Tina López started as an assistant seamstress and is now a seamstress in the costume department. She seems an unlikely candidate, though she might know someone from her gang past who would do the job. However, it's unlikely that Wells would have had much contact with her, since she's pretty far down the pecking order from a producer, especially one with his own company.

"Cato has worked at Centurion as a stuntman and wrangler for twelve years and Edwards for nine. Edwards's specialty is car work: chases, crashes. Former stock-car racer. The other three guys are in makeup, accounting and catering—like the woman, pretty far removed from Wells. I wouldn't think they would make good suspects."

"Okay, I'll talk to Cato and Edwards first. How do I find them?"

Bender did some more computer work. "They're both full-time employees: Cato at what we call the ranch, where animals are kept, out on the back lot; Edwards at the motor pool. When he's not doing stunt work, he's a mechanic. Neither is working on a film right now. Why don't I go along with you, lend a little studio authority to the interviews?"

"I'd appreciate that," Reese said.

Bender got his coat and put on a western straw hat. "Keeps the sun off my fair skin," he said. "A day in the sun means a trip to the dermatologist." He led the way outside, and they got into a golf cart. "It's how we travel on the lot," he said.

Reese had a good look at the studio as they drove down a long avenue with big hangar-like buildings on both sides.

"These are the soundstages, where interiors are filmed," Bender said. He stopped at an intersection and pointed. "Down there is the New York street set, which is the most-used standing set on the lot." He began driving again. "The studio commissary is over there, and down the side streets are the office buildings where the independent producers, like Wells, rent space. There are also bungalows that are dressing rooms for our stars."

He swung the cart into a large shedlike building and stopped. It looked like the workshop of an auto dealer, only larger. There were a number of hydraulic hoists, and along the rear of the building were two rows of parked vehicles with covers over them. "The cars back there are period stuff, everything from Packards to delivery vans to a fire truck."

A man in coveralls approached the golf cart. "Hey, Jeff," he said to Bender. "What can I do for you?"

"Hi, Ted. This is Alex Reese; we'd like to talk to Grif Edwards. He around?"

Ted pointed. "He's working on the car on the lift, last on the left."

Bender drove down to the lift and stopped. A man in coveralls was using a grease gun on what looked like a late-forties Ford. "Grif Edwards?" Bender called out.

The man turned and looked at Bender. "Who wants to know?"

 Cupie Dalton sat in front of his computer, looking at the Air Aware program. He picked up the phone and dialed a number. "Ed Eagle."

"Hi. It's Cupie."

"Hello, Cupie."

"Walter Keeler's airplane has made a move but only from Hayward to San Jose, a short hop."

"It doesn't matter anymore, Cupie; Walter Keeler is dead."

Cupie's jaw dropped. "She offed him already?"

"Apparently not. Keeler was killed in a collision with a gasoline tanker truck on the freeway while Barbara was in San Francisco."

"Holy shit. I hope he hadn't made a new will."

"I hope so, too, but it's possible. His lawyer wouldn't say. I gave him a letter for Keeler, but he didn't read it, so I had to fax the lawyer a copy."

"A letter about Barbara?"

"*All* about Barbara."

"So what's next?"

"My guess is that Barbara is going to be stuck in San Francisco for a few days at least, while she buries her husband and reads his will."

"You know what I think? I think a very rich Barbara would be more dangerous than ever."

"Yes, in my experience, the very rich tend to feel omnipotent, and an omnipotent Barbara is not a good thought."

"You have any instructions for me?"

"Yes. Bribe somebody in her building to keep an eye on her and let you know if she leaves town."

"I can do that; I got acquainted with the super on our last visit."

"Apart from that, just sit tight. I may have some work for you in L.A. soon. I've got a new client who might get charged with murder. His name is Donald Wells, and somebody killed his very rich wife and her son while he was in Rome. I think the cops and the D.A. like him for it. Wells is a movie producer based on the Centurion lot."

"I know the head of security at Centurion, Jeff Bender. You want me to pay him a visit?"

"Maybe you should. I would like to know as early in the game as possible if the Santa Fe police are investigating Wells."

"I'll give him a call."

"Okay. And keep me posted on Barbara's whereabouts."

"Will do."

GRIF EDWARDS LOOKED like a central-casting hoodlum out of a Warner Brothers noir movie—big, heavyset, broken nose, blue stubble—just the sort of guy who would beat up Bogart in act 1 and take a slug in the last scene.

"I'm Jeff Bender, studio security," Bender said. "This is Alex Reese, out of Santa Fe P.D. He'd like to ask you a few questions, and I'd like to hear your answers."

Edwards looked back and forth at the two men, then shrugged. "Okay."

"Mr. Edwards, where were you last weekend, Friday through Sunday?"

"I went down to Tijuana, to a bullfight," Edwards replied.

"What day was the bullfight?"

"Saturday and Sunday."

"Who was fighting?"

"I don't know. Some spic guys."

"Anybody get hurt?"

"Naw, I was hoping, but they all walked away. The bulls didn't do so good."

"What else did you do in Tijuana?"

"Drank some tequila, ate some tacos, got the runs."

"Who did you go with?"

"Buddy of mine."

"What's his name?"

"Jack Cato. He works on the back lot."

"Anybody else?"

"Just the two of us. We drove down in my car."

"Where'd you stay?"

"Some dump not far from the bullring."

"Its name?"

"Beats me. Some spic name."

"How many nights?"

"Friday and Saturday. We drove back Sunday, after the fight."

"You know a producer on the lot called Don Wells?"

"Sure, I worked three or four of his pictures. We're not exactly buddies, though."

"Ever see him socially? Have a drink or something?"

"Naw."

"Thanks for your time, Mr. Edwards."

Bender turned the golf cart around and headed out.

"I saw a rack of time cards near the door," Reese said. "I'd like to see what time Edwards clocked out last Friday."

"Okay." Bender stopped the cart, went to the rack and found Edwards's card, then he got back into the car. "Five eleven."

Reese wrote down the time.

"Now let's go see Jack Cato, and see if they've got their stories straight," Bender said.

The buildings were left behind them, and Reese found himself driving down the dirt street of a western town. They passed the saloon, the jail and the general store and came to a building with the fading words LIVERY STABLE painted in large letters on the side. Next to it was a corral with half a dozen horses in it.

"Here we are," Bender said. "This is both a set and a real stable." He led the way through the big doors to a small office inside.

A tall, wiry man in jeans and a work shirt looked up from a desk, where he had a hand of solitaire dealt out. "Hey Jeff," he said, standing up and offering his hand. His leathery skin and narrow eyes were right out of a B western. "What can I do you for?"

"Hi, Jack. This is Alex Reese, Santa Fe P.D. He'd like to ask you some questions."

"Questions? About what?"

"Just tell him what he wants to know, okay? It's lunchtime, and I'm hungry."

"Hell, all right."

"Mr. Cato, where were you last weekend?"

"Me and Grif Edwards—he works over to the motor pool—was down in Tijuana."

"When did you leave L.A.?"

"We got out a little early on Friday, to beat the traffic. Around three, I guess."

"What time did you get to Tijuana?"

"Well, shit, we didn't beat the traffic, so it was pretty near bedtime when we got there."

"What time was that?"

"I don't know, ten, maybe."

"Where'd you stay?"

"A little hotel called the Parador, down near the bullring. That's what we went down there for, the bullfights."

"Who was fighting?"

"Shit, I can never remember their names."

"How many bullfights did you go to?"

"Well, we went Saturday and Sunday, and there was three each afternoon. We came on back when they was over on Sunday."

"What time did you leave?"

"Around five, I guess. There was less traffic, so we were back in L.A. around nine."

"Do you know Don Wells, a producer on the lot?"

"Well, yeah, I've worked most of his pictures, either as a stunt-man or an extra."

"He's a buddy of yours, then?"

"Sort of. We play poker every Thursday night, when he's in town."

"Where do you play?"

"Over at his office."

"When was the last time you played?"

"Right before he went to Italy. That was a few weeks ago."

"Does Grif Edwards play, too?"

"Yeah, he's a regular."

"I guess that's it. Thanks a lot."

"Don't mention it. See you, Jeff."

The two men got back into their golf cart and drove away.

"Okay, I guess that went well," Bender said. "Cato lied about what time they left on Friday, and Edwards lied about not knowing Wells socially."

"It's a start," Reese said.

JOE WILEN TOOK the elevator up to Eleanor Keeler's apartment, accompanied by his associate, Lee Hight. Eleanor met him as he stepped directly into the foyer.

"Thank you so much for coming to San Francisco, Joe," Eleanor said, shaking his hand warmly and ushering him into the living room. "I don't even have a car. Walter was going to ship his two cars up here along with his household goods, but none of that has arrived yet."

"Eleanor, may I introduce my associate, Lee Hight?"

The two women shook hands, then Eleanor sat down on the living room sofa and offered them the facing chairs. "Can I get you anything? Coffee?"

"Thank you, no," Wilen said. "I'd rather get directly down to business."

"Of course. I must say, Joe, that you look a little grim this morning."

Wilen didn't respond to that. "Much has transpired since we met on your wedding day," he said, avoiding using her name.

"Well, yes, you're right about that."

"Including some events you don't yet know about. That's why I'm here." Wilen set his briefcase on the coffee table, opened it and placed the copy of the doctored Keeler will before her. "This is the will that Walter executed an hour or so before his death in the accident," he said. "It makes very specific bequests to you, and I want to tell you about the bequests and the conditions attached to them."

"Conditions?" Eleanor was looking wary now.

Wilen ignored the question. "Walter took me aside on your wedding day and gave me some notes for a new will. When I returned to the office, I gave the notes to Lee, here, along with my instructions, and asked her to draft the will while I was away for a couple of days in Santa Fe."

Eleanor's expression changed ever so slightly at the mention of Santa Fe.

"I played in a golf tournament in Santa Fe, and my partner was your former husband, Ed Eagle."

Eleanor's face became stony. "A very untruthful man," she said. "I hope you didn't believe anything he told you about me."

"Mr. Eagle wrote a letter to Walter and asked me to deliver it. He did not tell me of its contents but said Walter could, if he wished to."

"A letter?"

"This letter," Wilen said, handing her the copy from Eagle.

She glanced through it. "This is preposterous," she said.

"No, it is not," Wilen replied. "I took the precaution of having the state police check it out, and they confirmed all of the major assertions."

"You don't understand," she said.

"It doesn't matter whether I understand. Walter was at the point of signing his new will when I gave him the letter. When he had finished reading it, he showed me the letter and told me that he wished to make some changes in the will before he signed it. He dictated some new instructions to me, and I asked Lee to make the changes.

When Walter had read the new draft, he signed it in the presence of three witnesses, as you will see on the final page."

"Just give me the short version," Eleanor said, her face hard.

"Walter has left you a stipend of fifty thousand dollars a month for life, to be paid from a trust that now also owns this apartment. He has also given you lifetime occupancy of the apartment but not ownership. You may neither sell or rent the apartment or use it for any other purpose than your residence. You will be held liable for any damage to the apartment. Both the stipend and your residency in the apartment are contingent on noncriminal behavior on your part. Should you be convicted of any felony, the stipend will stop immediately, and you will be given thirty days notice to vacate the apartment."

Barbara had gone pale. "That was not what he gave me to believe," she said. "I was to get everything after his charitable bequests."

"He changed his mind after reading Mr. Eagle's letter," Wilen replied.

"This will not stand. I will break this will."

"I should point out that Walter also dictated a clause stating that, if any of his heirs contest the will or complain about its terms to the press, his or her inheritance will be reduced to one dollar."

"That's ridiculous," Eleanor spat.

"I assure you that it is perfectly legal, as is everything else in this will, and I can assure you, as Walter's executor, that, if necessary, I will expend whatever funds are necessary to uphold the will. I don't think you would be able to find a lawyer anywhere who would contest the will under these circumstances."

"What about Walter's airplane?"

"He sold it the day he signed his will. He planned to buy a better one but never had the chance."

"What about the vineyard we bought?"

"I spoke with Emilio Galiano, and he has released the estate from the sale and returned Walter's check."

"But that was to be mine!"

"A great deal might have been yours but for your dishonesty." Wilen closed his briefcase and stood up. "I want to make it perfectly clear that I in no way represent you legally. I do not wish to speak to you again. If you have any need to communicate with me, put it in writing and send it to my office. Do you understand?"

Eleanor stood up. "Get out."

Wilen turned to go, then stopped. "Oh, by the way, you have about ninety thousand dollars in your checking account, and you may keep that. Walter's household goods and cars will not be shipped here; they are now part of his estate. You will receive your payments on the first of each month, wired to your checking account. Good day." Wilen stalked out of the apartment, followed by Lee Hight.

They were out of the building before either of them spoke. "That was very good, Joe," Hight said.

"It was very satisfying," Wilen replied.

"I'm very glad that we acted as we did with regard to the will."

"If I had any doubts, they have all been resolved," Wilen said.

BARBARA PACED THE living room of her apartment, crying and swearing, cursing Walter Keeler, Ed Eagle and Joe Wilen aloud. "I will make you pay, Ed Eagle!" she cried. "And you, Joe Wilen, will eat dirt before I'm done with you!"

DOWNSTAIRS, the superintendent of the apartment building opened an envelope in his mail and found five one-hundred-dollar bills. A note told him that he would receive another five hundred each time he reported on the movements of Mrs. Walter Keeler. He put the money in his pocket, smiling. His wife didn't need to know anything about this.

———

BARBARA FELL ASLEEP on the living room sofa, and it was late afternoon before she woke. She was calm, now, and resigned to the terms of the will. At least she got six hundred thousand a year out of that fucking Walter, she thought, and the use of this apartment.

But while she was calm, her anger at Ed Eagle and Joe Wilen had shrunk into a cold, hard lump in her breast. She would deal with both of them.

CUPIE SAT AT his table in the garden at Spago Beverly Hills and waited for Jeff Bender to arrive. He had known Bender since he was a rookie detective in Beverly Hills, when Cupie was an LAPD detective, and they had always been friendly. Bender liked chic restaurants, and Cupie was happy to entertain him at one, especially since Ed Eagle was buying.

Cupie's cell phone rang, and he answered. "Cupie Dalton."

"Mr. Dalton, this is the superintendent at Mrs. Keeler's apartment building."

"Yes, what's up?"

"Mrs. Keeler left for the airport a few minutes ago. She said something to the doorman about being in Los Angeles for a few days."

"Right. Your money will be in the mail today." He hung up.

Cupie saw Bender enter the restaurant and work his way across the garden toward their table, waving at acquaintances and occasionally stopping to shake hands and chat for a moment. Finally, he reached the table, shook Cupie's hand and sat down.

"What are you drinking?" Cupie asked as a waiter appeared.

"Absolut martini, two olives, very cold," Bender replied.

"A Diet Coke for me," Cupie said. The waiter departed.

"You on the wagon, Cupie?" Bender asked.

"Nope, it's just that if I drink at lunch, I fall asleep in the afternoon. The golden years will come to you, too, Jeff."

"What are you up to these days?"

"I'm a busy bee, I am," Cupie replied. "I guess word must be getting around about what an ace P.I. I am."

"What sort of stuff you working on?"

"Oh, a widow who's been a bad girl; a husband who may have been a bad boy. That sort of thing."

"I wouldn't have thought you'd be interested in the domestic stuff," Bender said.

"Listen, I'm not kicking down doors and snapping Polaroids, kid; this is very important, big-money stuff."

Bender seemed to prick up his ears. "How much money we talking about?"

"Oh, a billion here, a billion there."

Their drinks arrived, and they raised their glasses and sipped.

"Tell me," Bender said, "would one or more of these billions relate to somebody at Centurion?"

Cupie grinned. "You're way ahead of me, Jeff."

"Well, I didn't think you were springing for Spago because you like a pretty face at your table."

"I suppose you already know the name of the gentleman."

"It wouldn't be one Donald Wells, movie producer and recent widower, would it?"

"The name has a familiar ring," Cupie said. "Seems there was something about the gent in the papers the last few days."

"Oh, it's big news and drawing attention from various places."

"What sort of places?"

"Santa Fe, of course, since that's where it all went down."

"Who in Santa Fe?"

"A detective specializing in homicides."

Cupie flagged down a waiter and ordered another round.

"Why, Cupie, I think you're trying to get me drunk."

"Come on, Jeff, a second martini never made you blink."

"I'm not resisting," Bender said, as the second drink arrived.

"What would the name of this detective be?" Cupie asked.

"Alex Reese."

"And what was he looking for?"

"Detective Reese is a very smart fellow," Bender said. He told Cupie about how Reese had combed the credits of Wells's movies for suspects.

"And who at Centurion did he find?"

"Two very likely candidates, I should think."

"Tell me about them."

"Two staff stuntmen, who double, in one case, as a wrangler and stable hand, and in the other, as a mechanic in our motor pool."

"Names?"

"Jack Cato and Grif Edwards, respectively."

"You know them?"

"I know Cato, and I've met Edwards."

"You think they're the kind of guys who would kill for money?"

"I think Edwards would kill for money," Bender said. "I think Cato would kill for money, then blackmail the guy who paid him to do it. He's the smarter of the two and the leader."

"And Reese is now a dog with a bone."

"You bet your ass he is. I'd give you odds that right now he's checking the guest list at the Parador Hotel in Tijuana, which is where these two boys claimed to have been on the relevant dates. It seems they're aficionados of the bullfight, though they couldn't come up with any of the names of the toreros in question on the dates in question. Also, Edwards lied about how well he knew Wells, and Cato lied about when they left for Tijuana. I'll bet Reeves is checking airline reservations between L.A. and Santa Fe, too."

"Are these guys smart enough to get away with it?"

"Cato may be; Edwards certainly isn't. In fact, I think that if this cop gets much closer to them, Edwards could meet with a fatal accident."

"Courtesy of Cato."

"If the boy has the balls to kill one of America's richest women, do you think he'd hesitate to cap Edwards, if he began to think he was a liability?"

"What about Don Wells?" Cupie asked.

"What about him?"

"Does he have the balls to cap Cato, in similar circumstances?"

"Well, now, that's a very interesting question," Bender said. "You know, all sorts of people are smart enough or crazy enough to hire somebody to remove a wealthy spouse from the scene, but could Wells point a gun at Cato and pull the trigger? I don't know. I really don't."

AFTER HE HAD poured Jeff Bender into his car, Cupie sat in his own vehicle and got out his cell phone.

"Ed Eagle."

"It's Cupie. The superintendent in Barbara's building says she left for Los Angeles this morning. She told the doorman she'd be away for a few days."

"Good to know. Let me know when she goes home. How did your meeting with the security guy go?"

"It went very well indeed; you'll get the bill from Spago. Sorry about that, but Bender has expensive tastes when somebody else is buying."

"Tell me it was worth the money."

"I believe it was. It seems that a cop from Santa Fe named Reese has questioned two studio stuntmen at Centurion; names Jack Cato and Grif-with-a-G Edwards."

"And?"

"Bender thinks they look good for it. They claim to have been in Tijuana when the killings took place, but he thinks Reese might punch holes in that."

"That's very interesting to know, Cupie."

"A strong hint that Bender is right could come if Grif Edwards meets with an unfortunate accident. He sort of predicted that. Cato is the smart one, and Edwards is not." He explained about the lies Reese had caught them in.

"Cupie, you can take anybody to Spago on my dime, anytime you think it's useful," Eagle said.

"You want me to pursue any of this further?"

"Not at the moment, but let me know if anything happens to Edwards."

"You betcha."

E D E A G L E A N D Susannah Wilde sat at their table at Santa Café and waited for Joe Wilen and his wife to arrive. "I told you about helping him find a house, didn't I?" Eagle asked.

"Yes, you did and about closing the sale, too."

"They're back to move in, I think," Eagle said. He looked up and saw them walk into the dining room. "Here they are."

"Hello, Ed. I'd like you to meet my wife, Sandi. Sandi, this is Ed Eagle and . . ."

"Susannah Wilde," she said.

The couple sat down.

"Good flight in?" Eagle asked.

"Yes, and the return trip will be my last in the King Air. I've sold it to an old friend."

"You must've bought something else," Eagle said.

"I bought Walter Keeler's CitationJet Three; I start training in it for my type rating next week."

"That will make the trips from the coast to Santa Fe quicker."

"I'm pleased about it, too," Sandi said. "I never liked the idea of propellers; I was always afraid that one would fall off. Or both."

They ordered drinks and dinner.

"By the way, Ed," Wilen said, "I can answer that question you asked me last time we spoke."

"What question was that?"

"The answer is yes, Walter did read your letter before signing his will, and as a result, his wife's inheritance was sharply limited. She gets a monthly stipend and the use of an apartment, and that's it."

"And how did she take the news?" Eagle asked.

"Not well. I had the pleasure of delivering it personally."

"Joe, I hope you got the message in my letter to Walter, that she is dangerous when crossed."

"Oh, at my suggestion, Walter included a clause cutting off her payments and evicting her if she is convicted of criminal activity, so I don't think she'll be out to get me."

"That was a smart move. Did you explain that to her, as well?"

"You bet I did and in no uncertain terms. I'm glad to see the back of that woman."

"I hope you have."

"Does she know about my letter?"

"Oh, yes. I showed her a copy when I delivered the news, so she knows that you were the cause of her downfall from billionairess to pensioner."

Eagle and Susannah exchanged a glance. "Oh," Eagle said.

"I hope I did the correct thing," Wilen said. "You didn't ask that I keep it confidential."

"You're quite right, Joe, I didn't, and nothing you did was incorrect."

"Are you in your new house, yet?" Susannah asked Sandi Wilen.

"In would be too strong a word, but we're got all the basic furniture, and before I go back to Palo Alto I expect to have it in pretty good shape. We'll be sleeping there from tomorrow night."

"I bought Walter Keeler's home furnishings from his Palo Alto house," Wilen said. "Had everything valued, then bought it from the estate, including two cars. The moving van will be here tomorrow."

"That should save a lot of time," Eagle said.

"Walter and I had similar taste," Sandi said, "so it's a good fit. It will remind us of him, too. We're going to miss him."

"I'm sure," Eagle replied.

"I've joined the golf club at Las Campanas," Wilen said, "so Ed, you and I will have to play before I start my jet training."

"I'd like that," Eagle said. "Joe, you said that Mrs. Keeler got occupancy of an apartment. Where?"

"In San Francisco. Walter bought it a week before he died, paid seven million dollars for it."

"Whew!" Susannah said. "She'll be well housed."

"She can't sell it, though?" Eagle asked.

"Nope, and she can't rent it, either."

"Well, Mrs. Keeler is going to be a very angry woman," Eagle said, half under his breath.

"What?"

"Nothing, Joe. Tell us about the house."

BARBARA/ELEANOR EAGLE/KEELER GOT off an airplane in Los Angeles and took a cab to Jimmy Long's house. Jimmy greeted her with a big hug.

"Hey, baby," he said. "I'm glad to see you."

"Oh, Jimmy, I'm glad to see you, too," she said.

He took her bags upstairs and had a drink waiting for her when she came down.

"God, I'm glad to be out of San Francisco," she said, sinking into a chair.

"I guess the memories are not good."

"Right, but not for the reason you think."

"I don't understand. The town made you a billionaire; why wouldn't you love it?"

She told him about Eagle's letter and Walter's change of heart. "I got fifty grand a month and the use—the *use,* mind you—of the apartment, and that's all."

"That's horrible, sweetheart," Jimmy said. "Still, you did all right for the work of a week or two."

"I guess so," she said, "but it's depressing." She took a long draw of her drink. "Jimmy, darling, can I ask you a question in confidence?"

"Of course."

"I mean it. This is just between you and me."

"Of course."

"You know a lot of people, a lot of different sorts of people, right?"

"Yes, I suppose I do."

"Did you ever run across anyone in your travels through life who would do anything for money?"

"Boy, have I! That pretty much describes everybody in this town!"

"I mean this quite literally, Jimmy."

"What, specifically, did you have in mind that somebody might do for money?"

"I suppose what I'm talking about is a hit man."

Jimmy looked at her for a moment. "Are you quite serious?"

"Quite."

Jimmy took a sip of his drink and looked thoughtful. "There have been rumors around town for years about a guy named Al who owns a gun shop on Melrose, but I'm not even sure he's still alive. And if he is, he's probably too old for that sort of work."

"Who else?"

Jimmy thought some more. "You know, I produced a western over at Centurion a couple of years ago. Remember *The Long Ride*?"

"Sure, I do. I loved it."

"There was a stuntman on that picture that I heard a rumor about. Somebody told me that he had arranged a car 'accident' some years back. Out on the Pacific Coast Highway, I think."

"What was his name."

"Jack . . . Cass. No, Cato. Jack Cato."

"I'd like to meet him," she said.

32

Alex Reese made a call to Tijuana, to a cop he knew on the federal police force there.

"This is Captain Rios," the voice said.

"Juan, this is Alex Reese, in Santa Fe. How are you?"

"Very well, Alejandro! And you?"

"I'm just fine. I'm working a case that requires some information from Tijuana, and I hope you can help me."

"Of course, if I can."

"There is a hotel near the bullring called Parador."

"Yes, I know it. It is one step up from a flea farm."

Reese gave him the dates. "I need to know if two men stayed there. Their names are Cato and Edwards. Could you find out for me?"

"I will do so immediately," Rios said. "Can you hold?"

Reese waited for three or four minutes, then Rios came back on the line.

"Alex? There were two American couples at the hotel on those dates, registered under those two names."

"Couples?"

"As in a man and a woman? Mr. and Mrs. Jack Cato and Mr.

and Mrs. Griffen Edwards. The clerk remembered that they paid in cash."

"Thank you, Juan, and it's good to talk to you again. Let me know if I can ever do anything for you in Santa Fe."

"I will do so, Alex. Good-bye."

"Good-bye." Reese hung up and pondered this information. Why did neither Cato nor Edwards mention women? He picked up the phone and called Jeff Bender at Centurion.

"Bender."

"Jeff, it's Alex Reese. I need some more information, and I wonder if you could get it for me?"

"If I can."

"I checked out the Parador Hotel in Tijuana, and there were two American couples registered under the names of Cato and Edwards on the relevant dates. Could you ask the two guys who the women were? I'd like to know if they have the names ready for the question, and, of course, who they were, so I can talk to them. I need phone numbers, too."

"Sure, Alex, I'll talk to them after lunch; I'm tied up until then."

"You've got my number." Reese hung up and went to work on airline reservations between L.A. and Albuquerque the weekend of the murders.

JACK CATO HAD a letter delivered by the studio mailman, an unusual event, since he got his mail at home. There was no return address, but the postmark was Los Angeles. He opened it and found a single sheet of paper.

Mr. Cato,

You come very well recommended. I have a highly paid job open that might interest you. If you'd like to know more, please be at the Seaside Café near the Santa Monica Pier at noon tomorrow. Take a table outside, sit fac-

ing the sea, and when I'm sure you've come alone, I'll join you. If you don't show, I won't contact you again.

Cato's first thought was that this was a setup, maybe by that cop from Santa Fe. His phone rang, and he picked it up. "Jack Cato."

"Hi, Jack. It's Jeff Bender. The Santa Fe cop called and asked me to check something with you."

"What's that?"

"Were you and Grif Edwards with anybody in Tijuana?"

"Yeah, there were a couple of girls."

"I need their names and phone numbers."

Cato gave him the names. "They're both in the L.A. phone book; they room together."

"Okay, Jack. Thanks. I don't think you'll hear any more from Detective Reese. He's already back in Santa Fe."

Cato hung up and read the letter again. What the hell, there was nothing incriminating about checking this out.

BARBARA AND JIMMY LONG arrived at the Seaside Café at eleven thirty and took a table that allowed them to view the outside tables. At one minute past twelve a pickup truck pulled up to the curb, and a man got out.

"That's Cato," Jimmy said.

They watched as he chose a table and took a seat facing the Pacific Ocean.

"Order me the lobster salad," Barbara said. "I'll be right back." She got up, took her handbag and walked outside.

CATO ORDERED A beer and began reading the menu.

"Sit still and close your eyes," a woman's voice said from behind him. She removed his sunglasses and put another pair on him. "All right," she said a moment later, "you can open your eyes, but keep the glasses on."

Cato opened his eyes, but he could see nothing. The glasses were large and tight fitting, and the lenses were black. "Who are you?"

"That's not important," she said. She had, apparently, sat down across from him.

"Who recommended me to you?"

"That person would prefer not to be known."

"All right, what is this about? I have to be back at work."

"There's an envelope on the table in front of you," she said.

He reached out and found it.

"It contains twenty-five thousand dollars in one-hundred-dollar bills," she said. "I want you to kill two men for me. They are in two different cities, and no one will connect them."

"You've got a lot of nerve, lady."

"Yes, I have. Now all that remains is to find out if you have enough nerve for this job."

"Are you a cop?"

"Certainly not, and no cop has anything to do with this. Now listen to me carefully. Inside the envelope is a sheet of paper with the names and addresses of the two men. There is also an untraceable cell phone number. You have two weeks to get the jobs done. I don't care how you do it. When you have killed the first man—it doesn't matter which one is done first—you will receive another twenty-five thousand dollars in the mail at your home address. When you have killed the second man, you will receive another fifty thousand dollars by the same means. Do you understand?"

"Why do you think I will do this?"

"Because it's not the first time you've done it, Jack, and you always need money. You have twenty-four hours to think it over.

When you've decided, call the cell phone number and tell me. If you don't want the job, we'll arrange for the return of the money. Now count slowly to twenty, then you can take off the glasses."

Barbara went back into the restaurant, sat down and began eating her lobster salad.

Jack counted to twenty and took off the glasses. He opened the envelope and found the money there, as she had said. There were two names, one in Santa Fe and one in Palo Alto, and directions on how to find them. He looked around at the other patrons of the restaurant and didn't see anyone he thought might be the woman, so he put a ten-dollar bill on the table, got into his truck and drove away.

He had been back in the stable office for an hour when the phone rang. "Jack Cato."

"Mr. Cato," a woman's voice said, "this is Ms. Bishop at GMAC. You're two payments behind on your truck loan, and unless we have payment immediately, we're going to have to take the truck."

Cato fingered the money in the envelope on the desk. "I'll send you a money order today," he said.

"Can we count on that?"

"Yes, you can." He hung up and dialed the cell number on the paper in the envelope.

"Yes?" a woman's voice said.

"This is the man you met in the restaurant."

"Yes?"

"I'll do the job."

"You have two weeks," she said. "If you're late, I'll have you killed." She hung up.

Cato hung up, too, and found that he was sweating.

33   ALEX REESE GOT a call from Jeff Bender, at Centurion.

"Hello, Jeff. That was fast."

"It only took a phone call. The two women's names are Tina López and Soledad Rivera. Cato says they're both in the L.A. phone book. Tina is the seamstress at Centurion who was on your list of possible suspects when you came to see me."

"Thank you, Jeff; can you tell me any more about them?"

"One of my people knows her and says she's a real looker, with a fabulous body. I haven't checked it out, myself."

"Maybe I'll check it out for you," Reese chuckled.

"You never know; it might be worth a trip back to L.A."

"If it is, I'll buy you lunch," Reese said. He said goodbye and hung up. Immediately his phone rang.

"Detective Reese."

It was the D.A.'s secretary. "He'd like to see you," she said.

"I'll be right there." He walked over to the D.A.'s office and presented himself.

"Take a seat, Alex," Martínez said. "Give me an update on your investigation into Donald Wells."

"My trip to L.A. was productive," Reese said. "Out of half a dozen crew members my research identified, two of them could very well be hired guns." He told Martínez about Jack Cato and Grif Edwards.

"You like them?"

"Yes, but they have an alibi I'm going to have to crack."

"Get on it."

"It may require another trip to L.A."

"Alex, you're not going Hollywood on me, are you?"

"Could be."

"All right. Send me the travel authorization. Any luck on tracing the Krugerrands from Wells's safe?"

"They're pretty much untraceable," Reese replied. "I've checked with some dealers, and finding a gold dealer in L.A. who would testify to cashing them in would be next to impossible."

"I was afraid of that," Martínez said.

"I'm having trouble putting Cato and Edwards in Santa Fe, too; the airlines have no record of them having flown into Albuquerque, and, as you know, there's no L.A.–Santa Fe connection."

"They could have driven it," Martínez pointed out.

"Possibly, but it's a long hike, and there's no way to prove it, unless we find a witness who saw them here, and that's not in the cards."

"Alex, I have to tell you, it's beginning to sound like, if Wells did it, he's going to get away with it."

"Not just yet, Bob. I'm still on it."

"Okay, Alex, but after talking to these two women, if you can't break the alibi, I think we're done."

Reese went back to his office and made an airline reservation to L.A.

JACK CATO STAYED in his stable office after work. He managed to catch Grif Edwards before he left work.

"Grif, I need a favor."

"What's that?"

"I need you to go over to my house right now and let yourself in. You know where the key is. Wave at the neighbors, if you see them; answer the phone if it rings. Tell anybody who calls that I'm down with something that seems like the flu: fever, chills, you know. If you need groceries or beer, pick them up on the way over there, because I don't want you to leave the house until well after I get home."

"You need an alibi, huh?"

"There's five hundred in it for you."

"Okay, will do."

Around eight Cato drove his golf cart over to the studio commissary and had dinner, then he went back to his office and slept on a cot in a back room until a little after midnight.

He opened the little lockbox in the bottom drawer of his desk and took out a ring of a dozen keys that he had collected over his years at Centurion, just in case, then he got back into the golf cart, drove back to the commissary and parked among three or four other carts there. From the commissary he walked a couple of hundred yards to a long, low concrete-block building, then, at the door, began trying keys. Finally, he found one that worked in the lock of the armory.

He let himself into the building and locked it from inside, then he took out a small flashlight and went into the armorer's office to a padlocked metal cabinet, where he began trying more keys, until one worked.

He opened the cabinet to display a wall full of handguns that were neatly hung on pegs. He selected a Walther PPK .380, and in one of the drawers at the bottom of the cabinet he found a silencer and screwed it into the Walther's barrel, checking for fit. When he was satisfied that the two mated properly, he unscrewed the silencer and put it into a jacket pocket, then he put the Walther into another pocket, locked the cabinet, let himself out of the building and re-locked the front door.

Keeping close to the building's wall, he walked back to the commissary and drove the golf cart back to the stable. Once there, he got into his truck and drove to a back gate of the studio, unlocked it with another of his keys and drove away.

He stopped for gas, paying cash, took the opportunity to enter the target's address into the GPS navigator in his truck, then began following its spoken directions. Soon he was on the freeway, headed north, and by early morning he was in Palo Alto.

The GPS navigator obligingly took him directly to the target's address, and Cato drove up and down the block a couple of times, checking it out. He parked on the street within sight of the residence and waited. He figured to take the day to identify the man, then follow him around until he had an opportunity. He loaded the Walther with hollow-point ammunition from his own supply, screwed in the silencer, then stuck it between the front seats of the truck and waited.

Shortly before eight A.M. the garage door of the house opened, and Cato saw a man loading a set of golf clubs into the trunk of a BMW 760. He backed the car out of the garage, closing the door with a remote control, and drove up the street past where Cato's truck was parked.

Cato's heart started beating a little faster. He started the truck, made a U-turn and followed at some distance. The neighborhood was slow to awake on a weekend morning, and there were only a couple of joggers and dog walkers to concern him. Then the target came to a traffic light and stopped.

As Cato approached, he checked ahead of and behind him. Both sides of the street were clear. He pulled up next to the BMW, in the left-turn lane, put it in park and rolled down his passenger-side window. He slid across the seat and shouted, "Excuse me!"

The man turned and looked at him.

"Mr. Wilen?"

The man rolled down the window. "Yes?"

"Are you Mr. Joe Wilen?"

"Yes, I am. What can I do for you?"

Cato pointed the gun at him. "Just hold still," he said. The bullet struck Wilen just above the left eye, and he went down immediately. Cato didn't feel the need for a second shot, since he was using hollow-point ammunition and since there were blood and brains all over the inside of Wilen's windshield and dashboard.

He put the truck in gear, and as the light changed, turned left. In his rearview mirror he saw the BMW coast across the intersection and come to rest against a curb. He checked his pulse: up maybe ten beats, no more. He took a few deep breaths and worked on settling down. Then a police car appeared behind him, its lights flashing, giving him a low growl of the siren.

Cato signaled a right turn, then pulled over to the curb, his hands on the steering wheel, and waited. The police car drove straight past him, not even looking at him, headed to some other destination.

Cato took some more deep breaths, drove a few more blocks, and, when he stopped at another traffic light, selected his home address in the GPS menu and pressed the direct button.

Once on the freeway he stopped for gas and made a call from a pay phone to the cell phone number he had been given.

"Yes?" the woman's voice said.

"The job in Palo Alto was completed an hour ago," he said.

"When I have confirmation on the news or in the paper, I'll send the next package. You have eleven days." She hung up.

THAT NIGHT, back in L.A., Cato drove to Centurion, let himself in through the back gate, cleaned and oiled the gun, then took a thin file and scored the barrel enough to change the ballistic markings it would produce. He returned it to its cabinet in the armory, wiped clean of prints, and went home for some rest.

Grif's car was parked on one side of the driveway. Cato let himself into the garage with the remote control and closed the door after him. It was dark outside, and he had seen none of his neighbors on the street.

Grif was sitting in front of the living room TV, eating chips and drinking a beer. "Hey," he said.

"Evening."

"Everything come out all right?"

Cato ignored the question. He peeled five hundreds off the roll in his pocket and handed them to Edwards. "Thanks for your help. Any calls?"

"Tina called. The cop from Santa Fe is coming to see her. She's got her story down pat, though."

"Good. Was that all?"

"There was a message from GMAC, saying they received your truck payment."

"Good. Anybody else?"

"That's everything. I saw your next-door neighbor when I got here yesterday with a sack of groceries. She asked after you, and I told her you were down with the flu. She wanted to bring over chicken soup, but I told her it wasn't necessary."

"All good," Cato said. "I'm going to go get some sleep; you can go home, if you want to."

"After the game," Edwards said.

Cato showered, dove into bed and slept well.

34 On Sunday morning, Eagle called Joe Wilen's new Santa Fe house and got his wife, Sandi, on the phone.

"Good morning, it's Ed Eagle."

"Good morning, Ed."

"Is Joe awake yet? I thought I'd roust him out for some golf."

"No, he went back to Palo Alto Friday night; he had a tournament to play there this weekend, and he starts his flight training tomorrow."

"Well, he'll be out of pocket for a couple of weeks, I guess. Tell him I'll see him when I see him."

"Okay, Ed. Tell Susannah I'll call her for lunch."

"Will do. Bye-bye." Eagle hung up and went to make breakfast. Susannah was up and in the shower.

He was about to start scrambling eggs when the kitchen phone rang. "Hello?"

"Ed?" It was Sandi Wilen, and she sounded shaky.

"Hi, Sandi. Anything wrong?"

"I just got a call from the Palo Alto police. They told me Joe is dead."

Eagle took a moment to digest this. "Are they sure it's Joe?"

"Yes, he had ID on him. He was shot in his car, on the way to the golf course."

"When did this happen?"

"Yesterday morning. They've been trying to reach me, but they didn't know about the Santa Fe house. A neighbor finally told them to try me here."

"Sandi, I'm so very sorry. I didn't know Joe very well, yet, but I was looking forward to getting to know him and having him as a neighbor."

"Thank you, Ed."

"Is there anything I can do to help?"

"No, I have to go back to Palo Alto. It's going to take me all day, what with the airline connections."

"Sandi, I'll be happy to fly you directly to Palo Alto. We can be there by lunchtime, and I'm sure you're going to need some help dealing with this when we get there."

"I wouldn't want to put you to that trouble, Ed, but . . ."

"I'll pick you up in forty-five minutes, okay?"

"Well, all right, Ed. I really appreciate this."

"See you then." Eagle hung up.

Susannah appeared in fresh jeans and a sweater, her hair wet. "I don't like the look on your face," she said. "What's happened?"

"Joe Wilen is dead, shot."

Susannah was shocked. "Is it Barbara, do you think?"

"Yes, I do think. I'm going to fly Sandi home and see if I can help there."

"Can I come?"

"Sure, if you want to. I could use some help with Sandi, I'm sure."

"I'll pack for a couple of days," she said, disappearing into the bedroom.

EAGLE LANDED AT San Jose and soon they were at Palo Alto police headquarters. A detective came down and met them, and introductions were made.

"I want to see my husband," Sandi said.

"Of course, Mrs. Wilen," the detective said. "We'll need your identification of the body. I'll get someone to take you over to the morgue." He picked up the phone and made a call. A moment later another detective appeared and escorted her away, with Susannah in tow.

"May I speak with you, Detective?" Eagle asked.

"Sure, let's use this room over here." The detective led Eagle into an interrogation room and closed the door. The two men sat down.

"Please tell me how Joe Wilen died."

"Your name again?"

"Ed Eagle. I'm an attorney, friend of the family. I may be able to help."

"Mr. Wilen was scheduled to play in a golf tournament yesterday morning. He left his house and a few blocks away, he stopped at a traffic signal. We think another vehicle drove alongside his car and someone shot him once in the head. The weapon was a .380, the bullet a hollow-point. One was all it took. A jogger found the car a few yards away; it had come to rest against a tree at low speed, and the engine was still running. The jogger didn't see another vehicle, but from the angle of the wound we think it was a taller vehicle, an SUV or a truck."

"I think I may have a suspect for you."

"Tell me who he is."

"It's a she, and she has more than one name: Barbara Eagle, sometimes; recently she was calling herself Eleanor Wright; and a couple of weeks ago, she married a Palo Alto man, Walter Keeler."

"I know who Keeler is, sure," the detective said. "He was killed last week in a car crash on the interstate."

"That's correct."

"What would Mrs. Keeler's motive be for killing her new husband?"

"I don't think she did that, but I think she either killed Joe Wilen or hired someone to do it."

"Okay, what was her motive for killing her husband's lawyer?"

Eagle explained about the letter he had written, that Wilen had shown to Keeler, causing him to change his will. "If Wilen hadn't shown him the letter, Mrs. Keeler would have inherited more than a billion dollars. After he read it, he cut her inheritance down to fifty thousand dollars a month for life and the use, but not the ownership, of their San Francisco apartment."

"So she was angry with Wilen?"

"Oh, yes, and she told him so to his face. He told me, and I warned him to be careful."

"Are you related to Mrs. Keeler?"

"She's my ex-wife. She was recently tried for a double murder in L.A. and got off—this was only a few weeks ago."

"And where can I find her now?"

"Maybe at her San Francisco home, but she could also be at the home of a friend called James Long, in Los Angeles."

There was a knock on the door, and the detective got up and opened it.

An attractive woman in her thirties stood there. "Detective Hayman?"

"Yes."

"I'm Lee Hight. I'm an associate of Joe Wilen—actually, his law partner."

The detective offered her a chair and brought her up to date.

"I was at the meeting where Joe told Mrs. Keeler about her inheritance," she said. "The woman looked as though she might kill him on the spot. It was scary."

"So you concur that Mrs. Keeler should be our chief suspect?"

"Without any doubt."

"Do you have the address of her San Francisco apartment?"

Hight gave it to him.

"Expect her to have a good alibi," Eagle said, "but she's responsible for Joe Wilen's murder, I promise you."

EAGLE AND SUSANNAH drove Sandi Wilen to her home, and she insisted that they stay overnight. They consented, and Susannah cooked dinner for them that evening.

"Ed, you think Walter Keeler's widow had something to do with this, don't you?" Sandi asked over dinner. "You told us at dinner the other night that she could be dangerous."

"I have no doubt that she is responsible," Ed replied. "She probably hired someone, because it would be too dangerous for her to do it herself, given the clause in Walter's will, cutting her off if she committed a crime."

"Did you tell the police detective about her?"

"Yes, I did, and Joe's law partner, Lee Hight, added her weight to the opinion."

"Lee is a good person and a good lawyer," Sandi said. "Joe made her a partner in the firm just this past week."

"Does the firm have a lot of clients?"

"One or two of Joe's friends. Most of the work was for Walter Keeler, and Joe said that would continue to be the case, because they'll be administering Walter's estate, which, as you can imagine, is considerable."

The doorbell rang, and Sandi went to answer it. She came back with Lee Hight. "Lee, you've met Ed Eagle; this is his friend, Susannah Wilde."

Lee sat down. "Mr. Eagle, you should know that, tomorrow morning, I'm going to cancel all payments from Walter Keeler's estate to Mrs. Keeler and issue an eviction notice for the apartment."

"Lee, do the terms of Keeler's will allow you to do that because you suspect Mrs. Keeler, or does she have to be convicted?"

"The will says she has to be convicted, but what the hell, she can sue us."

"Please don't do this," Eagle replied.

"Why not? Do you think she'll pursue it through the courts?"

"Yes, but more important, I think you would be placing your life in danger. If she has already had Joe killed, do you think she would hesitate to go after you? She's a very angry woman."

Hight looked worried. "I hadn't got that far in my thinking," she said.

"My advice is to continue to make the payments, and as soon as she's convicted, stop them."

"I guess that's good advice," Hight said. "I'm just so fucking angry about this, I'm not thinking straight."

"Sandi tells me Joe made you a partner last week. Do you have that in writing?"

"Yes, Joe took care of that."

"Then go run your law firm and don't worry about Mrs. Keeler. Let the police do that."

"All right, Mr. Eagle. I'll do that."

"And if I were you, I'd get a gun permit from your local police department, take some instruction, and carry it until Mrs. Keeler is locked safely away."

"I think that's good advice, too," she said.

———

THE FOLLOWING MORNING, Eagle called Cupie Dalton.

"This is Cupie."

Eagle told him about Wilen's murder.

"Man, she's something, isn't she?"

"Yes, and she's probably in L.A."

"So I should watch my ass?"

"So you should watch your ass."

"Do you know where she is in L.A.?"

"Probably at her friend Jimmy Long's house."

"I could tail her."

"Better somebody she doesn't know. I'm going to speak to the chief of police about that; maybe he'll authorize surveillance. God knows, the D.A. would like another crack at her."

"Good idea."

"You might look into who the hit man could be, Cupie. My guess is that Jimmy Long found somebody for her, since she doesn't really know a lot of people in L.A."

"I'll look into it."

Eagle said good-bye and hung up. Next, he called his friend, the Los Angeles Chief of Police, Joe Sams.

"Hello, Ed, how are you?"

"I've been better, Joe. You remember my former wife, Barbara?"

"The double murderess? How could I forget."

"Well, she's done it again."

"Not in L.A., I hope."

"No, in Palo Alto. I believe she hired someone from L.A. to kill a lawyer named Joe Wilen."

"Why from L.A.?"

"Because she doesn't know anybody in San Francisco, where she's now living. A couple of weeks ago, she married a very rich retired businessman named Walter Keeler."

"I knew Walter; I read about his death in the papers. Did she have anything to do with that?"

"No, it was a traffic accident." Eagle explained about the terms of Keeler's will and Wilen's part, as well as his own part in preventing her from inheriting everything.

"So she got Wilen, and you're next?"

"Probably. Don't worry, I'm carrying, thanks to your help with my license."

"Do you have anything on the woman that would give me probable cause to arrest her?"

"No. I think what your people could do best would be to find out who she hired to do it."

"And where do we start?"

"She has a friend named Jimmy Long, a successful movie producer. He was her alibi at her trial, and it was his story that got her off. He's her only friend here, as far as I know, so she might have turned to him to help her find a contract killer."

"Would this Jimmy Long be likely to know a contract killer?"

"He's in the movie business, Joe."

"Oh. All right, I'll assign some people to track down his connections and see if a likely hit man turns up. Anything else I can do?"

"If I can think of anything, I'll call you, Joe. Thanks for your help." Eagle hung up.

"You're carrying?" Susannah asked.

"You know I usually do, especially when I'm in L.A."

"Should I be carrying?"

"Maybe so. Barbara saw you at the trial, and she may have recognized you from the movies. Do you have a license for L.A.?"

"Yes. So you think she would really come after me?"

"Yes, because she knows it would hurt me."

**36** D̲ETECTIVE A̲LEX R̲EESE found the apartment building in West Hollywood where Tina López and her roommate, Soledad Rivera, lived and rang their bell.

The door was opened by a short, plump, pretty woman. "Yes?"

Reese flashed his badge. "I'm Detective Reese, Santa Fe Police Department. Are you Tina López or Soledad Rivera?"

"I'm Soledad," she replied. "What do you want?"

"I'd like to ask you and Ms. López some questions regarding an investigation I'm conducting. Is she here?"

"Maybe."

"May I come in?"

"What do you want to know?"

Before he could reply, another woman came down a hallway and approached the door. She was taller and quite beautiful, wearing low-cut jeans that exposed an expanse of belly from well below her navel to just below her deeply cut cleavage.

"Are you Tina López?"

"He's a cop from Santa Fe, Tina," Soledad said.

"What do you want?"

"I'd like to ask both of you some questions concerning an investigation I'm conducting. May I come in?"

"I guess so," Tina replied.

Reese took a seat in the small living room. "It's my understanding that you were both in Tijuana for the bullfights recently." He gave them the dates. "Is that correct?"

"Yes," Tina replied.

"Who were you with?"

"Grif Edwards and Jack Cato," Soledad said quickly.

"And where did you stay?"

"At the Parador," Soledad said.

"Before I ask you the next question I should tell you that my investigation is of a double murder, a mother and her son, in Santa Fe, and that anyone who gives false information to me with regard to those killings is liable to be charged as an accessory. Being an accessory to murder carries the same prison sentence as that for the actual murderer. Do you understand what I'm telling you?"

Both women stared at him blankly, and he thought he saw tears begin to well in Soledad's eyes.

"Do you understand?"

"We don't want to talk to you anymore," Tina said.

"Grif and Jack weren't with you in Tijuana, were they? It was two other men, wasn't it?"

"I don't . . ." Soledad began, but Tina elbowed her.

"We don't want to talk to you anymore," Tina said again.

"In that case, I'll have to have the Los Angeles police take you to police headquarters, and we can start all over again with a written record of your questioning." Reese changed his tone. "Ladies, let me give you some good advice: You don't want to go to prison for protecting these two guys. They're not worth it."

Soledad turned and looked at Tina, and tears began to roll down her cheeks.

"Shut up, Soledad," Tina said. She turned to Reese. "Now you get out of my house."

"I'll see you at the police station," Reese said, "and if I were you, I'd get a good criminal lawyer, and that's going to be expensive."

Soledad began to bawl.

Reese turned to her. "Soledad, do you want to talk to me and save yourself a lot of grief?"

"I told you to get out!" Tina cried.

"Soledad hasn't asked me to leave."

Soledad continued to cry loudly.

Tina jumped to her feet, went to the door and pointed outside. "Get out!"

Reese got up, taking his cell phone from his belt. As he walked to the door he made a show of calling a number. "LAPD? I'd like to speak to the chief of detectives, please." The door slammed behind him.

Reese went back to his rental car, got in and waited. Ten minutes later, Soledad Rivera ran out of the apartment building, carrying a nylon duffel bag, got into a Volkswagen Beetle and drove away. Reese started his car and followed at a distance.

Soledad drove to a neighborhood that seemed to be completely Hispanic, judging from the signs on the storefronts and the people on the streets. She turned into the driveway of a small, neat house, got out of her car and ran inside.

Reese noted the address. "Soledad has run home to Mama," he said aloud to himself.

ED EAGLE LANDED at Santa Monica Airport, picked up a rental car and drove with Susannah to her Century City apartment. Eagle called Don Wells at Centurion Studios.

"Ed? How are you?"

"Very well, thank you, Don. May we have lunch today?"

"Sure, why don't you come out to Centurion, and we'll go to the studio commissary."

"All right."

Wells gave him directions, and Eagle hung up.

"How long are we going to be here?" Susannah asked.

"One night, maybe two," Eagle replied.

Susannah went to a wall safe behind a picture, opened it and held up a small semiautomatic pistol. "This goes into my purse," she said.

"Good."

EAGLE WAS GIVEN a studio pass at the front gate and directed to the commissary. Don Wells was waiting at a table inside. He stood up and waved.

Eagle made his way across the crowded dining room to Well's corner table and sat down.

"Drink?" Wells asked.

"No, thanks, just some iced tea," Eagle replied, accepting a menu from a waitress. They ordered lunch.

"So, anything happening with the Santa Fe D.A.?" Wells asked. "Do they have any leads on the killer or killers?"

"They seem to be concentrating on you," Eagle said.

"You mean Jack Cato?"

"You know about that?"

"He told me he and Grif Edwards had a visit from a Santa Fe detective."

"Does that concern you?"

"Why should it?"

"It seems clear that the Santa Fe police are theorizing that you hired Cato and Edwards to kill your wife and son."

"Listen to me, Ed . . ."

Eagle held up a hand to stop him. "Before you say anything else, let me explain something, Don. Hypothetically speaking, if a client tells his lawyer that he's guilty of a crime, then when he is tried for it, the lawyer can't put him on the stand."

"Why not?"

"Because if the client, having told the lawyer he's guilty, claims innocence on the stand, then the lawyer is suborning perjury, since he knows his client is lying. Do you understand?"

"Yes, and don't worry; I'm not going to tell you I'm guilty."

"Good. What is your relationship with Cato and Edwards?"

"Not much of one. They've both worked on a number of my pictures as stuntmen or extras, and they're part of a group that plays poker at my office once a week when I'm in town."

"Do you think that these two men are the sorts who would hire out to commit murder?"

"Beats me," Wells said. "All I know about them is that Cato is hard to read at the poker table, and Edwards scratches his head when he draws good cards. Anything beyond that would be news to me."

"Ever heard any rumors about either of them?"

"What kind of rumors?"

"Rumors about their hiring out for murder."

"Nope. Stuntmen are a funny breed, though: a lot of swagger and big talk. It wouldn't surprise me if one of them bragged about something like that, whether he did it or not."

"From what you know of them, do you think they might become loose cannons if put under pressure by the police?"

"I honestly don't know, Ed. My impression of Cato is that he's the sort who's steady under pressure; I've seen that in his stunt work. Edwards? Who knows?"

"Don, at the very least, the police investigation of these two men means that they are taking you very seriously as a suspect. Have you ever given either of these men sums of cash?"

"Yeah, after a poker game, but I think I've won it back."

"You've said that you keep cash and Krugerrands in your Malibu safe, just as you did in Santa Fe. Is that money still there?"

"Yes, of course."

"See that it doesn't disappear. You may have to open that safe for the police, before this is over."

"I get it," Wells said.

Eagle hoped he did.

 BARBARA WAS SOAKING in a hot tub when Jimmy knocked on the bathroom door.

"Come in," she called.

Jimmy let himself into the bathroom. "There's what looks like an unmarked police car parked near the end of the driveway," he said.

"What kind of car?"

"A green Ford, I think."

Barbara stood up, allowing soapy water to cascade down her still beautiful, naked body. "Well," she said, "I think I'll take them shopping."

JACK CATO WAITED until the mailman arrived before leaving for work. He took the mail inside; among the overdue bills was a manila envelope. It bore no return address. He opened it and shook out the contents, a Ziploc bag containing two stacks of one-hundred-dollar bills. He stuffed the money into his jacket pocket, then got into his truck and drove to work. On the way, he stopped at a drugstore that took payments for the electric, gas and telephone companies and paid his bills in cash. He was now up-to-date on all his bills, and he intended to stay that way.

Once at the studio stables he found a pry bar and left the barn through a rear door. He looked around for spectators, and, seeing none, he opened the door of a prop outhouse, pried up some of the floorboards and, with his hands, scraped the loose dirt away, revealing a safe set in a concrete pad. He opened the safe and dropped the money into it, retaining enough for his day-to-day expenses. He closed the safe, raked the dirt back over it and hammered down the floorboards with the pry bar.

Soon he would have another fifty thousand dollars to add to his stash, and he had only ten days to accomplish his task. He had no doubt that this woman would make good on her threat to kill him if he didn't fulfill his mission on time. He had no idea who she was, so she could walk up behind him anywhere and put a bullet in his head. He began planning his work for the coming weekend.

He called Tina López at work, on her cell phone. "Hey," he said.

"Hey, yourself."

"You up for a trip to Tijuana this weekend?"

"Listen, Jack, we had a cop from Santa Fe come see us yesterday. Soledad went nuts and went home to her mother's house. She's scared shitless, and she might crack if she's pressed anymore."

"That's not good, sweetheart," he said. "You need to talk to her and tell her to get a grip. The story will hold, if she doesn't crack."

"I'll do the best I can. That's all I can promise. What the hell are you doing that I have to cover your ass again?"

"You don't want to know, Tina. Don't ever ask me that again."

"Look, we've got what we want. If you keep doing stuff, you're going to blow the lid off this thing, and we'll all go down."

"This is my last weekend's work," Cato said. "Just get your ass down to Tijuana on Friday, and don't come back until late Sunday night. There's five grand in it for you."

"You think I need five grand? I'm going to have more money than you could believe!"

"Yeah, but you don't have it yet, and you've got rent and car payments to make, right? Five grand should tide you over until it can come through."

She fumed for a moment. "All right, but this is the last time, you hear me?"

"I hear you. I'll give you your money on Monday."

"Right." She hung up.

Barbara noted the police car as she pulled out of Jimmy Long's driveway, and she made it easy for them, driving a steady thirty miles an hour and stopping for all the stop signs. She had never understood why there were all these four-way stop signs in Beverly Hills. Hadn't these people ever heard of right-of-way streets?

She drove down Rodeo Drive and gave her rental car to the attendant behind the Ralph Lauren store. She had not been inside the shop for more than a minute before she spotted a woman browsing whose cheap pants suit made her look out of place in the elegant store. Well, she could just eat her heart out, Barbara thought.

She tried on half a dozen things and chose a slinky, black dress and a couple of cashmere sweaters. She made sure the policewoman saw her black American Express card as she paid for them.

She walked out the front of the store and made her way down Rodeo, window-shopping, occasionally going inside and buying a dress or a pair of shoes. She had lunch alone in the garden at Spago, then worked her way back to the Ralph Lauren shop and retrieved her car. She was back at Jimmy's by midafternoon, and so was the police car. Let them report that!

JACK CATO REPEATED his actions of the weekend before, but this time he brought along a set of lock picks. What he wanted from the armory was locked in a large room that he had never been able to get a key to.

He let himself into the building and walked into a windowless hallway, closing the door behind him so that he could switch on the lights. He knelt before the double steel doors and took a close look at the lock. It was the sort of thing you'd see on the front door of a house, really, nothing special. He put on his reading glasses and unzipped the little case holding his lock picks. He selected two and began probing the lock, feeling it out.

It turned out to be a pain in the ass before he could get it open, but at least he knew the lock now, and it would be easier to deal with later. He swung open the heavy door and switched on the lights inside. The fluorescent fixtures flickered on, and he was staring at enough weapons to equip the SWAT teams of a city: assault rifles, machine guns, grenade launchers, even half a dozen mortars. He'd love to have sacked the whole room, but he wanted only one thing: an ordinary-looking aluminum briefcase, tucked away on a high shelf. He pulled up a stepladder and got it down.

It had two combination locks securing it, but it turned out that the combinations were just three zeros. He opened it and checked out the contents: a beautifully crafted, disassembled sniper's rifle that had been made by an old man named Al, a gunsmith who had a shop on Melrose, for a spy movie that had been made on the lot. Jack doubted if it had had more than half a dozen rounds put through it.

He closed the case and helped himself to a pocketful of .223 ammunition from a drawer. He knew the armorer didn't log ammo use, so he was safe. He relocked the steel door, let himself out of the building and returned to the stables.

He had already checked the shooting schedules for work under way. Nobody would need the sniper's rifle anytime soon, so he was good through the weekend.

He called a phone number and waited.

"Compton Flying Club," a woman's voice said.

"Hey, Sheila, it's Jack Cato."

"Hi, Jack. What can I do for you?"

"Is the Bonanza available this weekend?"

"Let me check."

He could hear her turning the pages of her desk calendar.

"All weekend," she said.

"Great, I'll take it Friday evening and have it back by Monday morning. I'm going up to San Francisco this weekend. Can you have it fueled and left on the line after about five on Friday? Leave the key under the nosewheel chock."

"Sure thing. Have a good flight."

Cato hung up. Everything was all set now.

38

EAGLE GOT A call from the LAPD a couple of days after his request to the chief.

"Mr. Eagle, this is Detective Barnes; the chief asked me to call you."

"Yes, Detective."

"We've had a team on Barbara Eagle for two days now, and all we're seeing is shopping trips in the daytime and restaurants in the evening. Mr. Long seems to work at home as much as he does at the studio. I don't know how much longer the chief will let us keep this up."

"Has she met anybody on her shopping trips or in the restaurants?"

"Hasn't spoken a word to anybody but store clerks and waiters and the diners, but we don't have the phone tapped, so who knows? Oh, I don't know if this is important, but she stopped in the Beverly Hills Post Office and mailed a package."

"What sort of package?"

"Just a manila envelope."

"She mailed a payoff to the hit man. Were you able to see an address?"

"No, sir, we couldn't get close enough."

"Okay, thanks very much, and thank the chief for me. Be sure and tell him about the envelope." Eagle hung up. The weekend was coming, and he had an idea the hit man was coming, too.

He called Susannah, who was at her house, dealing with a washing-machine repairman. "Hello, there."

"Hi, what's happening?"

"Barbara is still in L.A., and the cops are keeping an eye on her."

"That's reassuring."

"Don't let it be. She was seen at the post office, mailing a package. That has to be the payment for killing Joe Wilen. I have a feeling we're going to hear from her hit man this weekend, and I'd like you to stay at your house."

"Not going to happen," she said. "If the hit man shows up, you're going to need another gun. You already know I can shoot."

"Don't worry, sweetheart, I'll have help. I want you out of harm's way. Barbara saw you at the trial, and she may have recognized you from your movies. I hope you understand."

"I understand, but I don't like it."

"After the weekend, you can come home to me."

"Ed, I don't think you've thought this through."

"What do you mean?"

"Well, suppose you catch the guy, or kill him. Do you think that's going to stop Barbara?"

"Probably not," he admitted.

"I think what you're going to have to do is stop her before she gets to you."

"What are you suggesting?"

"I think you should take whatever steps are necessary."

"I'm not sure I like the sound of that."

"I don't like saying it, but you have to protect yourself. If you don't, she's going to keep trying until she wins."

"Right now, we have to think about this weekend, so let's

talk about this another time," Eagle said. "I'll call you tomorrow. Bye-bye."

Eagle called the district attorney.

"Bob Martínez."

"It's Ed Eagle, Bob."

"Hello, Ed."

"I need your help."

Martínez chuckled. "In court?"

"Thanks, no. That I can handle by myself."

"What, then?"

"I think Barbara is going to send a hit man to Santa Fe—the same guy who killed Joe Wilen in Palo Alto—probably this weekend."

"Why do you think that?"

"You know her history. What would you expect her to do?"

"You have any idea who he is? A description would help."

"No, no idea."

Martínez didn't speak for a moment. "You want some protection, is that it?"

"A couple of men will do, just for the weekend."

"Let me call the chief. I'll get back to you."

"Thanks, Bob."

DETECTIVE ALEX REESE was driving to Centurion Studios on Friday afternoon for his meeting when his cell phone buzzed. "Hello?"

"Hi, Alex. It's Raoul Hernández."

"Hi, Raoul." Hernández was a New Mexico state trooper who was also a pilot and who often flew state officials.

"Are you still in L.A.?"

"Yep, I've got one more interview, then I'll get a plane home later this afternoon."

"I'm in L.A., too, and I'll give you a lift back to Santa Fe, if you can be at Santa Monica Airport in a couple of hours."

"That would be great, Raoul. I'll be there."

"The airplane's at Supermarine."

"See you there." Reese hung up. This was a nice break; now he wouldn't have to fly to Albuquerque and take the shuttle bus to Santa Fe. He could be home for dinner.

At Centurion he went directly to Jeff Bender's office. Soledad Rivera was sitting in Bender's waiting room, and she glared at him as he passed through to Bender's office. He had summoned her there from the costume department, where she worked with Tina López.

"Hi, Alex. She's outside."

"Yeah, I saw her."

"Let's get her in here, then," Bender said, picking up his phone.

Soledad was more composed than she had been at their last meeting, Reese thought. "Good afternoon, Soledad," he said.

"What do you want?" she asked, sounding hostile.

"I wanted to give you a chance to talk to me without Tina being here," he said. "I think you're about to get into a lot of trouble, and I want to help you, if I can."

"You don't want to help me," she said, "and anyway, I don't need your help. I haven't done anything wrong."

"Think about that, Soledad. If you testify in court that you were in Tijuana with Cato and Edwards, you'll be in more trouble than you can imagine. Right at this moment, if you don't talk to me, you're obstructing justice."

"I don't have anything to say," she said.

"Soledad, you have a good job and a nice life. Why would you want to throw that away, risk going to prison for the rest of your life?"

"I haven't done anything wrong, and I don't have anything to say."

Reese and Bender exchanged a glance, and Bender shrugged.

Reese gave her his card. "If you change your mind, here's my number. I can keep you out of jail, Soledad."

She took the card but said nothing else, just walked out of the office.

"That didn't go too well," Reese said. "She was very emotional at our last meeting, and I thought she might break if I got her away from Tina, who is obviously in charge."

"That reminds me," Bender said. "A lot of gossip comes my way around here, and I heard something that might interest you."

"What's that?"

"This is just a rumor, mind you, and I can't prove it, but I heard that Don Wells has been fucking Tina López for a while."

"Before his wife's murder?"

"That's what I hear. I wish I could back it up, but I can't."

"That's very interesting, Jeff." He thanked the security chief for his help and left, headed for Santa Monica Airport.

As darkness approached, Jack Cato drove his car to the Compton airport, a small field southeast of Los Angeles International, then to the Compton Flying Club, where he had learned to fly fifteen years before and where he sometimes rented airplanes.

He parked his car and walked over to where the Beech Bonanza had been left parked for him. He opened the fuel caps and checked to be sure the airplane had been refueled, then he performed a preflight check and kicked away the chocks securing the wheels, finding the airplane's key under the nosewheel chock.

He tossed his duffel and hat and the briefcase containing the sniper's rifle into the rear seat, got the airplane started and taxied to the end of the runway. He called Socal Approach and gave them his tail number. "Departing Compton VFR, bound for Palmdale," he said into the headset. "Request a squawk code and vectors to the Palmdale VOR."

"Bonanza, squawk four-seven/four-seven cleared for takeoff. Fly runway heading and maintain VFR," the controller said.

Cato taxied onto the runway and shoved the throttle forward. A moment later he lifted off just in time to see the upper limb of the sun sink into the Pacific. Twenty minutes later, after a number of vectored turns, he was at the Palmdale VOR, a navigation beacon. He thanked the Socal controller, was authorized to change frequencies, then switched off the transponder and turned the radio volume all the way down. Now he didn't exist for the controllers, except as a primary radar target, so his tail number did not appear on their screens.

He entered 17,500 feet into the altitude preselect unit, entered SAF into the GPS computer, then climbed to his selected altitude, slipping on an oxygen mask at 10,000. He was flying across the Mojave Desert, direct to Santa Fe, at an altitude rarely used by general aviation aircraft, and although he had a screen display of other airplanes in the area, it was unlikely that any of them would ever come near him. All he had to do for the rest of the flight was to switch fuel tanks from time to time. He switched on the Sirius Satellite Radio, tuned in a country music station and opened a sandwich he had brought with him. The GPS told him he would be in Santa Fe in two hours and forty minutes.

Half an hour out of Santa Fe he took a sunglasses case from his pocket and opened it. Inside was something he had stolen from the makeup department during his last movie: a beautiful and voluminous handlebar moustache. He switched on the cabin lights, painted his upper lip with adhesive from a small bottle and, using a mirror, affixed the moustache.

He landed at Santa Fe, put on his large cowboy hat and went into the reception building at Santa Fe Jet. Using a fake driver's license with an Austin, Texas, address, he signed up for the rental car he had reserved, left a thousand-dollar cash deposit and placed his fuel and oxygen order, then he was on his way. The girl behind the counter would remember only a man with a big hat, a broad Texas accent and an outlandish moustache.

Cato knew Santa Fe fairly well, because he had made two pictures there and because he had studied a map and had located the route prescribed by the woman who had hired him.

He checked into a motel on Cerrillos Road, a busy, six-lane approach to the city, and watched TV until he got sleepy. He slept until past ten A.M., then donned his moustache and hat and had breakfast at McDonald's. He then drove to the northern outskirts of the city to a country road where he had once driven a stagecoach in a film.

He got out of the car and walked a couple of hundred yards into the desert, where he set up some stones as targets, then paced off one hundred yards. He assembled the rifle, loaded it and first from a prone position, then kneeling and standing, fired at the stones, making minute corrections to the telescopic sight until he was zeroed in. Then he disassembled the rifle, packed it into its case and walked back to his car.

He had some lunch at the Tesuque Market, a local grocery and restaurant, then he found the road where his target lived. He drove past the house, then turned around and drove back, checking it out again. Along the way he saw a little dirt track where he could park his car, unseen. Satisfied, he went back to his motel and watched a NASCAR race on TV.

He had a late dinner at a place on Canyon Road, still in his moustache and never removing his hat. A little past midnight, he got into his car and drove slowly out to the target house, parked his car and began to make ready.

EAGLE HAD DINNER in town with Susannah, made a lunch date with her for the next day, then drove her back to her house. He called a cell number he had been given.

"Yes?" a voice said.

"It's Ed Eagle. Can I come home now?"

"Yes. I'm in the house, and I've got a man patrolling the perimeter of the property."

"Thanks. I'll be there shortly." He drove back to his home, parked in the garage and let himself into the kitchen. A police detective was sitting at the counter, sipping coffee. "Good evening," Eagle said.

"I made myself some coffee," the cop said.

"Raid the refrigerator, if you're hungry. I'm going to bed. Long day."

"Good night, then," the cop said.

Eagle went into his bedroom and switched on the lights.

JACK CATO HAD seen the car drive in and the light go on. He worked his way around the house a couple of dozen yards until he could see, through a window, someone moving. He sighted through the scope and found his victim, as described.

He knelt beside a large boulder and rested the rifle on it, giving himself a steady shooting cradle. The target walked past a window, but he didn't have time to fire. Then the target came back and was satisfyingly still, framed by the window, undressing.

Cato needed only a single shot. He heard the glass break, and his target spun and fell, out of sight. Cato wasted no time. He walked quickly back to the car, disassembled the rifle, locked it in the trunk in the compartment with the spare tire, backed out of the dirt road with his lights off and drove away from the house. Using his map, he found another way back to town. An hour after the kill, he was in his bed, sound asleep, with the clock radio set for five A.M.

The following morning, Cato was back at the airport, just as Santa Fe Jet opened. He turned in his rental car and paid his fuel bill in cash, and half an hour later he was on his way back to Los Angeles.

After landing, he called the cell number he had been given.

"Yes?" she said.

"The job is done."

"I'll mail your money as soon as it's confirmed."

Cato hung up and drove home.

40 BARBARA TURNED OFF the cell phone and put it in her handbag.

"Well," she said to Jimmy Long, who was sitting up in bed, reading the papers, "my work here is done."

"You're leaving today?"

"Tomorrow," she said. "I want to see the papers before I leave."

"I'll miss you."

"Don't worry," she said, "I'll be back."

DETECTIVE ALEX REESE got the call at home, and he arrived at the house to find an ambulance parked at the front door and a stretcher being loaded. He got to the driver before the vehicle pulled away.

"What's the story?" he asked.

"Gunshot wound to the back of the head," the man said. "Still alive, though." He put the ambulance in gear and drove away.

Reese went into the house and found two deputy sheriffs placing yellow tape across a bedroom door. He ducked under the tape and walked into the master suite. Bullet hole through a windowpane, considerable blood on the carpet. There was nothing for him to do here, so he gave the deputies his card. "Tell the criminalist I want a copy of his report faxed to me the minute it's ready," he said.

Reese went into the study and found Ed Eagle on the phone.

"Cupie," Eagle was saying, "it's Ed Eagle. Call me as soon as possible on my cell phone."

"What are you doing here, Mr. Eagle?" Reese asked.

"We had a lunch date; I found her on the bedroom floor, unconscious and bleeding, and I called nine-one-one." He stood up. "I'm going to the hospital. If you want to talk more, I'll see you there."

"All right," Reese said.

EAGLE LEFT SUSANNAH'S house in a cold fury and drove to the hospital. He went into the emergency room and found a doctor he knew, who promised to let him know as soon as an assessment of Susannah's condition had been made, then he went and sat in the reception area.

Alex Reese came in and sat down beside him. "How is she?"

"They don't know yet."

"All right, Ed, tell me everything you know."

Eagle explained about the death of Joe Wilen and how he had expected to be attacked that weekend. "Bob Martínez sent two detectives out to the house. We were hoping to arrest the assassin and question him, but, as it turns out, he was after Susannah, not me."

"Who would have done this?" Reese asked.

"My ex-wife hired somebody to kill Wilen and, I thought, me. As it turns out, she had a plan to cause me a lot of pain first. Next, she'll come after me."

"Where is your ex now?"

"In Los Angeles. The police there have been watching her."

"Any other possible suspects?"

"None. You'd be wasting your time if you looked for any-body else."

A doctor approached them, and Eagle stood up. "Yes, Doctor?"

"Ms. Wilde has suffered a gunshot wound; the bullet creased the back of her skull and knocked her down. The scalp wound bled a lot, but she's not seriously hurt. She has a concussion, so we'll keep her overnight to make sure nothing further develops. She's awake, if you want to see her, but she's been sedated, so she's pretty groggy."

"Yes, please, I'd like to see her." Eagle was led into a curtained cubicle where Susannah lay on a gurney. He picked up her hand. "How are you feeling?"

"Dreamy," she said.

"I'm sorry this happened. I never believed she'd go after you."

"Ed," Susannah said, "come close."

Eagle bent over and put his ear near her lips.

"If you don't kill her," Susannah whispered, "I'm going to." Then she seemed to fall asleep.

EAGLE WAS DRIVING home when his cell phone vibrated. "Hello?"

"Hi, it's Cupie."

"Cupie, I thought Barbara's hit man would come after me this weekend, but he didn't. He went after Susannah Wilde instead."

"Oh, shit."

"She's all right; the shot clipped her but missed doing serious damage by half an inch."

"Do you think the hit man thinks she's dead?"

"Probably."

"Can you get a story planted in the Santa Fe paper saying she was shot and killed?"

"I know the editor, but I don't think he would print a false report."

"Tell him what's up. It's best if Barbara thinks she's dead. Don't use her name, just say an actress. Tell him to put it on the AP wire, too."

"I'll see what I can do," Eagle said. "In the meantime, I want you to start thinking about something." Eagle told him what he had in mind.

"That's going to be tough," Cupie said, "and it involves serious criminal activity on my part."

"You'll be well paid, Cupie. If you don't want to do this, tell me, and I'll get somebody else."

Cupie was quiet for a moment. "Let me get Vittorio in on this," he said. "I think it would appeal to him."

"All right, talk to him about it, then get back to me."

"Will do." Cupie hung up.

One way or another, Eagle vowed to himself, he was going to see Barbara taken out.

B ARBARA WOKE EARLY and went downstairs. The *L.A. Times* and *The Wall Street Journal* were on the doorstep. She took them into the kitchen, made coffee and started leafing through the *Times*. Nothing in the front section. She was well into the arts pages before she found it.

ACTRESS MURDERED IN SANTA FE

AP: Santa Fe police announced the death by shooting of a woman they described as "a member of the film community" at her home outside the city. She had apparently been shot through a bedroom window by a sniper, who is being sought by police. Police are withholding her name, pending notification of next of kin.

Barbara thought her coffee had never tasted better. In a rush of good feeling, she made breakfast for Jimmy and took it upstairs to him on a tray.

"Hey, the service is getting pretty good around here," he said. "You sure you have to go?"

"Well, maybe I'll stay on for a few days more," she said. What the hell, she thought. I'm not going to get laid in San Francisco.

"You're welcome as long as you'd like to stay," he said.

Barbara was pulling on some jeans and a cotton sweater. "You're sweet, baby."

"Where are you going so early?" Jimmy asked.

"I have to go to the post office," she replied. She went downstairs to his study, found a manila envelope, addressed it with a Magic Marker and stuffed it with fifty thousand dollars. The post office wouldn't be open yet, so she grabbed a roll of stamps from Jimmy's desk drawer, weighed the package on his postage scale and applied the postage.

DETECTIVE LUCY DIXON had just come on duty in her unmarked car when she saw the car, driven by the woman, come out of the Long driveway. She started her car and followed at a distance. Where the hell could the woman be going at seven forty-five in the morning? No shops were open at this hour.

She followed the car until it turned into the post office parking lot and watched as the woman deposited a manila envelope into the drive-thru mailbox, then left the parking lot and drove back the way she had come.

Dixon drove up to the mailbox and checked the schedule. A pickup was due at eight A.M., and it was already ten past. No time to get a federal warrant. She pulled her car farther forward and stopped, blocking the driveway, then got out of the car and waited.

Another ten minutes passed before the truck arrived and the driver got out.

Dixon approached him with a smile. "Good morning," she said.

"Good morning," he replied looking her up and down.

This was a good sign. She smiled more broadly and showed him her badge. "I'm LAPD," she said. "I wonder if you would let me look at a package that was mailed a few minutes ago?"

The driver shook his head. "Sorry, Detective, you can't mess with the mail without a federal warrant."

"It's Lucy," she said.

"Sorry, Lucy."

"I don't want to mess with it; I just want to see the address on it. It's a manila envelope, and it was mailed ten minutes ago, so it should be right on top."

He went around to the back of the box, shook open a mail bag and positioned it. Then he unlocked the box and raked the mail out and into the bag. "If you can see it, you can look at it," he said.

Dixon stepped over and checked the mail. There were two manila envelopes visible, but only one of them was without a return address. She got out her notebook. The address read: J.C., 129 Forrest Lane, Studio City. "Thanks, pal," she said. "You're a sweetheart."

"Hey, how about a movie and dinner this week?" he asked.

"Oh, I'm so sorry; I'm seeing somebody."

The man shrugged, got into his truck and drove away.

Dixon got back into her car and called her watch commander.

"Evans."

"Boss, it's Dixon. You know you said something about Mrs. Keeler mailing money to a hit man?"

"Yeah, that was the theory."

"Well, I just followed her to the post office and watched her mail a manila envelope at the drive-thru, so I waited for the truck to arrive, and I got the address off the envelope."

"Good work, Dixon. Give it to me."

She read him the address.

"I'll find a city directory and see who J.C. is."

"You know, boss, if you could get a federal warrant, I could intercept the envelope and open it."

"I'll see what I can do, Dixon."

"You want me back on Long's house?"

"Well, yeah. It seems to be working, doesn't it?"

"Okay, I'm gone." She got back into the car and drove back to the Long house, very pleased with herself.

DETECTIVE FIRST GRADE Tom Evans started to call the U.S. Attorney's office about the search warrant but realized the time. Nobody would be there just yet. He wrote a note to himself to call them and put it in a little tray where he kept reminders, since his short-term memory had started to go. He had only a year before his thirty years were up, and he wasn't about to get dumped on a non-work-related medical by reporting his memory loss. He could fake it for a year. He went back to work.

DIXON FINISHED HER shift at four o'clock and drove back to the station house to leave the patrol car and pick up her own. As she walked past the front desk to leave the keys, she saw Detective Evans. "Hi, boss."

"Hello, Dixon."

"What's happening with that federal warrant?"

Evans looked a little startled. "Huh? Oh, that's in the works," he replied.

"I'd love to go out to Studio City in the morning and serve that warrant," she said. Anything would beat sitting on Mrs. Keeler for another day, watching her shop and go to the beauty salon.

"I'll let you know," Evans said. What the hell was she talking about? He went back to his desk and went through the notes to himself in the tray on his desk. "Shit!" he said aloud. He turned around to see half a dozen detectives looking at him.

"You," he said, pointing to a cop. "Get your ass over to the U.S. Attorney's office and get me a federal warrant to search a mailbox in Studio City." He grabbed a form for the warrant and filled it out;

then he handed it to the detective and explained the circumstances. "Here's the request."

"Right, boss." The detective got his coat and left.

Evans looked at his watch: four thirty. "And move your ass!" he shouted after the detective.

DETECTIVE ALEX REESE had the weird feeling that he was starting a new investigation that was really an old investigation. Granted, the circumstances of the two cases were very different; granted, the weapons used were different; granted, he had not the slightest evidence to connect them. Still, they *felt* connected.

He had two people checking the airline schedules for likely killers—either one male or two males traveling together—and for forty-eight hours before the murder there had been a dozen single males traveling, and every one of them had checked out as legit.

Reese was driving in to work when he passed Airport Road, and he had a sudden thought. He made a quick U-turn and drove to the airport. He parked and walked into Santa Fe Jet, and approached the young woman behind the counter. "Hi," he said, showing her his badge. "Did you work this past weekend?"

"Yep, one weekend a month," she said.

"Do you remember any general aviation aircraft coming in with a single male pilot or two males?"

"Well, let's see," she said. "Best way would be to go through the fuel tickets to remind me. Here's a Learjet with two guys, in from

New York; here's a Bonanza with one guy, in from Austin, Texas; here's a guy in from Albuquerque in a Cessna 182. Everything else was groups, I think. The guy from Austin was kind of a hoot: a standard-issue Texan with a big hat and a big moustache. He looked kind of familiar, like that actor, Sam Elliot?"

"Are you sure it wasn't Sam Elliot?"

She flipped through the fuel tickets. "No, he was a Carl Timmons." She showed him the signature. "He flew in Friday night and left at the crack of dawn on Sunday morning."

"How'd he pay for his fuel?"

"In cash. That was kind of unusual."

"How often do people pay in cash?"

"Never, since I've been here. It's always a check or credit card."

"Did he rent a car?"

"Yes, he did."

"And how'd he pay for that?"

"Again, in cash."

"Where's the car?"

She looked at the list. "It's been rented again, not due back for a week."

Reese made a note of the address in Austin of Carl Timmons and of the tail number of the Bonanza.

"Has Timmons ever been in here before?"

"Not that I know of."

"How about the airplane?"

"Could be; we get lots of Bonanzas—very popular airplane."

"Is there anything else you can think of about Timmons? How was he dressed?"

"Like a cowboy: jeans, western shirt, cowboy boots. Alligator boots, come to think of it. Those things are expensive."

Reese handed her his card. "If you remember anything else about the guy, will you give me a call? It's very important."

"Sure, be glad to."

R EESE LEFT THE airport and drove back to his office. He went online to the website of the Federal Aviation Administration and checked the tail number of the Bonanza: It was registered to an Anthony DeMarco, M.D., of a Brentwood address in L.A. He found the office number of the doctor and phoned him.

"Dr. DeMarco's office," a woman's voice said.

"Good morning, may I speak with Dr. DeMarco, please?"

"Who's calling?"

"This is Detective Alex Reese of the Santa Fe, New Mexico, police department."

"I'm afraid Dr. De Marco is in surgery all day today," she said. "I can take your number and ask him to call you when he gets a break."

"Yes, please," Reese said. He gave the woman his number and cell number. "Any time of day. By the way, what sort of medicine does Dr. DeMarco practice?"

"He's a cosmetic surgeon; he operates three days a week, and this is one of them."

"Thank you. I look forward to hearing from him." Reese hung up and went back to work.

JACK CATO WAS shooting his first scene on a new movie, so he rose early, shaved and showered and had breakfast. The mailman arrived just as he was leaving the house, so Cato took the mail inside. A fat manila envelope was among the bills, and he took a peek inside. What he saw caused a wave of relief and elation to wash over him. He put the envelope into his briefcase and closed and locked it.

He was about to leave the house when the doorbell rang. He looked out the window and saw what appeared to be an unmarked police car. He put his briefcase into a drawer of a chest in the living room, then answered the door. A man and a woman stood there.

"Good morning," the woman said. "I'm Detective Lucy Dixon, LAPD, and this is Detective Watts." She handed him a document. "This is a federal search warrant to search your mailbox."

Cato looked at the document. "Well, okay, but I've already taken the mail out. You want to see it?"

"Thank you, yes."

"Then come inside." He led them into his little home office and pointed to the desk. "There you go, that's everything that came. You just missed the mailman."

The woman went through all the envelopes. "Are you sure this is everything, Mr. Cato?"

"That's it. Mostly bills, I'm afraid."

Dixon opened each envelope and perused the contents. She was particularly interested in the bill from GMAC. "Mr. Cato, are you acquainted with a Mrs. Eleanor Keeler, widow of one Walter Keeler?"

"Nope. I mean, I know who Walter Keeler was, because I use some equipment he made, and I read about his car accident a while back."

"You've never met Mrs. Keeler?"

"Not to my knowledge. A lot of people come on tours through the movie studio where I work, so I suppose she could have come through."

"Which studio?"

"Centurion. That reminds me, I'm shooting this morning, so I gotta go. Anything else I can do to help you?"

"I guess not. We'll be here again tomorrow morning, so don't open your mailbox; we'll do it for you."

"Okay, no problem. Can you tell me what this is about?"

"I'm afraid not." The two officers thanked him and left. He gave them a moment to get away, then retrieved his briefcase, put it into the toolbox bolted to his truck, locked it and drove to work.

Cato knew exactly what they were looking for: the money. How the hell could they know about that? He would have to be very careful with his spending. One good thing, though: Now he knew the name of the woman who had hired him. That might come in handy.

DIXON AND WATTS were driving back to their station, empty-handed.

"Anything of interest in his mail?" Watts asked.

"I thought it was interesting that there were no past-due balances on any of his bills," she said, "and his bill from GMAC showed he had recently been three months behind on his truck payments, but he had brought the account up to date in the past week or so. Still, he had only a little over three hundred bucks in his bank account. I think we should pull a credit report on Mr. Cato."

 **J**ACK **C**ATO **TOOK** his golf cart over to the studio commissary at lunchtime. He looked around the dining room and spotted Tina López and Soledad Rivera at a table together. He went through the cafeteria line, took his tray over to their table and sat down.

"Hey, Jack," Tina said.

"Hey, Tina, Soledad. How was Tijuana?"

"You tell me," Tina said. "You were there, too."

"Drunk, I guess."

"You got something for me?"

He picked up her napkin, stuffed an envelope into it and put it in her lap.

She groped around, found the money and smiled.

"Need any help down there?" he asked, nodding at her lap.

"Thanks, but I'm all fixed up for that."

"He's back, huh?"

She shrugged.

"I'll see him at poker tonight, then."

Soledad spoke up. "Am I going to hear from that cop again?"

"What if you do?" Cato asked, digging into his lunch. "You know what to tell him."

"Everything turn out all right this weekend?" Tina asked.

"I don't know what you're talking about," Cato replied, shoving a chunk of meat loaf into his mouth.

LUCY DIXON SAT down at her sergeant's desk. "Boss, we came up dry at Cato's house; he got to the mailbox first."

"Who?"

"Jack Cato. That's his name. J.C.?"

He shuffled through some slips of paper in a tray on his desk. "No money, huh?"

"Well, I think it came, but like I said, he got to it first. The mail-man comes early in Studio City; we were about a minute late. I went through what mail there was, mostly bills and a bank statement. All his bills are current, but he's only got a few hundred bucks in the bank."

"So what? That's all I've got, too."

"I pulled a credit report on him: very spotty, lots of payments a month or two late. And yet, everything is current now. What does that tell you?"

"You tell me."

"It tells me that all his bills are paid because he came into some money."

"That makes sense."

"I checked with the studio. He's on a base salary of fifty-two grand a year, but he gets paid for doing stunt work in movies on top of that."

"So, if he makes two or three movies a year, he's flush, huh?"

"He hasn't worked on a film this year, until this morning, when he started one."

"All this makes sense to me, Dixon, but you've got nothing that the D.A. would want to take to court. Stay on this woman, what's her name?"

"Keeler."

"Like Ruby Keeler. I liked her movies when I was a kid."

"I'll stay on her, boss." Dixon went back to her patrol car and drove back to Beverly Hills.

CATO THOUGHT ABOUT it for a while, then he picked up the phone and called the cell number she had given him.

"Yes?"

"I got your package this morning," Cato said. "Thanks."

"Then we have nothing further to talk about. Good-bye."

"Wait! I've got a heads-up for you."

"What?"

"About a minute after I opened your envelope, two LAPD cops showed up with a federal warrant to search my mailbox. Fortunately, I had already put it away, but they opened all my mail. I think you can guess what they were looking for."

"How would they know about that?"

"Well, they didn't hear about it from me, Mrs. Keeler. You'd better look to yourself."

"What did you call me?"

"It's what they called you. They asked me if I knew you."

"And what did you tell them?"

"What do you think I told them? I blew them off. Now I'll say good-bye; I just thought you ought to know about this." He hung up.

BARBARA PUT THE cell phone away and retraced her steps for the past couple of days. That female cop had followed her to the post office, and she must have seen her mail the envelope. But how did she know it had been sent to Cato? Then the penny dropped. Oh, shit, she thought. She waited for the box to be opened and found the envelope, and I have no one to blame but myself.

And, as a result, Jack Cato now knew her name, and he must think that she was very, very rich.

CATO'S FIRST SCENE wrapped late in the afternoon, and at six, he went over to Don Wells's offices. Grif Edwards and a couple of other players were already there. Wells came in from the set, and the poker table was set up.

"Give me five hundred," Cato said to the banker, tossing five hundreds onto the table.

Wells looked at him sharply but said nothing.

Cato won two hundred and twenty dollars, and when the game wrapped at midnight, he got into his golf cart and went back to the stable to get his truck. As he got out of the cart, a Mercedes with its headlights off pulled up next to him, and the window slid down.

"You're getting careless, Jack," Wells said.

"What do you men?"

"Throwing hundred-dollar bills on a poker table. Did that money come from my safe?"

"No, Don, it didn't."

"Then where'd you get it?"

Cato shrugged. He realized now that he had made a very big mistake.

"A guy owed me some money, and he paid in hundreds."

"You find a bank where nobody knows you, and you get some small bills, you hear me?"

"Okay, Don."

"Don't be caught anywhere at any time with anything bigger than a fifty in your pocket, and not many of those."

"You're right, Don; I should have thought."

"Think more, Jack. The cops have already talked to you once."

"My alibi is tight, Don."

"Yeah, I heard about how Soledad cut and ran when the cop showed up."

"Tina's got her straightened out."

"Yeah, I know. She'd better stay straightened out, and so had you."

"Don't worry about me, Don."

"I will, Jack. I will," Wells said. Then he put up his window and drove away.

Cato stood looking after him, sweating.

44 EAGLE PICKED UP Susannah at the hospital and drove her to her house to pick up some clothes. Her shoulder-length hair covered the bandage on the back of her head. "Are you in pain?" he asked.

"No, they gave me something for it, but I haven't had to take it. I have a nice little bald spot on the back of my head, though."

"Susannah, I'm so sorry I let you stay here alone." They pulled into her driveway and went into the house.

"Ed, you don't need to say that to me again. It's not your fault; it's *her* fault." She walked into her bedroom and looked at the window. "Where's the bullet hole?"

"I had the windowpane replaced."

"Thank you, Ed, that was very thoughtful." She filled a large suitcase with clothes and cosmetics, then a smaller case. "I think that's it. Let's get out of here."

Eagle put the bags into his trunk and started the car. "I'm not letting you out of my sight until this is over," he said.

"And when will it be over? Do you know?"

"Soon," Eagle said.

———

DON WELLS CALLED Ed Eagle.

"Good morning, Don," Eagle said.

"Ed, what's going on with the investigation? When are they going to clear me?"

"I don't want to ask Bob Martínez about that, Don; he'll think we're getting nervous, and we don't want that. I'm sure they're still investigating, but when their leads don't turn up anything, they'll drop it."

"Will they send me a letter clearing me?"

"I think the best we can hope for is that they'll release a statement to the press, saying that you're no longer a suspect."

"When?"

"Don, it might be a few days; it might be a few weeks. If I don't hear from them in, say, a month, I'll get somebody from the press to call and interview Martínez. That will give him an opportunity to clear you."

"Should I proceed to probate with my wife's will?"

"Of course. Do anything you'd normally do in the circumstances."

"What sort of leads do you think they're following?"

"Well, we know they're looking for anyone you might have hired to do the job. Detective Reese has already interviewed your two stuntmen, and I'm sure he's checked their alibis."

"I suppose you're right."

"I know you want to be out from under this, Don, but you're just going to have to be patient."

"All right, Ed. Let me know if you hear anything."

"Of course I will. Goodbye."

EAGLE HUNG UP. He was beginning to think that Don Wells was awfully nervous for an innocent man.

ALEX REESE WAS momentarily stumped. He'd checked out all his leads; now he was waiting for a break. Then he remembered something he hadn't checked out. He called a friend of his at the NYPD.

"Hi, Alex. How you doin'?"

"Pretty good, Ralph. Could you check something out for me on your computer?"

"Sure thing."

"There was a street killing in Manhattan, a mugging gone wrong, some years back. I'd like to speak to the lead detective on the case."

"What's the victim's name?"

Reese consulted his notes. "William John Burke."

"Hang on."

Reese heard the sound of computer keys tapping.

"Got it," Ralph said. "It's still open. The lead guy was a detective in the One-Nine named Dino Bacchetti. I know him. He's a lieutenant now, runs the detective squad over there. Here's his number."

Reese wrote down the number. "Thanks, Ralph. I appreciate it." Reese dialed the Nineteenth Precinct.

"Bacchetti," the man said.

"Lieutenant Bacchetti, my name is Detective Alex Reese, Santa Fe, New Mexico, P.D."

"What can I do for you, Detective?"

"You worked a homicide some years ago. Victim was one William John Burke. You remember that?"

"Yeah, I remember. I was never able to clear it. It looked like a mugging, but the guy had a rich wife, and that always interests me."

"Do you remember the name Donald Wells, in connection with that case?"

"Yeah, I do. He was a friend of the couple—more of an acquaintance, really. He had been at a dinner party with the two of them the night before Burke was killed. I talked to him, but he had a solid alibi, and he struck me as uninvolved. Until . . ."

"Until what?"

"A year later—no more than that, a year and a half, maybe—I saw Mrs. Burke and Donald Wells at a restaurant together, looking very interested in each other. Not long after that, I saw in the papers that they had gotten married."

"Did you interview him again?"

"No. I went over my notes, and, like I said, he had a solid alibi. He was at some sort of awards ceremony at a table of eight. I couldn't find any substantive reason to talk to him again."

"Did he seem like the kind of guy who might have the connections to hire somebody to mug or murder Burke?"

"I thought of that at the time, but no, he didn't seem like that kind of guy, and none of his acquaintances I talked to thought so, either. They were a pretty straight crowd. But you never know, do you? There might be somebody in anybody's past who would commit murder for enough money."

"That's right. You never know."

"You looking at Wells for something else?"

"Yeah, somebody murdered his wife and stepson."

"The same one? The rich one?"

"Same one."

"Ahhhhh," Bacchetti breathed. "Now, *that's* interesting."

"And this time I've found a possible hit man—two of them, in fact."

"Would you do me a favor and find out how long he's known these two guys?" Bacchetti asked.

"Not long enough to go back to your case. They're both stuntmen at Centurion Studios, and, as far as I can tell, he hasn't known them for more than four years."

"Tell you what, Alex. I'll put a couple of men on the Burke homicide. You never know what they might come up with."

"Thanks a lot, Dino." Reese hung up wishing he had some way to help Bacchetti tie Wells to the Burke killing, too.

 Bob Martínez had just returned to his office from court when his secretary buzzed him. "Yes?"

"Mr. Martínez, there's a man on the phone named Jason Bloomfield, who says he's the executive director of the Worth Foundation. Will you speak to him?"

"Worth Foundation? Is that the one that Donna Wells's will mentions?"

"Yes, sir."

"Put him on."

"Mr. Martínez?"

"Yes, Mr. Bloomfield, what can I do for you?"

"You're aware that I run the Worth Foundation?"

"Yes, my secretary just told me."

"I'd like to talk with you about the investigation into the murders of Donna Worth Wells and her son."

"Well, I can confirm that we're investigating that case, but I'm afraid that's all I can tell you, until our investigation is complete."

"Let me explain my problem, then you can tell me if you can help."

"All right, Mr. Bloomfield, go ahead."

"I believe you've seen a copy of Mrs. Wells's will."

"Yes, I have."

"Then you know that the foundation is one of her beneficiaries."

"Yes."

"And you know that, since both she and her son are dead, Donald Wells becomes the principal beneficiary."

"Yes, I do."

"You would also know that, should Mr. Wells be found responsible for his wife and stepson's deaths, he would not be able to inherit, and the foundation would become the principal beneficiary?"

"In addition to being district attorney, I'm an attorney, Mr. Bloomfield."

"Can you tell me whether Donald Wells is a suspect in the murders?"

Martínez didn't speak for a moment, and when he did, he was careful. "Mr. Bloomfield, I expect that you've seen enough TV shows to know that in any homicide of a female, the first suspect is usually the husband or boyfriend."

"Yes, I do."

"And that's the case, even when hundreds of millions of dollars are not at stake?"

"I can understand that."

"Then I think you can draw your own conclusions about Mr. Wells's status in the investigation."

"I need just a little more than that, Mr. Martínez. If I know that Mr. Wells is a suspect, then, when he files for probate, I can ask the judge to stop any further action, until it's clear whether Mr. Wells is implicated in the homicides."

"That's a civil matter, Mr. Bloomfield, and thus outside the jurisdiction of this office."

"Let me put it another way, Mr. Martínez: It's my understanding from watching all those TV shows, that putting pressure on a suspect is sometimes an investigative technique used by the police and the district attorney."

Martínez thought about that. "All right, Mr. Bloomfield, you can tell a judge that I said that Donald Wells is a suspect—no, the *only* suspect—in the homicides of his wife and stepson."

"Would you give me that in writing?"

"You can refer the judge to me for confirmation."

"Thank you very much, Mr. Martínez."

"You're very welcome, Mr. Bloomfield."

DONALD WELLS WAS at his desk when he got a phone call from an old friend in New York.

"Don, this is Edgar Fields."

"Hello, Edgar, long time. How are you?"

"Very well, thanks. Don, I just wanted to tell you that I had a visit this morning from two police detectives investigating the death of John Burke."

"Oh?"

"Yes, and Bessie Willoughby had a visit from the same two detectives last evening."

"Yes?"

"Don, you will remember that Bessie and I were two of the seven people who established your whereabouts the evening of Burke's murder."

"Yes, Edgar, I remember."

"Well, it seems that the police have reopened the case and are reinterviewing everybody at that table."

"It does seem that way, doesn't it?"

"Well, I just wanted to let you know, Don."

"I wouldn't worry about it, Edgar; after all I *was* at that table that evening."

"Except for about half an hour or forty-five minutes, when you went out for a smoke."

"I don't remember that, Edgar."

"I do, and so does Bessie. I'm sure the others do, too."

"Did you mention that to the detectives?"

"They specifically asked both of us if you left the table for more than five minutes during the evening. I had to tell them that. They also asked me if you smoke. I told them I didn't know, I assumed so."

"Well, that's all right, Edgar; I have nothing to fear in all this, so there's no need to worry."

"I'm glad to hear it, Don. I wish you well."

"Thank you, Edgar." Wells hung up. Why the hell would they be reopening that investigation? He didn't like this at all.

His secretary buzzed him again. "Your lawyer, Marvin Wilson, is on line one."

Wells picked up the phone. "Yes, Marvin?"

"Don, I just got served with some papers. The Worth Foundation has filed a petition with the probate court to stop probate of Donna's estate."

Wells was alarmed. "On what grounds, Marvin?"

"On the grounds that the Santa Fe district attorney says that you're the only suspect in the murders."

"That's preposterous!" Wells said.

"Of course it is, Don, but I now have to appear at a hearing to argue against their petition."

"Well, sure, go ahead."

"Don, I'm not sure that's a good idea."

"Why not?"

"It's not going to look good in the press if a judge stops probate because you're the only suspect in a double homicide."

"Well, I guess not. What do you recommend?"

"I think it would be better if I called the foundation's attorney and agreed to withdraw our petition for probate, if they will withdraw their petition. We can probably deal with this on a handshake."

"How long before we can file for probate, Marvin?"

"It will depend on the Santa Fe district attorney's actions in the case. If he gets you indicted or if you're arrested, then we couldn't file until you're cleared or tried and found not guilty."

"What can we do in the meantime to resolve this?"

"Well, after some time has passed, we can have your Santa Fe attorney press the D.A. for some sort of statement of nonculpability that would satisfy the probate judge."

"How much time?"

"A few months, at least."

"And you feel strongly that this is our best course of action?"

"I do. And if word of this gets leaked to the press, you can take the position that you have no objection to waiting for probate, and you're anxious to see the case resolved."

"All right, go ahead and call their attorney." Wells hung up, and there was a sick feeling in the pit of his stomach. He had a big project in preproduction, and he had planned to finance it himself, once the will was probated. Now that had to come to a screeching halt, and he was left holding the bag for the preproduction costs. He would have to go to the studio for the money.

Wells reviewed his prospects. There were four people out there who could hurt him, if too much pressure were put on them: Jack Cato, Grif Edwards, Soledad Rivera and, of course, Tina. He was going to have to find a way to see that none of them cracked.

**46** Detective Alex Reese was about to leave his office for lunch when his phone rang, and he picked it up. "Detective Reese."

"Detective Reese, this is Luisa, you remember?"

"Give me a hint."

"Out at the airport? Santa Fe Jet?"

"Oh, of course, Luisa. What's up?"

"Well, you gave me your card and asked me to call you if I thought of anything else?"

"Yes, I did. Have you thought of something?"

"Not exactly, but I know where I saw that Timmons guy from Austin."

"Where?"

"Driving a stagecoach."

"A stagecoach?"

"In a movie. I remember that I knew the movie was made in Santa Fe, because I could see the Jemez Mountains in the background. I can see the Jemez from my mother's house."

Reese drew a quick breath. "Do you remember the name of the movie, Luisa?"

"No, it was several weeks ago, and it was on TV, on one of the cable channels, because there weren't any commercials."

"Thank you, Luisa," Reese said, "you've been a big help, and I appreciate it." He hung up and ran down the hall, where three other detectives were leaving for lunch. "Hang on, everybody, we're ordering in, on me."

"What's up, Alex?" one of the detectives asked.

"We're going to the movies. Hal, get those DVDs of the Donald Wells productions. You can draw straws for this, but I want somebody sitting there with a remote control on fast forward. Stop when you see a stagecoach. I'm looking for a stagecoach driver with a handlebar moustache and a big hat. When you find it, get a very good print made from the best frame, then go to the credits and look for the name, Jack Cato. He should be the driver."

Everybody shuffled into the conference room, where a TV set was set up. Reese was elated. He called the D.A. with the news.

BOB MARTÍNEZ WAS pleased. "What about the airplane you think he used?"

"It's registered to a plastic surgeon from L.A.; he hasn't returned my calls yet."

"Keep on him."

JACK CATO HAD finished his day's shooting, which involved being dragged behind a horse for four takes. He went back to the livery stable to shower in the rough bathroom there, then he put on some clean clothes and went back to his little office. He retrieved an item he had bought and tore the plastic wrapping off, then inserted batteries.

He tried it; it worked. Then he put it back into the drawer. He wanted to get Mrs. Keeler on tape.

DON WELLS DROVE by the stable and saw Cato's truck still there. He pulled up to the building and stopped. There was a light on in the office. He got out of the car and walked inside. Cato was sitting at the desk, writing checks, and he looked up. "Hey, Don."

Wells sat down.

"I'm just paying some bills; today was payday."

"Go ahead, Jack. I'll wait."

Cato wrote two more checks and sealed them into envelopes. "Okay, I'm done. What's up?"

"I want you to take a little trip, Jack."

"Where to?"

"I don't much care, but out of the country. You like Mexico, don't you?"

"Well, yeah, but I'm not sure I can afford a vacation right now."

Wells tossed some bundles of money on the desk. "That'll give you a running start. It's twenty-five grand. With what you've got saved, you should be able to live well down there."

"How long do I need to be gone, Don?"

"I think you should look at this as a permanent change of address."

"But what about my job?"

"That's going to have to go. I'll be shooting in Mexico from time to time; you can work then, and I'll put you in speaking parts. Also, I'll make some calls to a couple of people I know in the film business down there. You should be able to make a good living playing gringos in Mexican pictures. You'll live a lot better there than here."

Cato opened a desk drawer and put the paid bills inside, then he pressed a button on his new purchase and left the drawer open. "Don, what's going on? Why do you want me to leave the country?"

"Because I have a feeling the Santa Fe police are on to you."

"You mean on to *you*, don't you?"

"It's the same thing, Jack. If one of us goes down, we all go down. You see that, don't you?"

"Don, I think if we just hang tight, everything will be fine."

"If it gets to be fine, I'll let you know," Wells said. "Then you can come back. But in the meantime, we have problems."

"What kind of problems?"

"I'll take care of Tina and Soledad, send them away for a while, but then there's Grif Edwards."

"You don't have to worry about Grif, Don. I mean, he's not the smartest guy in the world, but he'll stand up."

"Let me describe a situation, Jack, and you tell me what you think about it. You're Grif Edwards, and you get arrested. The cops tell you they've got evidence that puts you in my house in Santa Fe at the time of the murders; they tell you that they'll go easy on you if you'll implicate others, maybe even tell you you'll walk if you turn state's evidence. You're Grif Edwards; what would you do?"

"Okay, I get the point. What would make you feel more comfortable, Don?"

"Get Edwards to meet you in Mexico; see that he doesn't come back."

"You know, Don, if I stay at Centurion, I can retire with a pension in a few years."

"Here's what I'll do, Jack: Right now, I can't probate my wife's will, because I'm still a suspect. But with the four of you unavailable to the police, I'll be cleared in a few weeks or months. Once that happens, and her estate is settled, every year, the first week in January, I'll send you twenty-five grand in cash. That's a lot of money in Mexico, Jack, and it's as much as you'd get from a pension. A buck goes a long way down there."

"How long will you send the money?"

"For as long as we both shall live," Wells said. "If I die, you'll have to go to work. If you die, well, you won't need the money. Fair enough?"

"Well . . ."

"Let me mention one other thing, Jack: If you stay in L.A., or anywhere else the cops can find and extradite you, you're looking at life with no parole, at a minimum. And in New Mexico, they still have the death penalty."

Cato sighed. "Okay, Don. When I finish this picture, I'll go."

"You finish the picture tomorrow, Jack. I want you to go home now, pack up your stuff and load your truck. Throw away what you can't take with you. Tell the neighbors you've got a job back east, or you inherited some money. Write your landlord a letter; pay him anything you owe him. Tomorrow, when the picture wraps, don't go back to your house. Give the employment office your resignation, leave the studio and don't be seen in this country again. We've both got untraceable cell phones. If you have to communicate with me, do it that way. Don't leave any messages. If I don't answer, try me later, late at night."

"That's pretty final, Don."

"It can get a lot more final, Jack." Wells shook his hand, went back to his car and drove home to Malibu. He hoped to God that Cato had taken him seriously, because if he hadn't, Cato was going to have to go, and Don Wells was going to have to see to it himself.

JACK CATO SAT at his desk and thought it through. He called the motor pool, and Grif Edwards answered.

"Hey, it's me."

"How you doin'?"

"Pretty good. I hear we've been cleared on that thing."

"Yeah? That's great news. How do you know?"

"Let's don't talk about it on the phone. Are you working late?"

"Yeah, I've got a ring job on a '38 Ford, and I need to finish it tonight. I should be done by ten, ten thirty."

"When you finish, come over to the stable. I'll tell you what's going on. There's going to be more money, too."

"See you around ten."

Jack got his pry bar and went out to the privy behind the barn. He got the floor up, brushed back the dirt and opened the safe. He removed all the money and put it into a small, plastic trash bag, then locked the safe, rearranged the dirt and hammered down the floorboards.

He returned to the stable and went through his desk drawers to see if there was anything he wanted to keep. He stuffed a few things into the trash bag, then he typed out a letter of resignation, saying he had gotten a better job offer and was leaving Centurion immediately.

He got into his truck and left by the main gate, taking particular care that the guard recognized him. He drove around the studio property to the back-lot gate and let himself in with his key, then returned and parked the truck in the stable, out of sight.

He put on a pair of thin driving gloves and typed two letters. He put one into an envelope but didn't seal it, then put it into his inside coat pocket. He put the other letter, the money from the privy and the small tape recorder in a lockbox welded to the underside of his truck, then he wiped the typewriter clean of any of his old fingerprints that might remain.

Around ten o'clock, Grif Edwards showed up. "Hey, Jack," he said.

"C'mere a second and try out this typewriter." He handed Grif a sheet of paper.

Grif put the paper into the machine and typed, Now is the time for all good men to come to the aid of their country. "Yeah," he said, "it's okay."

"You want it? I'll give it to you."

"Thanks. I guess I can use it." Edwards picked up the typewriter and put it into his car, then came back. "Why are you getting rid of it?"

"Because I'm moving to Mexico. You want to go with me?"

"Why are you moving down there?"

"Because Don Wells told me if I don't, I'm going to end up in prison."

"Holy shit! I thought you said we were in the clear."

"I thought we were, until Don came by here after I called you and told me the cops were on to me. That means you, too."

"Jesus, Jack, I thought our alibis were airtight."

"Something broke along the way. I don't know what."

"So you're going to Mexico?"

"Tomorrow after work. I'm gonna go home tonight and load up my truck. You want to go?"

Edwards shook his head. "I don't know, Jack."

"Well, you let me know tomorrow. In the meantime, I want to give you a present."

"What's that?"

"Come on, I'll show you. You're gonna like it."

The two men got into Edwards's car and drove over to the armory. Cato let them in and led Edwards to the little office, where he opened the steel gun cabinet. He picked up a Colt Officer's .45, shoved a clip into it and racked the slide. He picked up a soft cloth on the desk, wiped the gun down, picked it up with the cloth and handed it to Edwards. "Remember this? You always liked it."

"Oh, yeah, I used it in that cop thing we did, remember?"

"It's yours, now. They'll never have any idea where it went."

Edwards hefted the gun in his hand and aimed it.

"Let me show you something about this weapon," Cato said, taking it from him. Quickly, he held the gun, wrapped in the cloth, an inch from Edwards's temple and pulled the trigger. Blood and brains sprayed on the wall behind him, and the force knocked him to the floor.

Cato picked up Edwards's right hand and put some more of his prints on the weapon, and on the letter and envelope from his pocket, then he put the armory key into Edwards's pocket. Still wearing his driving gloves, Cato took the typewriter from the backseat of Edwards's car, then walked back to the stable, showered again and rolled his clothes into a tight wad. He put on clean clothes, collected the remaining stationery and envelopes in his desk drawer, then got into his truck and drove to the back-lot gate and let himself out, chaining it shut again.

He drove to Edwards's house, found the key under the flowerpot and let himself in. He put the stationery into a drawer in Edwards's desk, then set the typewriter on the desktop. He removed the envelope from his pocket and leaned it against the telephone on the desk.

He let himself out, then, on the way home, he ditched his blood-spattered clothes in a street trash basket.

ALEX REESE WAS sitting at his desk the following morning when the phone rang. "Alex Reese."

"Detective Reese? This is Dr. Anthony DeMarco in Los Angeles, returning your call. I'm sorry I didn't get back to you earlier, but I've had a busy week."

"Thank you for calling, Dr. DeMarco. Do you own a Beech Bonanza?" He gave him the registration number.

"Yes, I do."

"Have you recently flown your airplane to Santa Fe?"

"No, I haven't, but I lease the airplane to the Compton Flying Club at Compton Airport, and one of their members may have rented it and flown it there. I'll give you their number."

Reese wrote down the number. "Thank you very much, Dr. DeMarco," he said, then hung up and phoned the club.

"Compton Flying Club. This is Margie," a woman's voice said.

"Good morning. My name is Detective Alex Reese, from the Santa Fe, New Mexico, Police Department."

"What can I do for you?"

Reese gave her the relevant dates. "Did you rent Dr. Anthony DeMarco's Beech Bonanza to a member that weekend?"

"Hang on, let me check the log." She came back. "Yes, we rented it to a member named Jack Cato."

Reese's heart leapt, then he had another thought. He gave her some earlier dates.

"Yes, we rented the Bonanza to Mr. Cato then, too."

"Were you there when Mr. Cato took off?"

"Not the second time; he asked me to fuel the airplane and leave the key under the nose wheel. But the first weekend I was there when they left."

"Someone was with him?"

"Yes, another man."

"Do you know the other man's name?"

"Jack called him Grif. I don't know his last name."

"Would you be kind enough to write me a letter to that effect?" Reese gave her his address, then hung up. He went immediately to the D.A.'s office.

Bob Martínez waved Reese to a chair. "What's up?"

"You're not going to believe this: Jack Cato and Grif Edwards killed Donna Wells and her son, *and* Cato fired the shot that struck Susannah Wilde."

"They did *both*?"

"Well, I think Cato worked alone on the Wilde thing, but Edwards was with him for the Wells murders. I have a witness that saw them take off together in the Bonanza from Compton Airport, in L.A. I don't have a witness yet who saw them in Santa Fe, but I've got one at the airport who puts Cato in the Bonanza the second time. She made him from a movie he was in, one of Don Wells's pictures."

"This is fantastic work, Alex, but I don't get the Susannah Wilde thing. What connection does Wells have with her?"

"Well, they're both in the movie business; maybe they know each other that way. That's going to take some more investigating."

"Oh, another thing," Martínez said. "There's a break in the murder case of Donna's first husband. Wells's alibi for that occasion now has a crack in it."

"Wonderful! Will you get me a murder warrant for Jack Cato and Grif Edwards? I'll get the LAPD to pick them up, and then we'll extradite them."

"I'll not only get that warrant; I'll get you extradition papers, too. I want you to go back to L.A. and be in on the arrest; it'll look good in the papers."

"What about Don Wells? Shouldn't I pick him up, too?"

"We've got a problem there," Martínez said. "We can connect Wells to Cato and Edwards, but we don't yet have any evidence that he hired them to kill his wife and son. We're going to have to break Cato or Edwards—or both—to get that."

"There are also the two girls who gave Cato and Edwards their alibi. I've learned that one of them is sleeping with Wells, and has been for some time."

That will sound good at trial, but we don't have enough to arrest the girls yet. Maybe Cato and Edwards will give them up, too."

"I'll question them again after we've arrested Cato and Edwards. The problem is, when Wells hears about it, he might run. God knows, he has the money."

"Yeah, that could be a problem. I'll request LAPD surveillance on him." Martínez looked at his watch. "Can you make the eleven o'clock plane from Albuquerque?"

"No, I have to stop at home and pick up some things. I'll make the three o'clock plane, though."

"I'll have the warrants and extradition papers for you in an hour," Martínez said. "I'll get the LAPD to get search warrants for their homes and places of work, too."

———

REESE LEFT, and Martínez dictated the warrant and extradition details to his secretary, called a judge and sent his secretary to him for his signature. He called the L.A. Chief of Police and requested surveillance on Don Wells, then he called the LAPD office for search warrants. Then he made another call.

"Ed Eagle."

"Ed, it's Bob Martínez."

"Morning, Bob."

"I have some news. Call it disclosure."

"Yes."

"You recall the two stuntmen who worked for Don Wells, the ones we questioned in L.A.?"

"Yes."

"We can put them in Santa Fe at the time of the murders of Donna Wells and her son."

"Lots of people come to Santa Fe for a weekend, Bob, especially from L.A."

"There's more, Ed."

"What more?"

"We can put one of them, Jack Cato, in Santa Fe at the time of the shooting of Susannah Wilde."

There followed a stunned silence.

"That doesn't make any sense, Bob. Wells has no motive to kill Susannah; they don't even know each other. No, it was Barbara who sent the shooter to Susannah's house."

"Well, it's looking like the same shooter as the one who committed the Wells killings."

"Then we've got two different people hiring the same hit man."

"Happens all the time, Ed. The pros will work for anybody."

"Are you arresting Cato and Edwards?"

"Yes, the warrants are being issued now. Alex Reese is flying to L.A. this afternoon to serve them and make the arrests."

"What about my client? Are you arresting him?"

"No, we have insufficient evidence for that. On the other hand, if he tries to run, we'll bring him in. You might convey that to him, Ed."

"I'll pass on the message. Thanks for calling."

48 JACK CATO STAYED up late packing most of his belongings and stuffing others into trash bags. He unloaded the trash bags into a Dumpster at a construction site a few blocks away, then he went home and loaded everything else into his truck.

He got a couple of hours sleep and was on the set at Centurion at seven A.M. Don Wells walked past him, stopped and consulted a clipboard. "I'm going to shoot your stuff first, Jack; you'll be out of here by noon. Are you ready to move?"

"Yep, everything's in my truck."

THEY HAD BEEN working for a little over an hour when the director called for a change of setup. "Where are my guns?" he yelled at an assistant director.

"They're late," he said. "I'll call the armory." The young man pressed a button on his cell phone, talked, listened, then came back to the director, who was talking with Don Wells. "You know that stunt guy, Grif Edwards?"

Both men nodded.

"Well, he's dead. Shot himself over at the armory. That's why the guns aren't here; the cops are crawling all over the place."

"We can't shoot this scene without guns," the director said.

"Come on," Wells replied, "let's go over there and see what we can do." The two men got into a golf cart and drove over to the armory.

There was yellow tape over the door, and as they looked in, a detective approached them. "Can I help you gentlemen?"

"We heard there was a shooting over here," the director said. "We're shooting the final scenes of a film, and we need our guns."

"Do you gentlemen know a man named Griffin Edwards?"

"Sure," the director said, "he's worked on our films as a stunt-man. Did he kill himself?"

"Do you know any reason why he would?"

"Not me," the director said.

"Me, either," Wells chimed in. "Is the guy who runs the armory here?"

"Yeah, just a minute."

They waited until the armory manager came outside. "You heard?"

"Yes," the director said, "and we're sorry, but we need half a dozen Winchesters and six-guns. I ordered this stuff last week."

Another detective came outside and introduced himself as the officer in charge of the investigation. The manager explained the situation.

"Well," the detective said, "Edwards didn't use a Winchester or a six-gun, so I guess you can give them to these people."

"We'll have them back this afternoon," Wells said. They loaded the guns and blank ammunition into the golf cart and returned to the set.

Wells waved Cato over. "Seems Grif Edwards has shot himself over at the armory."

STUART WOODS

"Jesus!" Cato said. "Why would he do that?"
"Who knows?" Wells said. "Let's get back to work."

ED EAGLE AND Susannah Wilde took off from Santa Fe and headed for Los Angeles. They were halfway there before Eagle put it all together in his mind. "I've got it," he said.
"Got what?"
"Wells had nothing to do with the attempt on your life; that was Barbara, as we've always thought. But she used the same hit man that Wells used."
"How would Barbara and Wells be using the same hit man?"
"The connection is the movie business. Barbara's pal, Jimmy Long, is a producer, too, and he works out of Centurion. I'd be willing to bet that Jack Cato worked in at least one of his pictures."
"That makes sense as a connection, I guess. What are you going to do about all this?"
"First, I'm going to talk to two P.I.s who work for me sometime, then I'm going to talk to Don Wells, then I'm going to talk to the chief of police."

THEY WERE MET at Santa Monica Airport by Cupie Dalton and Vittorio. Eagle made the introductions, then he talked with the two men while Susannah went inside to freshen up.
"How are you progressing?" Eagle asked.
"We can get it done," Cupie said, "but first, we've got to solve a problem."
"What problem?"
"The LAPD has got surveillance on Barbara; we can't get to her as long as that's the case."
"Well, shit," Eagle said. "That's my fault; I asked Joe Sams to have her watched."

236

"Can't you ask him to call off his men?" Cupie asked.

Vittorio spoke up. "That's not very smart," he said. "If you do that, and then we do our job, Sams will make the connection."

"You're right, Vittorio," Eagle said. "Let me think about how to do this. You two just keep an eye on her and let me know if she starts looking like she's leaving L.A."

"Whatever you say, Ed," Cupie said. The two men got into their car and drove away.

Eagle went inside the FBO, found an empty conference room and called Don Wells.

"Hello, Ed," Wells said.

"Don, there have been developments."

"Tell me."

"The Santa Fe police have been able to place your two stuntmen, Cato and Edwards, in Santa Fe at the time your wife and son were killed."

"I don't think those guys would do something like that."

"Well, the police do, so you'd better expect to hear from them."

"Ed, there's nothing connecting me to those two, except work and a few poker games."

"Don, here's how the police think: They're looking for motive, means and opportunity. As far as you're concerned the motive is your wife's money, the means is those two stuntmen and the opportunity is their presence in Santa Fe at the time of the murders. Do you see where this is heading?"

"Ed, I've got nothing to fear in this, unless somebody's planning to frame me."

"Good, I'm glad you feel that way. Just be sure that you don't leave town or give them any other reason to believe that you're involved."

"Oh, there's something you should know, Ed: One of the stuntmen, Grif Edwards, committed suicide at the studio armory last night."

"Swell," Eagle said. "Don't look at this as good for you; it sounds like Cato killed him to keep him from talking."

"I didn't think of that," Wells said.

"There's something else, Don: Do you know who Susannah Wilde is?"

"The actress? Sure."

"She also lives with me, most of the time. It looks as though Cato tried to kill her, too."

"Christ, Cato is a busy guy, isn't he?"

"In the circumstances, Don, what with my connection to Susannah, I think you should get yourself another lawyer."

"You think I had something to do with an attempt on Ms. Wilde's life?"

"No, Don, but I'd feel uncomfortable continuing. Please get yourself another lawyer. I'll recommend somebody, if you like."

"That won't be necessary, Ed; I know lawyers in L.A."

"Well, then I wish you well, Don. Goodbye." Eagle hung up.

Susannah came looking for him and found him in the conference room. "Ready to go?"

"Yes," Eagle said, "and I've just washed my hands of Don Wells."

49 JACK CATO HAD just wrapped his last scene when two detectives arrived on the set, took him to one side and sat him down. One of them read him his rights.

"What's this about?" Cato asked.

"It's about the death of Grif Edwards."

"I heard he committed suicide."

"You want a lawyer, Mr. Cato?"

"Nope, I don't think I need one."

"You knew Grif Edwards pretty well, didn't you?"

"Yes, I did."

"When did you last see him?"

"Last weekend, when we went down to Tijuana for the bull-fights."

"Anybody with you?"

"Yeah, Tina López and Soledad Rivera. They both work in the wardrobe department."

"Did you notice anything unusual about Edwards's behavior?"

"Yeah, he was very depressed, but he wouldn't talk about it. He just drank a lot of tequila and didn't say much."

"Did you see Edwards at all yesterday or in the evening?"

"No, I left work a little after six and went home."

One of the detectives consulted a clipboard. "He's on the front-gate list; drove out at six-oh-nine P.M."

"What do you think Edwards was doing in the armory last night?"

"Well, from what I've heard, that's pretty obvious, isn't it?"

"Did Edwards own any firearms?"

"Not that I know of."

"How would Edwards have gotten a key to the armory?"

"I have no idea. I didn't know he had one; those keys would be pretty tightly controlled, I expect."

"So you think he broke into the armory to get a weapon to shoot himself with?"

"Makes sense to me." The detective's cell phone rang, and he answered it. After a brief conversation, he hung up. "Edwards left a note at his house," he said to his partner.

"A suicide note?" Cato asked.

"That's what it sounds like. Typed it on his own typewriter."

"All right, Mr. Cato, we're done; you can go."

Cato got into his golf cart and stopped by the personnel office to leave his resignation, then made his way back to the stable. His money was stowed in a steel box welded under the frame of his truck, and everything was packed. It was nearly five o'clock. Just one more thing to do.

He dialed a number on his prepaid cell phone.

"Yes?"

"Good afternoon, Mrs. Keeler."

"Who is this?"

"You know who this is; I ran a couple of errands for you, re-member?"

"The second one didn't work out; you were ineffective."

"What are you talking about? It was a head shot."

"I just heard she's alive and well, and you owe me fifty thousand dollars."

Cato laughed. "Well, I'm gonna give you some good news and some bad news, lady. First, the good news: I'm calling from out of the country, so I won't be around to implicate you."

"That is good news. Now what about my fifty thousand?"

"That's the bad news. I shot the lady in the head, as you requested. She lived; that's your problem. More bad news: You're going to pay me twenty-five thousand dollars every year, starting in about a week. I'll call you and give you an address to send it to. If I don't get it, every year and on time, my next call will be to the D.A.'s in Palo Alto and Santa Fe. And if you send somebody after me, he won't find me. I'm a careful man."

"You're scum, Cato."

"That's what you get when you hire somebody to do your dirty work for you, lady. I'll say goodbye . . . for now. Get the money together." He hung up.

He took one more look around the stable, went through his office one last time to see if he'd forgotten anything, then he got into his truck and headed for the front gate.

ED EAGLE WAS having lunch with his friend, Joe Sams, the police chief. He had explained about the connection of Jack Cato and Grif Edwards to the two shootings in Santa Fe.

"I don't know if you've heard, Ed, but Cato's buddy, Grif Edwards, committed suicide last night."

"I hadn't heard, but I'll give you odds Cato killed him."

"Well, we don't have any evidence of that. Why don't you give all this to the Santa Fe cops? It's their jurisdiction and they've already got warrants."

"They already know about it, and I expect they're on their way to L.A. to pick up Cato. They probably don't know about Edwards's suicide yet. If I were you, I'd want to hang on to Cato until you have enough evidence against him in the Edwards killing. And one more thing: My ex-wife very probably hired Cato to kill her husband's lawyer, Joe Wilen, in Palo Alto."

"We have constant surveillance on Mrs. Keeler," Sams said.

"If you pick up Cato, he'll implicate her in Wilen's killing."

"The Santa Fe police are picking him up, Ed."

"And what are you going to do if he bolts?"

"They can track him down and bring him back."

"They can't bring him back from Mexico."

"Ed, you're getting too exercised about this."

"Joe, if you don't get exercised about it you're going to be left holding the bag that Cato slipped out of. And he's the only one who can give you Don Wells for hiring him to kill Wells's wife and son."

"Again, New Mexico jurisdiction."

"But wouldn't you rather break the case than let them do it?"

"Well, it would look good in the papers, I guess. But I'm not going to pick up a phone and order the arrest of Jack Cato right now. If Santa Fe wants him, let them come and get him."

"Then why don't you pull your surveillance off my ex-wife and give her a little room to operate. Maybe she'll make a mistake."

"That's just the opposite of what you asked me to do a couple of weeks ago. What's changed?"

"Hell, Joe, it's okay with me if your people tail her, if you want to keep applying those resources, but she's not going to make a move while you're watching her."

"Oh, all right, I'll pull my people off."

"As you wish, Joe. Like I said, it doesn't matter to me."

HALF AN HOUR LATER, Eagle was on the phone with Cupie Dalton. "Okay, Sams is going to pull his people back."

"Good news, Ed."

"I suggest that, from a distance, you watch the cops who are watching her. When they go away, then you can make your move."

"And make it we will," Cupie said. "You sure you want to play it this way, Ed? You can still change your mind and let the law do the work for you."

"The law is never going to get her, Cupie. I'm sure this is the way to go."

"Then Vittorio and I are on it," Cupie said, and hung up.

 ALEX REESE ARRIVED at Centurion Studios and asked to see the head of security. As he waited, a black pickup truck pulled up next to him in the outbound lane, but from his tiny economy rental car he could not see the face of the driver high above him.

The guard handed Reese a pass for his dashboard and waved him in. Reese went directly to the security office and was shown immediately into Jeff Bender's office. The two men shook hands.

"What can I do for you, Alex?" Bender asked.

"I'm here with a warrant to arrest Jack Cato for the murder of Don Wells's wife and stepson," Reese said. "I thought, as a courtesy, I should see you first."

Bender grabbed his jacket. "Let's go," he said. He led Reese to his golf cart, and the two men took off through the big lot at top speed, which was about 16 mph. Shortly, they arrived at the stable.

The two men got out of the cart, and Reese unholstered his Glock. They walked into the stable and found it quiet. Bender opened the door to the little office and looked around. "This looks emptier than usual." The phone on the desk rang, and Bender picked it up. "Hello?"

"Mr. Cato?"

"Who's calling?"

"This is studio personnel," the woman said.

"This is Jeff Bender, studio security. Cato isn't here; can I help?"

"No, I just wanted to get a forwarding address. Mr. Cato handed in his resignation about an hour ago, and he didn't leave one."

"I suggest you write to his old address and see if it gets forwarded," Bender said. "And I'd like to know about it when you find out."

"Yes, sir."

Bender hung up. "Jack Cato resigned from his job an hour ago," he said.

"Oh, shit."

Bender dialed a number. "Front gate? This is Jeff Bender. Has Jack Cato left the lot?" He listened for a moment. "What was he driving? Do you have his plate number on file? Thanks."

He handed Cato's license number to Reese. "Cato left the lot less than fifteen minutes ago, driving a black Chevrolet Silverado pickup."

"Shit again. I'd better call the LAPD and ask for an APB on him."

"They're not going to give you an APB on an out-of-state warrant," Bender said. "Protocol is to call your chief and have him call Chief Sams."

"May I use the phone?" Reese said.

"Sure."

Reese called his HQ, asked for his chief and was told he had just entered a meeting and wasn't expected out for some time. Reese left his cell phone number and asked to be called back on an urgent basis. He hung up and turned to Bender. "Cato seems to have a fondness for Tijuana. How long would it take him to drive down there?"

"Man, it's rush hour, and it's rush hour in every city from here to the border, including San Diego. Who knows? If Cato is on the freeway, he's parked, like everybody else. If he's smart he'll use the surface streets for a couple of hours, then, when traffic starts to thin out, get on the freeway again. When your chief calls back, ask him to call the Border Patrol and get Cato stopped when he tries to leave the U.S. Also, ask him to get that warrant on the wire right away, so that if Cato gets stopped by the highway patrol for a traffic violation they'll detain him."

"What do you hear from the LAPD on the Grif Edwards suicide?"

"They were here for several hours today, talking to everybody."

"Do they suspect Cato?"

Bender shook his head. "Edwards left a note at his house, so right now they're treating it purely as a suicide. They wouldn't have put out an APB on Cato, if that's what you're thinking."

Reese's cell phone vibrated, and he answered it.

"Detective Reese, this is Captain Ferraro; I saw your message for the chief, but he just left the building with some people. Can I help?"

Reese told him what he needed. "I think the LAPD APB is the most important thing. If we could nail him before he leaves the city, life would be simpler. The California Highway Patrol should hear about it, too." He recited the description of Cato's truck.

"I don't have the authority to do that on my own, but I'll grab the chief at the first opportunity and press your case."

"Thanks, Captain. You can reach me on my cell." Reese hung up. "Damn! If I'd just made the earlier plane!"

"Don't blame yourself, Alex. This'll work out; it'll just take some time. It's a big system, and it'll nail Cato."

"Not if he makes it to Mexico," Reese said.

BARBARA EAGLE KEELER was watching Judge Judy on TV when Jimmy Long came home.

"Your cop car is gone," he said.

"Really?"

"First time in days I haven't seen it parked out there."

Barbara stood up. "Jimmy, Jack Cato is headed for Mexico, which means that somebody's after him. I'm going to disappear for a while, until I'm sure he's not talking to the cops. I don't know how he found out my name, but he knows it, and I can't take the chance of staying here any longer."

"Okay. How can I help?"

"Just keep an eye on the papers and an ear on the TV news. If you hear anything about Cato, call me on my cell phone."

"Where are you going to now?"

"You don't want to know that, Jimmy."

"Maybe not. What do you want me to tell the police, if they call?"

"Tell them I went back to San Francisco." Barbara went upstairs and started packing. When she was done, she came back downstairs. "I forgot," she said, "I don't own a car."

"You want me to drive you to a car rental place?"

"Tell you what, drive me to a Mercedes dealership."

"Okay, babe."

CUPIE DALTON SAT up straight. "Here we go," he said to Vittorio. "First, the cops leave, now there goes Barbara."

"That will be Long driving, I guess," Vittorio said.

"I don't think she has a car," Cupie replied. "Two to one, they're on the way to the airport."

"Probably. Where do you think she's going?"

"Back to San Francisco is my guess."

"We don't want that, do we?"

"Nope."

"But we can't do it while she's with Long."

"Nope. We need to find her in some nice, quiet place, even if it's in San Francisco."

**51** Barbara walked into the Mercedes dealership and was immediately greeted by a salesman.

"Good evening," he said. "May I show you something?"

"I'd like to see a list of every new car in stock that's ready to drive away," she said.

The salesman went to his desk, offered her a chair and took an inventory from a drawer. He removed a page from the list and handed it to her. "That's everything on the lot," he said. "A couple need prepping before they go out."

Barbara ran down the list and stopped at a silver E55. "Let's take a look at this one," she said.

"It's right over there," the man said, pointing across the showroom. "You know about the E55? It's the fastest Mercedes."

"I know about it," she replied.

"We're about to have a model change," the salesman said, "so I can offer you a good deal on it."

Barbara sat in the car. "Is it prepped?"

"Ready to drive away."

She got out of the car and checked the equipment list.

"Just about every option," the salesman said. "Do you have a trade-in?"

"Nope, just cash."

He looked at the list price on the car and quoted her a price.

She counteroffered and they settled on a price. "Check or credit card?" she asked.

"Which credit card?"

She handed him her black Amex card and her driver's license.

He compared her to the photo on the license. "Is the address on the license current?"

"It is."

"Let me speak to our finance guy." He noted her checking account number and walked into a private office with her credit card. Five minutes later, he was back.

"We'll be happy to take a check," he said. He added in the sales tax and gave her the amount.

Barbara sat at his desk and wrote the check.

The printer on the man's desk began to spit paper. "The bill of sale is printing out right now." He handed it to her. "Thank you very much for your business."

A man in Mercedes coveralls appeared and drove the car out of the showroom and onto the lot. Twenty minutes after arriving, Barbara gave Jimmy a good-bye kiss.

"Take care of yourself, baby."

"I'll be in touch," she said, then she got into her new car and moved out into traffic.

"THAT WAS FAST," Vittorio said.

Cupie put the car into gear. "It sure was. If I'd tried to buy a Mercedes, they'd have tied me up for an hour, running credit checks and probably taking a blood sample."

"It helps if you're Mrs. Walter Keeler and beautiful."

They followed as Barbara got onto the freeway, headed south.

"I guess she ain't going to San Francisco," Cupie said.

BY SEVEN O'CLOCK, Jack Cato was sick of driving in the heavy traffic. He exited the freeway and found a steakhouse, and as he got out of his truck, he found something else, too. Parked two spaces away, shielded from the view of the restaurant by shrubbery, was a black Silverado pickup, identical to his, except that it didn't have the toolbox bolted into the bed.

Cato had a quick look around, then found a screwdriver in his glove box and removed the license plate from the other Silverado. Moving fast, he exchanged it with the plate on the other Silverado, then he went inside, got a table and ordered a New York strip. An hour later, he was headed south again in lighter traffic, in a vehicle nobody was looking for.

IT WAS NEARLY midnight when Alex Reese got the call.

"This is Captain Ferraro. Sorry to take so long, but the chief went out to dinner with some people, and his cell phone was turned off. You got your L.A. and statewide APB's."

"Thanks, Captain."

"And both departments have your cell phone number for when they find him."

Reese thanked him again, then went to bed. He slept better knowing that every L.A. cop and CHP officer was looking for Jack Cato.

Barbara reached La Jolla, a San Diego suburb, before midnight and drove directly to La Reserve, a spa where she had spent time before. Half an hour later she was having a late supper in her suite, watching an old movie on television.

————

"I KNOW THIS PLACE," Vittorio said. "She's been here before, and I know a woman who works here as a masseuse."

"Good," Cupie said. "We might as well find a motel; she's not going anywhere for a few days, and we have arrangements to make."

JACK CATO FOUND a motel in San Diego and used his Texas ID and credit card. He would cross the border in the morning, during rush hour. As soon as he got to his room he turned on the television, and not five minutes had passed before he saw his own face. "Shit!" he yelled. Fortunately, the picture they were showing was one from the western, with the handlebar moustache.

Cato was nearly asleep when his cell phone rang, and he picked it up. "Yeah?"

"It's me," Don Wells said. "Are you in Mexico yet?"

"Almost . . . tomorrow morning."

"Have you got backup ID?"

"Yes."

"I have another, very lucrative job for you in Mexico."

"How much?"

"One hundred K."

"Who?"

"Two people, traveling together."

"Where?"

"Tomorrow morning, cross the border and take the noon flight from Tijuana to Acapulco. Book it tonight. You'll be met by a man in a red straw hat carrying a sign saying 'Mr. Theodore.'"

"I'll need a piece."

"The man will provide that and anything else you need, including twenty-five K, U.S."

"How long will this take?"

"Up to you; shouldn't be more than a day. You'll follow two people; do it; then take their money and valuables. Call me on this cell phone when it's done."

"When do I get the rest of the money?"

"I own a little beach house; the man will take you there. I'll arrive with your money after the job is done."

"All right. I'll see you tomorrow." Cato hung up, elated. He would add another hundred grand to his nest egg.

THE FOLLOWING MORNING, Cupie called a man he knew in L.A., a con man and sometime actor named Ron Gillette, who was fiftyish, handsome, beautifully dressed and too charming for his own good.

"Hey, Cupie, how's it going?"

"Extremely well, Ronnie. Could you use a few days' work at two grand a day and expenses?"

"What does it involve?"

"Being yourself, seducing a woman, a day or two in the sun."

"Does anybody get hurt?"

"Of course not," Cupie lied.

"When and where?"

"Be in San Diego by five o'clock today." Cupie gave him the address of his motel. "I'll have a room for you."

"Clothes?"

"Blue blazer, white trousers, business suit, dinner jacket and your passport. You'll be using your own name."

"Done."

"I want you to make a stop in Marina del Ray and have your

253

picture taken. Wear your blazer." Cupie gave him a name and a number. "Bring some postcard-size prints with you."

"Okay."

"One more thing: Do you know any beautiful women in San Diego?"

"Will La Jolla do?"

"Sure. Make a dinner date for tomorrow night, and pick her up at seven thirty."

"In that case, I won't need the hotel room."

"Good. See you at five." Cupie hung up.

Vittorio was on his own phone, speaking Spanish, making arrangements. He hung up. "We're good to go," he said. "I'll make one more call when it's time."

Cupie nodded and called Ed Eagle.

"Hello, Cupie. Is everything happening?"

"Yep. Expenses are going to run to fifteen, twenty grand, plus our daily fees."

"It's worth it. Where are you?"

"Do you really want to know, Ed? Don't you like surprises?"

Eagle sighed. "All right, Cupie, I'll trust you."

"Always the best thing. Why don't you go back to Santa Fe, Ed? It's better to be as far away as possible from the scene. I'll call you in a couple of days."

"Maybe you're right," Eagle said.

Cupie hung up and made some more arrangements.

Alex Reese hung around his hotel room, waiting for a call, but none came. He called Santa Fe and got Captain Ferraro on the phone.

"It's Alex Reese, Captain. Have they picked up Jack Cato?"

"I haven't heard a word, Alex," the captain replied.

"I don't understand it; they should have had him by this time."

"Got a pencil? I'll give you a contact number at the California Highway Patrol."

Reese wrote down the name and number, then hung up and redialed. "Colonel Tom Pace," he said to the operator.

"This is Tom Pace."

"Colonel, I'm Detective Alex Reese, Santa Fe P.D. Captain Ferraro gave me your number."

"Oh, yes. No joy on that APB, I'm afraid."

"I think he must be out of L.A. by this time. My best guess is, he'll cross the border at Tijuana."

"We had a word with the border patrol; they've got his photo and his license number. He won't get across."

"Will you call me when you hear something?"

"Of course. I believe I have your cell number."

Reese thanked him and hung up. He went out, looking for breakfast.

JACK CATO STARTED the day early at a barbershop, with a much shorter haircut and a shave. By nine thirty, he was approaching the Mexico border, and he had his ID ready when the agent approached. "Good morning," he said with a smile. "Beautiful day."

"Yes, it is," the man said, studying his ID. "How long are you staying in Mexico?"

"I'm house hunting down there," he said. "My stuff is in the back. You want to see it?"

"Not today," the man said, returning his ID to him. "Move on, please."

That had been easier than he had anticipated, Cato thought, but now he looked ahead to the Mexican side of the border and saw something he didn't like: A police officer had a mirror on a pole, and he was examining the underside of vehicles as they approached the border. He had not anticipated this. He had a lockbox welded under his truck with his money in it, and he tried to remember if he had driven through any mud since he last had the truck washed. He hoped to God he had; he needed the camouflage.

A policeman waved him forward to a barrier and asked him for his ID and vehicle registration. Cato complied, and as he did, he heard a scrape from under the truck. The man was there with his mirror.

"What is the purpose of your visit to Mexico?" the policeman asked him.

"Pleasure."

"What is in the back of the truck?"

"My personal belongings. I'm planning to look for a holiday casa to buy."

"Please step out of the truck and come with me," the cop said. He led the way to the rear of the truck. "Please remove the cover."

Cato unhooked the tarp over his goods and rolled it back.

"Open this box," the cop said, pointing.

Cato opened it to reveal some of his clothes. He was instructed to open two other boxes, while another cop put a Labrador retriever into the back of the truck, who went happily to work with his nose. The other boxes contained pots and pans and some lamps.

"You can secure the cover again," the cop said. The dog jumped down and went on to the next vehicle with his handler. The policeman handed him back his ID. "Thank you, Mr. Timmons. You may enter Mexico."

Cato got into the truck and drove across the border. He parked his truck in a garage near the crossing, grabbed an overnight bag and took a cab to the airport. An hour later he was boarding his flight to Acapulco. It departed on time.

Vittorio was having a very nice lunch on the beach at La Jolla with Birgit, his friend, the masseuse, at La Reserve. She was a good six feet tall, blonde, and beautiful in a sweet way.

"So, Vittorio, you've come to visit me at last."

"Yes, and I've been looking forward to it."

"How long can you stay?"

"A day or two. I'll do the best I can."

"Is your visit connected with your work this time?"

"Yes. In fact, it's connected with the same work I was doing last time."

Birgit laughed. "Yes, she checked in last night. I should have known you would not be far behind."

"Do you know what name she's using?"

"Keeler," she said. "I gave her a massage this morning, and the staff has been talking about her. Apparently, her rich husband recently died."

"Yes, that's true. Do you know what her plans for the day are?"

"I believe she's staying close to her cottage. She made a dinner reservation in the dining room while I was there. Eight thirty this evening."

"That's good to know," Vittorio said, then he set about seducing Birgit, an action she received with alacrity.

 **53** B ARBARA DAWDLED OVER her lunch, thinking. She still had something to clean up before she could be at peace. Jack Cato was no longer of any use to her, so she needed fresh talent, someone closer to the scene. She got out her untraceable cell phone and made a call to Santa Fe, to a woman she had been intimate with when she had lived there.

"Hello?"

"Hello, little one."

"Barb . . ."

"*Shhhhh,* let's not use names on the phone."

"What's up, baby?"

"Tell me about you, first."

"Oh, business is slow, and there's not much love in my life at the moment." Betty Shipp was a small, beautiful woman who liked sex of all sorts but preferred women.

"Not in mine, either."

"Let's get together, then."

"I'm afraid I'm a long way from you right now, but maybe later. If business is slow, maybe you could use a nice chunk of money."

Betty laughed. "Sure, who do I have to kill?"

Barbara said nothing.

"*Oooooh,* I was on the mark, huh?"

"You were."

"Let me guess: the tall guy."

"And his girlfriend. It'll be easy; they live together."

"When?"

"A Sunday morning would be perfect."

"How?"

"Two each to the head would be nice. Something small will do, maybe a .22."

"I never did two people before. Come to think of it, I've done only one just the one time, and God, the bastard deserved it. You're the only one who knows."

"I know; I was your alibi, remember? Here's how you'll do it." Barbara explained in detail. "Got it?"

"Sounds simple enough. You mentioned money?"

"I'll wire you twenty-five thousand today, another twenty-five when I read about it in the papers."

"I'll give you my account number."

"No. Just go to the Western Union office on Cerrillos Road, you know it. Give me a couple of hours to get it there."

"You got a deal. I never liked him anyway."

"You'll like her even less, baby."

"When will I see you?"

"We'll need to wait a few weeks for things to cool down, then I'll bring you to a place you'll love. Bye-bye, sweetie."

"Bye."

Barbara hung up and went to her suitcase for the cash.

JACK CATO WALKED through the Acapulco airport, his eyes darting everywhere.

Ahead and to his right a man in a red straw cowboy hat held up a sign. Jack caught his eye as he passed and nodded, then continued outside. He stood on the curb and watched the man cross the road to the parking lot, then he followed.

The man in the red hat walked to a van, opened the rear doors and got in, leaving the doors open. Jack looked around, then got in, too.

"Good day, señor," the man said.

"Good day."

"I got some things for you." He unfolded a map. "You know Acapulco?"

"Pretty good."

The man pointed with a stubby finger. "Here is the airport. You leave, turn right, take the coast road. A few miles, you pass a bar, El Toro Loco, then you take your first right turn and follow the road to the beach and turn left. It's the boss's house, número 1040. You can remember that?"

"Easy." He remembered that he was going to have to do something about filing his tax return, unless he wanted another government agency searching for him.

"You park your car here," the man said, pointing.

"Car?"

The man rapped on the side of the van. "Parked just here." He handed over the keys. "Every afternoon, five o'clock, about, the two women go to El Toro Loco for a margarita, then they go to town for shopping, on this road, here. It's a quiet road; you can hit them going or coming, take your pick. Must look like a robbery, yes?"

"Yes, I know."

The man handed him a very small semiautomatic pistol. "Is .380, plenty big?"

"Yes."

"Comes with this," the man said. He handed over a Ziploc bag containing two magazines, a silencer and a pair of latex gloves, and, using a handkerchief, he dropped the gun into the bag.

"Gun and bullets don't have no prints on them. You use gloves when you handle and when you drive car, got it?"

"Got it."

"When you are finished, you drive into Acapulco and park car somewhere, walk away, leave nothing. Get a hotel. You call the man. He will arrange to meet you with the money; he will tell you where. Then you go back to Tijuana. Go now. Any questions?"

"Do the two women have names?"

"You know them: Tina and Soledad."

He knew them. Wells was leaving no loose ends. He thought maybe he would like to fuck them first, as he had before. He took the plastic bag and his overnight bag, got out of the van and into the car, a well-used Toyota. He ignored the latex gloves and put on his own leather driving gloves.

First, he found the bar, then the house, then, using the map, he drove the road into Acapulco. There were two very sharp bends in the dirt road, a couple of miles from the bar, and a good ditch along the road. He saw only one car the whole time.

He didn't want to be seen anywhere by anybody, so he avoided El Toro Loco and drove back to the beach. He found a narrow track off the road behind some bushes that gave him a view of the house. He backed in and left the engine running, the air-conditioning on. He checked his watch: three forty.

HE WAITED LESS than an hour before he saw the two women pull out of the driveway. He put the car in gear and waited until they passed and got some distance, then he followed. At El Toro Loco, they didn't stop but turned toward Acapulco on the road he had just driven. He made the turn and accelerated to catch up; he wanted them at the first curve.

It was not to be; a battered pickup truck was passing in the other direction. Cato swore, then caught up for the next curve. As they made the turn to the left, he stepped on the gas and went for the "pit," a maneuver he had used in the movies. He struck their left rear bumper hard enough to throw the rear end of their car off the road, which pitched the whole vehicle into the ditch, turning it upside down.

He took one last look around, then got out of the car and ran to theirs. "Tina? Soledad?" he called out.

"Yes, we're in here! Who is it?"

"It's Jack," he called back. He ran around the upside-down car to the driver's window and looked inside. The two women were still in their seat belts, their heads touching the ceiling.

"Jack," Tina said, smiling, "I don't know what the hell you're doing here, but get us out of this car!"

"Don't worry, Tina," he said. He shot her in the side of the neck, under the ear. Soledad began screaming, so he shot her, too, near the heart. She kept moving a little, then stopped. He felt both women for a pulse and found none.

Their handbags were lying on the ceiling next to their heads. He grabbed them both and checked the road again for traffic. Nothing. He emptied both bags on the ground next to the car and took two wads of pesos and American currency, then tossed the handbags onto the pile of things. Then he remembered that Tina wore a gold Rolex that Don Wells had given her, and he went back and took it off her wrist.

A moment later, he was driving off toward Acapulco, and he didn't see another car until he reached the outskirts of the city. He drove into the center of town, grabbed his overnight bag, stuffed the gun and the plastic bag into it, locked the car and walked away. He found a cantina with a garden and ordered a Dos Equis, then got out his cell phone and dialed Wells.

"Yes?"

"It's done."

"I told you to call me late at night."

"Sorry, I forgot."

"What else did you forget?"

"Nothing. It went perfectly."

"Meet me at three o'clock tomorrow afternoon at the FBO next to the main terminal at the airport. Be there early. When you see me get off the airplane and enter the building, go to the men's room. I'll meet you there and give you your money."

"See you then," Cato said and hung up. I wonder what else you're going to give me, he thought, seeing that I'm the last loose end.

54 CUPIE AND VITTORIO were still making phone calls when there was a knock on the door of their motel room. Cupie answered the door. A tall, handsome man stood there.

"Ron! How are you? Come on in." Cupie introduced him to Vittorio.

"I'm great, Cupie." Gillette found a chair and settled down, looking way too good for his plain surroundings. "We all set to go?"

"We are. You have to take your girlfriend to dinner at a place called La Reserve at eight thirty. Give me her address, and a car will pick you up shortly before that." Cupie made a note of it.

"What do I do there, just eat?"

Cupie showed him a photograph. "This woman will be having dinner there at the same time, probably alone. Her name is Eleanor Keeler, but she sometimes goes by the name of Barbara Eagle. I want you to see her, and above all, I want her to see you. Vittorio has arranged through a friend for you to be seated near her, and if possible I want you to chat her up. If that doesn't work, follow her when she leaves and introduce yourself. You can use your real name; it won't matter. That's all you have to do, until tomorrow night."

"Okay, got it."

"Sorry, there's also the postcard. Did you bring the photos I asked you to?"

Gillette took an envelope from his pocket and handed it to Cupie.

"They came out great."

Cupie looked at the postcard prints, selected one and handed it to Gillette. "I want you to write what I tell you to on the back of the photo."

Gillette took a handsome fountain pen from his pocket, uncapped it and took Cupie's dictation.

"Keep the postcard, then tonight, when you leave La Reserve, leave it in an envelope with Barbara's name on it at the front desk. Then wait for her call."

"What do I do tomorrow night?" Gillette asked.

"She'll accept your invitation, so welcome her, make her comfortable, give her a drink, then tell her it's just going to be the two of you. Fuck her, if you can; it won't be hard. Vittorio and I will be at hand, but she won't see us. After that, just go along with the play. That's all there is to it."

"And what's the play?"

"It's better you don't know." Cupie gave him a few more instructions, then sent him on his way.

JACK CATO FINISHED his cerveza, then left the cantina, looking for a hotel. He nearly threw the gun and the plastic bag into a Dumpster but thought better of it. He wasn't out of this alive yet, and he wasn't going to take any chances. By the weekend, he should be free and clear; he'd collect his truck from Tijuana and vanish into Mexico. He had a couple of ideas about where he might settle, and the money Wells was bringing him would move him into a better real estate bracket. He was beginning to feel good about his new country of residence.

He found a hotel and was delighted to find a whore working the bar who looked a lot like Tina López. He hadn't had a chance to fuck her before the end, so he made up for it with the girl from the bar.

Ron Gillette and his girl, Lauren Knight, arrived at La Reserve on time. Eleanor Keeler wasn't in the restaurant yet, so they had a drink at the bar and caught up.

"You're looking gorgeous, Lauren," Gillette said.

"You, too, Ron. What have you been up to?"

"A little picture work, a little of this and that; you know my drill."

"I do. How long can you stay?"

"Only tonight, I'm afraid. I'll have to leave you tomorrow afternoon." He looked up to see Eleanor Keeler being shown to her table. "Finish your drink," he said to Lauren. "I'm starving."

Eleanor Keeler was sitting on the banquette at one side of the dining room, and the headwaiter seated them next to her, at a corner table. Gillette slipped the headwaiter a fifty. "Good evening," he said to Barbara as he slipped into his seat.

"Good evening," she said, giving him a smile. Women always gave him a smile. He ordered another round of drinks and asked for a menu, then watched as a waiter poured Barbara a glass of champagne from a bottle of Veuve Cliquot Grand Dame.

"That's my favorite champagne," he said to her.

"Mine, too," she said.

"I'm Ron Gillette, and this is Lauren Knight," he said, offering his hand.

"Eleanor Keeler," she said, squeezing his hand. "Do you two live in La Jolla?"

"Lauren does. I'm in town on my yacht, cruising."

"Where are you cruising?"

"Oh, back up the coast," he said. "I'm based in L.A. most of the time."

"Is it Gillette, as in razor blades?" she asked.

The woman didn't waste any time, he thought. "Yes, but I sold the company after I inherited some years back. Now I'm free as a bird." He could see her becoming more interested.

He turned back to give Lauren some attention, since he wanted to get laid that night, but from time to time, they both talked more with Ms. Keeler. She finished dinner first.

"It was such a pleasure meeting you both," she said, shaking their hands, then she said, more pointedly, to him, "I hope I'll see you again sometime."

"I hope so, too," he said.

"What was that all about?" Lauren asked. "That stuff about the yacht?"

"I didn't want her to think I lived here," he replied. "She might have been hurt when I didn't call her. Excuse me a minute, I have to go to the men's room."

"Don't you dare follow her," Lauren said.

"I'm headed in the opposite direction," he replied, and did so.

He stopped at the front desk and asked for an envelope, then he inserted the postcard into it, wrote Eleanor Keeler's name on it, sealed it and asked that it be delivered to her room. Then he returned to the dining room and collected Lauren.

The car was waiting for them and delivered them back to her La Jolla beach house, where they spent a very pleasant night together.

Barbara was getting ready for bed when an envelope was slid under her door. She opened it, read it and smiled broadly. What a nice invitation, she thought. She called the cell number and left a voice-mail message, accepting. "And I'm looking forward to it," she said.

**55**

ALEX REESE WALKED around his hotel's neighborhood with his cell phone in his pocket, waiting for the call. He walked all morning, had some lunch, then walked most of the afternoon. He didn't know what else to do.

Finally, he called Captain Ferraro. "Afternoon, Captain. I've heard nothing from the CHP; how long should I wait?"

"I don't know, Alex. You'd think they'd have him by now. Tell you what, give it until tomorrow morning, and if nothing happens, come on home. You can always go back for Cato. By the way, I took a call from a Lieutenant Dino Bacchetti of the NYPD. He says they've cracked Donald Wells's alibi for the time of his wife's former husband's murder, and the case is wide open again. They're reviewing all the work that was done in the original investigation, and he hopes they'll have enough for an arrest."

"I hope not," Reese said. "I want to get my hands on Cato and get him to implicate Wells in his family's murder before New York shows up and snatches him away."

"You've got a point. Keep in touch." The captain hung up.

Reese switched on the TV in his room and searched for something to watch that would take his mind off Jack Cato.

JACK CATO WAS at the FBO at the Acapulco airport half an hour early. He read an aviation magazine and waited nervously for Don Wells to show. He checked inside his overnight bag for the position of the gun inside.

At five minutes past three a Cessna CitationJet taxied up to the space in front of the terminal, and the door opened. A car pulled up to the airplane, and a crew member got off with some luggage and loaded it into the car. Then Don Wells stepped into the sunshine, a briefcase in his hand, and walked down the stairs and onto the tarmac. He said something to the crew member, then headed toward the FBO.

Cato got up and went into the men's room. He kicked the stall doors open to be sure they were empty, then busied himself washing his hands. A moment later, Wells walked into the room. "Are we alone?" he asked.

Cato set his overnight bag on the counter and unzipped it. "Yes, we are."

Wells walked over, took some paper towels from the holder and wiped water from the counter, then set his briefcase on it and snapped open the locks.

Here it comes, Cato thought. He put his hand inside the bag and gripped the pistol.

Wells opened the briefcase, removed a manila envelope and handed it to Cato.

Cato didn't want to let go of the pistol, but he needed both hands to open the envelope. It was filled with stacks of hundred-dollar bills. He riffled through some of them to be sure they weren't hiding newspaper, then he put the envelope in his overnight bag. For a tiny moment of panic he realized the envelope blocked his access to the pistol, but Wells closed his briefcase and stuck out his hand.

"Thanks, Jack. You lie low down here until I get in touch with you."

"I'll do that, Don. Thanks for the money."

"Don't spend it all in one place," Wells said, then he turned and walked out of the men's room.

Cato splashed some water on his face and dried it, then he took the gun from the bag and stuck it in his belt under his jacket, and walked back into the lobby. He turned and walked toward the sidewalk and outside, his eyes sweeping every person in sight. He felt that if he could just get into the terminal building he'd be safe.

It was a two-minute walk, and he made it unmolested, then he realized he had to go through security. He found the men's room, waited until it was empty, then wiped the gun clean and dumped it into a stainless-steel waste basket along with the plastic bag containing the extra magazines. Then he went to the Aero México counter and checked in for the next flight to Tijuana. He had an hour and a half to wait, so he bought some magazines and made himself comfortable, but he still kept a watchful eye on other people.

Suddenly, he heard a Mr. Timmons being paged over the public-address system, and he looked around again for danger and found none.

"Mr. Timmons, please come to the Aero México desk," a woman's voice said again.

Cato presented himself at the desk. "I'm Mr. Timmons."

"Oh, good, Mr. Timmons. We have an extra seat on the earlier flight to Tijuana, which leaves in ten minutes, and I wondered if you would like to have it?"

"Yes, thank you."

She changed his ticket, gave him the gate number and said good-bye.

Things seemed to be going his way, Cato reflected, as he buckled his seat belt. He'd get back to Tijuana, put the money into the lockbox under his truck and get a good night's sleep before heading south. There was a letter in there, too, that he wanted to burn. It no longer seemed necessary.

 DONALD WELLS DROVE his car to his beach house, nervous about what he might find there. He turned into the drive, half expecting to find the place swarming with Mexican police, but there was only the housekeeper's car. He let himself into the garage with the remote, removed his luggage from the trunk and walked in through the kitchen door.

"María!" he called out.

"*Sí, sí,*" his housekeeper called back from another room, then entered the kitchen, carrying a vacuum cleaner. "*Buenos días,* Señor Wells," she said. "Did you have a good trip?" Her English was good, if heavily accented.

"Very good, María. Are the ladies here?"

"No, señor, and their beds were not slept in last night."

"That's odd," Wells said, trying to sound worried. "Did you see them yesterday?"

"Yes, señor. They were lying on the beach when I came, and I changed both their beds. The linens are still fresh and unwrinkled; that's how I know they did not sleep here."

"Did they have a car?"

"Yes, señor, a green Honda from renting."

"Will you unpack these bags for me, please, María? I'll see if I can reach Tina on her cell."

María left with the luggage, and Wells went into his study and called Tina's cell phone, which went straight to voice mail. "Tina, it's Don Wells. I just got into town, and María says you and Soledad didn't sleep here last night. I'm concerned about you, so please call me at the house and let me know you're all right." Then he looked up the number for the police and dialed it. "Capitán Morales, please," he said when it was answered.

"This is Morales," the capitán said, in Spanish.

"Capitán, this is Don Wells. How are you?"

"Oh, Señor Wells, I am quite good, and you?"

"I'm fine. I just got in from Los Angeles, and I expected to find my house guests, two young women, here, but they are not in the house, and my housekeeper tells me their beds were not slept in last night. I don't want to be an alarmist, but I am concerned about them."

"Ah, Señor Wells, I will come out to your casa to see you about this. In about an hour?"

"I don't want to put you to any trouble."

"No, no, señor, no trouble. I will see you in one hour."

Wells hung up, went into the kitchen and got himself a beer, some of María's guacamole, and some chips. He took them into the study and ate them on the leather couch in front of the big TV.

Sometime later the doorbell rang, and María escorted Capitán Morales and two men in plainclothes into the study. Wells seated them and noticed that one of the men was holding an envelope.

"Now, Señor Wells," the capitán said, "please tell me about these two young women."

"Their names are Tina López and Soledad Rivera; they work in the wardrobe department at the movie studio where I have my offices. They have often worked on films I have produced. They both had some vacation time coming, so I let them use this house. I believe they arrived three or four days ago."

"I see. And when did you arrive?"

"A few minutes before I spoke to you on the phone. I flew into the airport on a private aircraft, and we landed at three o'clock."

One of the other men spoke up. "May I have the registration number of the airplane and the names of the pilots?"

"I'm afraid I don't know the registration number, since it is a chartered airplane. The pilot's name is Dan Edmonds; I don't know the copilot's name."

"And the name of the company you chartered from?"

"Elite Aircraft, at Burbank Airport, in Los Angeles."

The man took all this down. "May I use a telephone in another room?"

"Of course. There's one in the kitchen."

The man left, and his partner resumed the questioning. "When you arrived at the airport, did you speak to anyone?"

"No, my car was waiting, and I went inside the FBO to use the men's room while the pilots loaded my luggage into it."

"Was there not a toilet on the airplane, señor?"

Wells smiled. "Yes, but our approach was very bumpy, not conducive to aiming well."

The other detective came back and nodded to the capitán, who spoke up again. "Señor Wells, can you describe the two young women?"

"They are both in their late twenties or early thirties. Tina is about five feet seven inches tall and a hundred and thirty pounds; Soledad is smaller, about five-four and a hundred and thirty pounds. They are both Hispanic and speak Spanish but were born in Los Angeles, I believe."

The capitán held out his hand, and one of the detectives put the manila envelope in it. He opened the envelope and handed Wells two photographs. "Are these the two women?"

Wells looked at the photos and let his eyes widen. "What happened to them?"

"Are they your two friends?"

"Yes, they are. What happened?"

"They were apparently driving from this house into Acapulco yesterday afternoon. They were found in their car, upside down in an arroyo, both dead."

"That's very upsetting," Wells said, frowning, "an awful accident."

"It was not an accident, Señor Wells," the capitán said. "Their car was apparently run off the road and into the ditch; both women were shot once each, with a small-caliber handgun."

"Good God! Why would anyone harm them?"

"Apparently to rob them, señor. Both their handbags had been removed from the car and emptied on the ground beside it. There was no money or jewelry among the belongings. Also, one of the women, the driver, showed marks on her left wrist of having worn a watch, which was missing."

"I'm going to have to get in touch with their families," Wells said.

"Perhaps it would be better if I did that," the capitán replied. "If you will give me the number."

Wells looked at his wristwatch. "I'll have to call the studio," he said and went to the phone. After speaking to personnel he handed the capitán the names and numbers of their next of kin.

"May I ask, Señor Wells, why you did not have these numbers yourself?"

"I don't know their families, Capitán; I have only the number of the apartment they share. When you speak to the families, would you please convey my condolences and tell them I will bear any expense involved in returning their remains to Los Angeles?"

"Of course, Señor Wells. If you will permit me, I will place these arrangements in the hands of a mortuary known to me, and they will send you a bill. Normally, in cases of this kind, the remains are cremated, which makes transport more convenient."

"Whatever their families wish, Capitán, and I am very grateful for your help in this matter. Tell me, do you have any idea who did this?"

"No, señor, not yet. We found a stolen car abandoned in Acapulco that had paint from the women's car on its bumper, but the car had been carefully cleaned of fingerprints."

"I would appreciate it if you would keep me informed on the investigation," Wells said. "And when you have spoken to their families, would you ask to whom and where I should send the belongings they left here?"

"Of course. And now we would like to speak to your housekeeper, if we may, and see their belongings."

"This way," Wells said, rising.

Half an hour later they were gone, seeming satisfied. With the women silenced and Jack Cato disappearing into Mexico, Wells began to breathe easier.

 **EAGLE AND SUSANNAH** got back to his Santa Fe house by late afternoon and unpacked. They were having a drink when the phone rang, and Eagle answered.

"Ed, it's Bob Martínez."

"Hi, Bob."

"An update for you: Detective Reese is in Los Angeles with an arrest warrant for Jack Cato, on a double-murder charge."

"Donna Wells and her son?"

"Yes. We can put him in Santa Fe when Susannah was shot, too, but we still have more work to do on that."

"Are you arresting Don Wells? By the way, I am no longer representing him."

"When we get Cato in custody and back to Santa Fe we'll make him an offer in the hope of getting him to turn on Wells. Grif Edwards is dead."

"I heard."

"There are still the two women who alibied Cato and Edwards, but they seem to have left L.A., so Cato is our only shot right now at implicating Wells. New York may have a chance, though."

"Why?"

"They think Wells may have murdered his wife's first husband, but they were unable to make a case at the time. Now they've cracked his alibi for the time of the murder, so they're reopening the case. Of course, we'd rather see him go down in Santa Fe."

"Of course."

"The LAPD has lifted surveillance on your ex-wife, and, quite frankly, we don't know where she is; maybe gone back to San Francisco. I'm not sure you can rest easy while she's on the loose."

"Thanks for calling, Bob. Please keep me abreast of developments." He hung up and told Susannah the details of the conversation.

"Ed," Susannah said, "do you think we're safe now?"

"Yes, I do."

"With Barbara still out there somewhere?"

"I don't think we're going to have to worry about Barbara anymore."

"I don't like the way you said that. You haven't done anything stupid, have you?"

"That remains to be seen," Eagle said.

A CHAUFFEURED MERCEDES called at La Reserve for Barbara at seven o'clock and drove her to a local marina. The driver held her door for her. "Madam, I'm told the yacht is on slip one hundred, at the end of the main pier," he said, pointing.

She tipped and thanked him, then walked through the gate and down the pier. As she came to the pontoon at the end and turned a corner, the yacht came into view. Oh, gorgeous, she thought. Not only is this man the heir to a great fortune, he has impeccable taste in yachts.

A uniformed crew member stood at the end of the gangplank. "Mrs. Keeler?"

"Yes."

"I'm Captain Ted," the man said. "Welcome aboard *Enticer*. Mr. Gillette is waiting for you on the afterdeck. This way, please."

He led her down the port side of the yacht, and she noted the gleaming varnished mahogany and the teak decks. As she rounded a corner, Ron Gillette stood up to greet her, resplendent in a blue blazer and white linen trousers.

"Barbara! Welcome aboard!" He offered her a comfortable chair, then a steward appeared with a bottle of Veuve Cliquot Grand Dame and poured them both a glass.

"Ted," Gillette said, "I think we can get under way now." He turned back to Barbara. "The other couple I mentioned in my card who were meant to join us are having sitter problems and won't be coming. I hope you won't mind dining alone with me."

"Not in the least," she said, giving him her best smile.

Lines were taken in, and the yacht moved, nearly silently, away from the dock, and headed toward the Pacific.

"Where are we cruising?" she asked.

"I've left that to our captain, Ted; he knows these waters well."

"The yacht is very beautiful. Tell me about her."

"My grandfather had her designed in 1935, by John Trump, and built in New Jersey; she's been in the family ever since. Last year, I put her through a complete renovation—electrics, engines, navigational equipment—so she's now virtually a new yacht."

"New yachts aren't this beautiful," Barbara said.

The steward appeared with hors d'oeuvres: bits of foie gras on toast and beluga caviar with little buckwheat cakes and sour cream.

"Would you prefer iced vodka with your caviar?" Gillette asked.

"Thank you, I prefer the champagne. You were kind to remember that I liked it."

The yacht turned northward and cruised along slowly as the sun sank into the Pacific and Ron Gillette coaxed information from her and talked on and on about his family and his life as a world traveler. Barbara believed she might have met her fifth husband.

When darkness fell they moved into the saloon, where a sumptuous dinner was served by the steward and the chef. Soft piano music played from a hidden sound system, and the stars came out.

Slowly, as they dined, the yacht turned toward the west and continued until it was on a southerly heading. With the sun down, this was not obvious from the saloon.

After dessert they moved to a comfortable sofa while the dishes were taken away. The steward served them cognac. "Will that be all, Mr. Gillette?"

"Yes, thank you, Justin. We'd like to be alone now."

"Certainly, sir. You won't be disturbed." He vanished.

Gillette and Barbara clinked glasses and sipped their brandy, then he leaned over and kissed her lightly under the ear.

"What lovely perfume," he said, nibbling at her earlobe.

"What a lovely kiss," she said, raising her lips to him.

"I don't believe I've shown you the owner's cabin," he breathed into her ear.

"I'd love to see it," she replied.

They rose, and he led her down the companionway to the after-stateroom, which was large and comfortably furnished with a king-size bed. The lights had already been lowered, and they could still hear the lovely music.

"This is wonderful," Barbara said as they sank into the bed.

"The evening is yours," Gillette said. "You have only to tell me what you desire."

And she told him.

58 JACK CATO BOARDED his flight, and through his window he saw lightning in the distance. His first instinct was to get off the airplane, but he wanted out of Acapulco before he had to have a conversation with the local police.

Five minutes after takeoff, while the airplane was still climbing, it was buffeted by turbulence and lit periodically by lightning flashes. Cato knew, from his flight training, what thunderstorms could do to an airplane, even one as large as this, and if he had been offered a parachute, he would gladly have jumped.

He wanted a drink desperately but wasn't going to get one unless he could snag it from the unmoored cocktail cart that was careening up and down the aisle, and he had a window seat so could not reach it. The woman next to him vomited into her lap, and the stench was awful.

A man two rows ahead got out of his seat, trying to go God knew where, and had to be restrained by the flight attendant and another passenger. Here and there, an overhead locker flew open and pillows, blankets and luggage spilled onto the heads of the passengers. Women were screaming, and so were some of the men. The flight attendant, once again strapped into her seat, sat as if in a catatonic state, white as marble, her lips moving, without sound.

And then, suddenly, they were on top of the clouds, and the flight, in a matter of seconds, became perfectly smooth. He could see the array of stars as they made their way north.

"Ladies and gentlemen," the pilot said over the PA system, "I wish to apologize for the roughness of our ascent, but I want you to know that we were never in any danger."

"Lying son of a bitch," Cato said to himself.

The flight attendant came and led the woman next to him to a toilet, and she returned after a few minutes, stinking less badly. The seat-belt sign remained on, and no drinks were served.

The flight attendant reached over and tapped him on the shoulder, and he started. "May I put your bag in the overhead compartment?" she asked.

He realized that he was hugging the soft leather bag with his money in it. "No," he said. "Can I have a drink?"

"I'm sorry, sir, but the seat-belt sign is still on and will probably remain that way. Please be sure to put your bag under the seat in front of you for landing." She went on her way.

Cato willed himself to relax and had nearly done so, when the airplane began its descent into Tijuana. Shortly they were in clouds, and the lightning started again. It was as if someone in some great video center was replaying their ascent, except the descent was, if anything, worse. The pilot announced final approach, and Cato knew he was flying the instrument landing system. The airplane yawed, bumped, made sharp ascents and descents, and he knew the pilot was hand-flying the approach, because the autopilot couldn't operate in such turbulence.

They broke out of the clouds, but rain was streaming down Cato's window, and the airplane was still bucking. Then, miraculously, they were on the ground and braking. Cato didn't know how the pilot found the taxiway in the downpour, but he did. The moment the airplane stopped moving, Cato was on his feet, and the hell with the attendant's instruction to remain seated. He was the first person off the airplane, and he nearly ran to the bar in the terminal.

It took two shots of tequila to begin to calm him; the third one he sipped more slowly. Finally, he weaved his way out of the terminal, and while his fellow passengers were still waiting for their luggage, he slung his bag over his shoulder and began waving for a taxi in the heavy rain. He was soaked before one finally stopped. He instructed the man to take him to the garage near the border crossing.

"Ah, yes, señor," the man said. "I know the one. You would, perhaps like a clean hotel for the night? My cousin has a very nice place not far from this garage."

"No, no thanks," Cato said. He had an almost panicky need to be sure his truck was safe, then he would go to the Parador, where he had stayed before. He would have some dinner and a couple of drinks, and maybe a whore, then he would get a good night's sleep and be on his way south the following morning.

The cab stopped in front of the garage, and Cato made his way to the elevator, since he had parked on the roof. The rain had begun to ease when he stepped out onto the upper deck and looked around for his truck. Then he saw something that chilled his soul. All the boxes that had been loaded into his truck bed were scattered around the roof. They had been cut open, and the contents—his clothes and belongings—were being blown about in the wind and rain. He heard tires squealing and looked wildly around, then saw his truck speeding onto the down ramp. The thief didn't know about the lockbox welded into the truck's chassis, the box with most of his money and the letter that he must destroy.

He had a chance, he thought. He stopped the elevator doors from closing and leapt back into the car. The ride down was painfully slow; it seemed to take half an hour to reach the ground. He ran from the elevator and into the street, looking up and down the block for his truck.

Then he saw it, at the Mexican side of the border crossing. The thief was driving it into the United States. He began to run, but the tequila was catching up with him. By the time he reached the Mexican side, the truck had been cleared and was driving toward the American side of the border. There were few cars waiting to cross, and he knew that soon the truck would be gone and that he would never find it.

He cleared the Mexican side and began to run again. "Stop that truck!" he yelled. "Stop that truck! It's stolen! That's my truck!" One of the American border patrol officers turned and looked at him. "Stop that truck!" he yelled again. "It's stolen!"

The officer yanked open the truck door and pulled a young man out of the cab. "What did you say?" he asked Cato, as he wobbled up to the truck.

"That's my truck; he stole it!" Cato puffed. "He threw all my stuff out and stole it from the garage." Unable to continue, he sank to a cross-legged sitting position on the wet pavement and watched the officer handcuff the thief, then the man walked over to him.

"Are you all right, sir?"

"Gimme a minute," Cato said, gulping in new air.

"What is your name, sir?"

"Ca . . . ah, Timmons," Cato said.

"May I see the registration for the truck and your driver's license?"

Cato reached into his right hip pocket for his wallet, then changed his mind and reached into the left pocket for his Timmons license. He handed it to the officer. "The registration is in the armrest of the truck," he said.

"You got here just in time, Mr. Timmons," the officer said. "Another ten seconds, and he would have been gone with your truck."

"Thank you for stopping him," Cato said, struggling to his feet.

The officer walked around the truck slowly. "You said the thief removed your belongings from the truck?"

"Yes, they're scattered all over the roof of that garage over there," he said, pointing. "Can I take my truck back and get my things now?"

The officer was looking at the truck registration. "First, let's clear up something. Why is the license plate on your truck not the one listed on your registration, Mr. Timmons. And who is John W. Cato?"

Cato's legs failed him again.

 CUPIE AND VITTORIO stood on the foredeck of *Enticer*, staring toward the shore. "Where the fuck is he?" Cupie asked.

"He'll be here," Vittorio said. "He promised me, and he owes me."

"Owes you?"

"He accepted a gift: I gave him a beautiful Colt .45 the last time I saw him," Vittorio explained. "I couldn't cross the border with it, so I thought, what the hell, it couldn't hurt to keep a capitán sweet."

"You're sure he's coming?"

"She cut off his nephew's dick. He'll be here."

"He'd better; the yacht has to be back at Marina del Rey tomorrow morning, or it will cost Eagle another five grand, and I don't want to have to explain it to him."

Cupie went to the bridge, where Captain Ted was lounging, letting the autopilot take them south at a leisurely eight knots.

"What's up?" Ted asked.

Cupie grabbed the microphone of the VHF radio and tuned it to channel 16. "Capitán Rodríguez, Capitán Rodríguez, this is the yacht *Enticer*. Do you read?"

Static. Then a voice, very loud. "*Enticer*, this is Rodríguez. What is your position?"

Cupie looked up at the GPS and read off their latitude and longitude.

"That is not very far away. Are you wearing lights?"

"Yes, we are," Cupie said. He turned to Ted. "Give me a white flare," he said.

Ted dug into a locker and handed him the flare.

Cupie picked up the microphone again. "Watch for a bright light," he said, then he walked back on deck, peeled the seal off the flare, struck it and held it overboard, so the phosphorous wouldn't drip on him. The whole world lit up.

BARBARA WAS RIDING Ron Gillette as if he were a circus pony, and making a lot of noise doing it. She was suddenly reined in by a hammering on the door.

"Mr. Gillette!" a voice called out.

"Huh? Yes?" Gillette said.

"Please come on deck and bring Mrs. Keeler; the police want to inspect the yacht and see the crew's papers. Please bring your passports!"

"Yeah, give us a couple of minutes, okay?"

Barbara sighed and rolled off Gillette. "What's going on?"

"It's just a routine thing," Gillette replied. "Happens all the time; homeland security and all that. Let's get dressed."

They got into their clothes, and Barbara took a moment to apply lipstick. She grabbed her handbag. "Okay, I'm ready."

"They're going to want to see our passports," Ron said, taking his from an inside pocket of his blazer and holding it up.

Barbara dug into her handbag and came up with her passport. "Got it."

"Don't worry," Ron said. "We'll be back in bed in ten minutes."

"I'll look forward to it," Barbara said, smiling.

He led her up the companionway stairs and onto the afterdeck. A brightly lit motor vessel was moored alongside *Enticer*, bobbing on the small waves. It was flying a Mexican flag.

"Ron," Barbara said, "that's a Mexican flag." She pointed.

"Yes, it is," he replied.

"Are we in Mexico?"

Ron looked toward shore at some lights. "I guess so." He pointed. "That must be Tijuana over there."

Barbara looked around, as if for a way out, but there was no escape; she'd just have to brazen it through. Then two men appeared from forward on the yacht, and she knew one of them. "Cupie? What the hell are you doing here?"

"Hi, Barbara," Cupie said cheerfully. "You remember Capitán Rodríguez, don't you?"

Barbara stared in horror at the Mexican policeman. "No," she said, "I don't."

"Well then," Cupie said, "you remember his nephew . . ."

"Ernesto," the capitán said, helpfully.

"I've no idea what you're talking about."

"May I see your passport, Mrs. Eagle?" Capitán Rodríguez said. "I'm sure we can straighten this out very quickly."

"My name is Mrs. Walter Keeler," she said, handing the capitán her passport. "You must have me confused with someone else."

"Oh, he's not confused, Babs," Cupie said.

"No, señora," the capitán replied, "I am not confused." He removed a piece of paper from his tunic pocket and handed it to her. "I have a warrant for your arrest on three charges of attempted murder."

"What on earth are you talking about?" she demanded.

Vittorio appeared on the afterdeck. "One," he said, raising his hand. "Attempted murder by drowning."

"Two," Cupie said, raising his hand. "Attempted murder by gunshot."

"And three," the capitán said, "counting my nephew, who will be very happy to see you, Mrs. Eagle."

"I tell you I am not this Eagle person!" Barbara said desperately. "My United States passport will tell you that!"

"Yes," Cupie said, "she is."

"Right," echoed Vittorio.

"You are all insane!" she shouted. "Ron, do something!"

Gillette took the paper from her hand and glanced over it. "Well," he said, "this appears to be a valid warrant. Did I mention that I'm a lawyer?"

"Well, if you're a lawyer, do something!"

"I'm afraid I'm not licensed to practice in Mexico," Gillette said. "I'm awfully sorry about this, Barbara, but it looks as though you're going to have to go with this policeman."

As if on cue, two other policemen, bearing automatic weapons, appeared behind the capitán.

"If you please, señora," the capitán said, indicating that she should board his boat. "I hope it will not be necessary to handcuff you." He took her by the wrist and elbow and began dragging her toward the other boat.

"This is outrageous!" Barbara shouted. "I want to speak to the American ambassador at once!"

"Unfortunately," the capitán said, "we did not bring his excellency with us, but as soon as we reach my office you may telephone him."

The two policemen stepped forward, lifted Barbara off her feet and handed her over the rail to two more policemen on the other boat.

The capitán gave Captain Ted a smart salute. "I think we need not detain you further, Captain," he said. "I bid you all a good evening," he said to the others, then, assisted by his officers, he climbed over the railing and reboarded his boat.

"Cupie!" Barbara shouted from the police boat, "call Ed Eagle! Tell him I need a lawyer!"

"Oh, don't worry, Barbara. I'll call Ed Eagle. You have a nice evening, now." He waved as the police boat pulled away. "Well, Captain Ted," he said, "if you could drop us in La Jolla, then you can be on your way back to Marina del Rey."

"Sure, Cupie," Ted replied.

"Oh, and may Vittorio and I have some dinner, please?"

"Of course. I'll tell the chef."

"I assume you've already eaten, Ron."

"Yes, I have," Gillette said, "but I'll join you for a drink. Tell me, did that beautiful woman actually cut off somebody's dick?"

"She certainly did," Cupie said. "Probably more than one." He got out his cell phone and speed-dialed Ed Eagle.

"Wow," Gillette said, "I guess I got out lucky."

The yacht slowly turned back toward La Jolla and her speed increased.

ED EAGLE PICKED up the phone. "Hello?"

"Hi, it's Cupie."

"What's the news?"

"Mrs. Keeler is in custody."

"Where?"

"In Tijuana, Mexico, though I think she will shortly be transported south, to the scene of the penilectomy. By the way, she asked me to call you, and I assured her I would."

"Call me? Why?"

"It seems the lady needs a lawyer."

Eagle laughed. "Well, she hasn't lost her sense of humor," he said. "Send me your bill, Cupie, and thank you so very much." He hung up.

"What is it?" Susannah asked.

"It's over," Eagle said. "Let's spend tomorrow in bed."

"You talked me into it," she said, melting into his arms.

**ALEX REESE GOT** out of his car at the border patrol station and ran inside. A man wearing captain's bars got up from a desk and came toward him. "May I help you?"

"I'm Detective Alex Reese, Santa Fe P.D."

"Oh, of course, Detective. I'm Captain Taylor."

"The California Highway Patrol tells me you've got Jack Cato."

"Either Cato or Timmons, take your pick."

"Sorry?"

"He had two sets of ID but only one registration for his truck, in the name of Cato. I don't know how he got across the border. One of our people must have slipped up. The CHP says you can have him, though."

"I'd like to see him," Reese said.

"Come this way." He led Reese down a hallway and opened a door. Jack Cato was visible in the next room through a one-way mirror. "He was drunk as a skunk when we got our hands on him; he's probably just hungover by now." He indicated a pile on a table behind them. "That's all the stuff we found on him and in his truck. He had a kind of safe welded to the underside of the chassis."

Reese turned and stared at the pile. "How much money is that?"

"Something over two hundred grand; each of those bundles holds ten thousand dollars. He had more than a hundred thousand in the shoulder bag, there, and at least that much in the safe under the truck."

Reese produced a pair of latex gloves and pulled them on. "Have you catalogued all this stuff?" He poked among the contents of Cato's pockets.

"Yep, here's a list. If you agree, then sign it, and we'll give you a box to put all this stuff in."

Reese went through the two wallets, then counted the bundles of money. "Looks good to me," he said, signing the list and handing it to the captain.

The captain went to a locker and produced an evidence box. He raked all the money into it, revealing an envelope and a small dictation recorder that had been under the pile.

Reese picked up the envelope, opened it and looked at the letter inside.

"What's that?" the captain asked. "I didn't see that before."

"It appears to be Cato's confession," Reese said in wonder. He picked up the dictating machine and pressed the play button. Immediately, he recognized the voice of Don Wells, speaking with Cato. "Well, I'll be damned," Reese said.

"What?"

"I think I just cleared another couple of murders."

"Congratulations. You want us to put Cato in your vehicle?"

"I've got an airplane coming from Santa Fe; it should be at Montgomery Field in San Diego by now. Could you give us a lift over there and turn in my rental car for me tomorrow morning?"

"Sure thing."

"And can I borrow some leg shackles?"

Reese left the room and went next door. "Hi, Jack," he said, offering his hand. "Remember me?"

"Reeves," Cato said, disconsolately.

"Reese. Call me Alex."

"What are you doing here?"

"You and I are going to take a plane ride to Santa Fe," Reese said, taking a document from his pocket. "You can sign this waiver, and we'll be on our way."

Cato looked at the document through bleary eyes. "Extradition?"

"Unless you'd rather do your time at San Quentin or Pelican Bay. Our place in Santa Fe is cozier, though." Reese put a pen on the table.

"Oh, what the hell," Cato said, then signed the document. "I would have liked one last Saturday night in Tijuana, though."

"You'll have a nice Sunday morning in Santa Fe, instead. The weather forecast for tomorrow is perfect."

THEY WERE SOMEWHERE over the Mojave Desert in the state's King Air, and Cato was gazing down at the moonlit landscape.

Reese went forward and tapped the copilot, a New Mexico state policeman, on the shoulder. "Can you come back here for a few minutes without the airplane crashing, Rico? I need a witness."

"Sure," the man said. He came back and took a seat across the aisle, while Reese settled into one opposite Cato.

"How much longer?" Cato asked.

"An hour and a half," the copilot replied, "give or take."

"You'll be housed in Santa Fe for a while," Reese said. "It's not so bad, as jails go."

"Will they go for the death penalty?" Cato asked.

"I think you can count on that, Jack."

Cato nodded.

"But if you tell us everything, and I mean *everything,* and in court, I think I can get the D.A. to take the death penalty off the table."

"You want me to give you Wells?"

"And the woman called Mrs. Keeler, and everything else you know."

"I'll give you Wells on a platter," Cato said. "He hired me and Grif Edwards to do his wife and the boy. Our payment was what was in his safe in the Santa Fe house."

"Just a minute, Jack." Reese took a small recorder from his pocket, switched it on and placed it on the table between them. "My name is Detective Alex Reese, and I'm on a New Mexico State airplane with suspect Mr. Jack Cato. Sergeant Rico Barnes is a witness to this interrogation. Mr. Cato, do you agree to have this conversation recorded?"

"Yes, I do," Cato said.

"For the record, I have offered to intercede with the district attorney to waive the death penalty in these cases, in return for your complete cooperation. Is that your understanding?"

"Yes, it is."

"Have you been offered anything else for your cooperation, or have you been coerced in any way?"

"No," Cato said.

"Now, let's start at the beginning. Did you take the lives of Mrs. Donna Wells and her son, Eric?"

"Me and Grif Edwards," Cato said. "We each shot one of them; Grif shot the boy. Don Wells hired us to do it and paid us with the cash and gold in his safe in the Santa Fe house, a hundred thousand. He gave us the combination."

"Are you acquainted with a Mrs. Walter Keeler?"

"Yes, she hired me to kill a guy in Palo Alto, a Joe Wilen, and a woman in Santa Fe. I don't know her name, but she's a blonde. I shot her in the head with a rifle through the window of her house."

"How much did Mrs. Keeler pay you?"

"A hundred thousand dollars for the two of them."

"Can you identify her, if you see her?"

"No, I never saw her; I just talked to her on the phone. Oh, I killed Grif Edwards, too, and the two women."

Reese blinked. "Two women?"

"Tina López and Soledad Rivera. I killed them this afternoon . . . yesterday afternoon, I guess it was . . . outside Acapulco. Don Wells paid a hundred grand for the two of them."

"Holy shit," Reese muttered under his breath. "Anybody else?"

"Nah. Oh, there was that one girl about four or five years ago. I fixed the brakes on her car, and she was killed in the crash. Another guy paid me for that. I can't think of his name right now, but it will come to me."

"Good, Jack," Reese said. "That's good. Just take your time. Now let's go over the details."

**61** EARLY SUNDAY MORNING Don Wells got up, dressed and drove to the Acapulco airport. He handed his car over to a lineman for parking, then got aboard the CitationJet. While they were taxiing, he called Capitán Rodríguez at his office and was told that the capitán didn't come in on Sundays.

"Please give him a message for me when he comes in tomorrow," Wells said. "This is Donald Wells. Tell him that I have had to return to Los Angeles unexpectedly, but that if he needs any further information or assistance from me he can reach me at my office any time." He gave the officer the number and hung up.

As the jet climbed out of Acapulco and turned toward Los Angeles, Wells allowed himself to relax in a fashion he had not known since he had made the phone call to Ed Eagle from Rome. Things had not gone as smoothly as he had planned, but he had met every twist and turn with the right moves, and now he could inherit the nearly one billion from his wife's estate that was free and clear of other bequests, and with Jack Cato losing himself in Mexico, he could enjoy his new wealth without the nagging presence of his wife and the constant attention demanded by his stepson.

Jack would call him before long and let him know where to send his next payment, and when Jack went to meet the messenger, he would cease being of any concern to Wells. All doors to his past would be closed, and he would be safe.

He accepted a Bloody Mary from the copilot and gazed out the window at the Mexican beaches far below. This would be his last trip to Mexico and his last trip anywhere in anything but the Gulfstream 550 jet he had already ordered.

Life was going to be sweet.

THEY LANDED AT Santa Monica, and his car was waiting as he came down the air stair. He tossed his briefcase into the front passenger seat and waited for a moment while his luggage was loaded into the trunk by the lineman, then drove out of the airport and headed home to Malibu.

He had his eye on a lot in the Malibu Colony, where he would build himself a new house, one designed only for him and not for a meddlesome wife and child with their own needs.

He would finance his own films from now on; he would never again have to make a pitch for studio money. He would move to new offices, too, and the Hollywood community would know that he was a force to be reckoned with. Membership in the Academy of Motion Picture Arts & Sciences would follow, maybe even an Oscar or two.

He would get rid of the Acapulco beach house and buy something in the South of France, something close enough to Cannes to allow him to throw major parties every year during the film festival. The new Gulfstream would transport him and his friends effortlessly to and from his new home in France.

Maybe a major house in Aspen, too, a real showplace. Maybe he'd start his own film festival there, become a patron to new directors and writers, people who could make him more money in the future.

He pulled into the garage of his Malibu home, closed the garage door and walked into his kitchen with his bags, then froze. Someone in dark clothes was bending over, looking into his refrigerator.

Wells stood and stared at this rather large ass. Burglar, had to be a burglar; go back to the car, leave the house, call the police.

"Mr. Wells?" a voice said from another direction.

Wells turned and stared at another man, who was wearing a business suit, latex gloves and a badge, hanging from his coat's breast pocket.

"What's going on?" Wells asked.

The man walked toward him, holding out two folded pieces of paper. "I am Detective John Ralston, of the Los Angeles Police Department. I have a warrant to search your premises . . ."

"Search my house? Why would you do that?"

". . . and a warrant for your arrest on two charges of first-degree murder." The man set the two documents on the kitchen counter and produced a pair of handcuffs. "Turn around, please, and put your hands behind you."

Wells stood, frozen in place, so the detective spun him around and cuffed him.

"Now listen, please, while I read your rights. You have the right to remain silent . . ."

Wells immediately thought of Tina and Soledad. That's what this is about, he thought. Keep your mouth shut and call a lawyer.

"Do you understand these rights?"

"Yes," Wells said. "I want to call my lawyer."

"Come with me; I'll get you a telephone." The detective led him into his study, uncuffed one hand and cuffed him to his chair. "There you go. Make your phone call and just wait here." He started to leave.

Wells needed to know something. "Detective, whom am I charged with murdering?"

"Why, your wife and son, of course. The extradition process is under way. I'll be back in a minute." He left the room.

Wells had to reorient his thinking before he took his address book from an open drawer, looked up Ed Eagle's home number in Santa Fe and dialed it.

"Hello," the deep voice said.

"Ed, it's Don Wells."

"Good morning, Don. What can I do for you on a Sunday morning?" he asked drily.

"Ed, my house is full of cops, searching it."

"What for?"

"I don't know, but they also have an arrest warrant."

"On what charge?"

"Murder of my wife and son. This is crazy, Ed! They're extraditing me to Santa Fe, and I need you to represent me again."

"Well, first of all, Don, it's not crazy. I had a call a few minutes ago from Bob Martínez—you remember him—the district attorney here?"

"Yes, of course."

"And Bob tells me they've got Jack Cato in jail here in Santa Fe, and he's singing like a bird."

"But that's not possible; Jack's in . . ."

"Mexico? I'm afraid not, Don. There was some sort of kerfuffle at the border, and Cato made the mistake of reentering the United States, where an arrest warrant was waiting for him. They flew him back here overnight."

"Ed, will you represent me?"

"No, Don, I've already resigned from that job, remember?"

"But I need the best possible Santa Fe lawyer, Ed, and that's you."

"Don, let me give you some free advice, something your next lawyer may not be too anxious to explain to you, since he will want to milk as much money as possible out of you before he does the deal."

"Deal?"

"That's my advice, Don. Make the best deal you can. Martínez is not unreasonable; he'll take the death penalty off the table, if you give him a complete confession."

"You're advising me to send myself to prison?"

"It's that or send yourself to death row for a few years until your appeals are exhausted and they execute you. You're done, Don. Cato has cooked your goose to a fine turn. He even has you on tape. Now, if you want me to represent you just to make the deal, I'll do that, but I won't stand up in a courtroom and plead you not guilty. You've already lied to me repeatedly, and I don't like clients who lie to me, even if a lot of them do."

"I don't want to take a deal," Wells said.

"Then I suggest you call Raoul Samora, who is the second-best trial lawyer in Santa Fe, or James Parnell, who is nearly as good. You can get their numbers from Information. Anything else I can do for you, Don?"

"No," Wells said, "there isn't." He hung up the phone and slumped in his chair. He looked around the room at the beautiful elm paneling in his study, at the books and papers that the police had scattered in their search, at the picture that had covered his safe, which stood exposed. He fought nausea.

With a trembling hand, Wells dialed 411 and got the usual recorded message. "Santa Fe, New Mexico," he said, "residence of Raoul Samora."

62 ED EAGLE HUNG up the phone just as Susannah entered the bedroom bearing a tray for him containing eggs Benedict. A moment later, she was back with her own tray and adjusting the rake of the electric bed. "Who was that, calling on a Sunday morning?"

"Don Wells," Eagle said. "They've arrested him, and he's looking for a lawyer again."

"Not you, I hope."

"That's what I told him. I gave him a couple of names. With Cato's testimony facing him he's going to have to plead guilty to save his life."

"Which is pretty much over."

"Who knows, maybe they'll let him do a prison film."

They both dug into their eggs.

"It really is over, isn't it? Confirm that for me just once more."

"It really is over. Barbara's in a Mexican jail, Don Wells will soon be in a New Mexican jail, and Jack Cato, the man who shot you already is."

"Nobody's ever going to shoot me again," Susannah said.

"I sincerely hope not."

The front doorbell rang the bedside phone intercom.

"Who the hell would be here on a Sunday morning?" Susannah asked.

Eagle pressed the speaker button on the phone. "Yes?"

"Flowers for Mr. Eagle and Ms. Wilde," a woman's voice said.

"Flowers?" Susannah asked. "Who would send us flowers?"

"Just leave them on the front doorstep," Eagle said.

"I'm sorry, sir. I need a signature."

"Who are they from?"

"I'm sorry; I'm not allowed to read the card."

"Hang on a minute," Eagle said. He switched off the speakerphone, set his tray aside and got out of bed, naked.

"Just tell her to go away," Susannah said.

"This will just take a minute," Eagle said, getting into a robe and slippers. He walked through the house to the front door and opened it. A small woman stood there, mostly hidden by an elaborate bouquet of flowers.

"Where would you like me to put them?" the woman asked.

"On the table over there," Eagle said, "to your right." He stepped back and allowed the woman to enter. As she passed, he snagged a small envelope hanging from the bouquet, opened it and read the card:

Thanks for everything, Ed. You deserve this.

Barbara

"When did you take this order?" Eagle asked the woman, who had set down the bouquet and was turning to face him. He heard the noise before he saw the gun in her hand. He flinched as something struck his left ear, then he ran for the front door, hoping to close it between them before she could get off another round.

"Susannah, get out of the house!" he yelled as another shot struck the doorjamb.

Then he heard another, louder noise, just once, and everything went quiet.

"Ed?" Susannah called.

"She's got a gun!" Eagle yelled, flattening himself against the outer wall of the house.

"Not anymore," Susannah said. "You can come back in."

Eagle peeked through the front door. The flower woman was lying, spread-eagled on her back, her chest pumping blood. Susannah still stood in a combat stance, holding the .45 that he kept in his bedside drawer.

"Who is she?" Susannah asked.

"I have no idea, except that she delivered a message." He picked up the card from where he had dropped it and handed it to Susannah.

She glanced at it but kept the pistol pointed at the flower woman. "She's still bleeding, so she must still be alive. You'd better call an ambulance and the police. Make that two ambulances; you're bleeding like a stuck pig."

Eagle put a hand to his ear and walked over to the flower woman, kicking her small pistol away from her. "She's stopped bleeding," he said, bending over and putting two fingers to her throat. "She's dead."

Susannah walked to the nearest phone, called 911, and spoke to the operator, then she went to the fridge in the kitchen and came back with some ice wrapped in a dish towel and applied it to Eagle's ear.

"You've got a nice, clean notch there," she said. "A battle scar in the Barbara wars."

"Which are now, officially, over," he said.

"That's what you said five minutes ago," she replied, kissing him. "I'm going to keep going around armed for a while."

"So am I," he said, putting an arm around her and leading her back to the bedroom. "We'd better dress for the police."

"When they're gone, I'll start over with the eggs Benedict," she said.

"When they're gone, we'll start over with everything," Eagle replied.

Epilogue

LEE HIGHT SAT at her desk in Joe Wilen's old office, drafting a document in connection with his charitable foundation. Margie, Joe's old secretary and now Lee's, walked into the room, holding a newspaper.

"Did you see this?" she asked, placing the San Francisco morning paper on her desk. She tapped a story at the bottom of the front page.

Lee looked up to see the headline:

WALTER KEELER'S WIDOW
CONVICTED IN MEXICO

Acapulco (AP) Barbara Eagle Keeler, widow of Palo Alto billionaire Walter Keeler, was convicted today in an Acapulco court of three counts of attempted murder. In spite of a brigade of expensive Mexican lawyers, the testimony of the three victims, Cupie Dalton of Los Angeles, Vittorio (only one name) of Santa Fe, New Mexico, both private investigators, and Ernesto Rodríguez, the nephew of the chief of police of Acapulco, proved convincing to the all-male jury.

Mrs. Keeler's attorneys moved for a stay of sentencing, pending appeal, but the judge rejected their motion and immediately sentenced her to a term of twenty-five years to life and ordered her to prison.

A two-attorney delegation from the Palo Alto district attorney's office presented an extradition request and arrest warrant on one count of murder, that of Joe Wilen, a business associate of and attorney for Walter Keeler, but the judge told them they would have to wait at least twenty-five years to serve the papers.

A man, Jack Cato, who alleges that Mrs. Keeler hired him to kill Mr. Wilen, has been giving testimony in another murder trial in a Santa Fe, New Mexico, court, that of film producer, Donald Wells, who is charged with arranging the murders of his wife, a pharmaceuticals heiress, and her son.

The article continued inside the paper, but Lee stopped reading. "This is all I need," she said. "Margie, I'll dictate a letter to our bank, cutting off the woman's monthly payments, then you get hold of a San Francisco realtor and put the apartment on the market. Tell them to clean out her clothes and personal belongings and give them to some charity."

"Love to," Margie replied, sitting down, steno pad in hand.

Author's Note

I am happy to hear from readers, but you should know that if you write to me in care of my publisher, three to six months will pass before I receive your letter, and when it finally arrives it will be one among many, and I will not be able to reply.

However, if you have access to the Internet, you may visit my website at www.stuartwoods.com, where there is a button for sending me e-mail. So far, I have been able to reply to all of my e-mail, and I will continue to try to do so.

If you send me an e-mail and do not receive a reply, it is because you are among an alarming number of people who have entered their e-mail address incorrectly in their mail software. I have many of my replies returned as undeliverable.

Remember: e-mail, reply; snail mail, no reply.

When you e-mail, please do not send attachments, as I *never* open these. They can take twenty minutes to download, and they often contain viruses.

Please do not place me on your mailing lists for funny stories, prayers, political causes, charitable fund-raising, petitions or sentimental claptrap. I get enough of that from people I already know. Generally speaking, when I get e-mail addressed to a large number of people, I immediately delete it without reading it.

Please do not send me your ideas for a book, as I have a policy of writing only what I myself invent. If you send me story ideas, I will immediately delete them without reading them. If you have a good idea for a book, write it yourself, but I will not be able to advise you on how to get it published. Buy a copy of *Writer's Market* at any bookstore; that will tell you how.

Anyone with a request concerning events or appearances may e-mail it to me or send it to: Publicity Department, Penguin Group (USA) Inc., 375 Hudson Street, New York, NY 10014.

Those ambitious folk who wish to buy film, dramatic or television rights to my books should contact Matthew Snyder, Creative Artists Agency, 9830 Wilshire Boulevard, Beverly Hills, CA 98212-1825.

Those who wish to make offers for rights of a literary nature should contact Anne Sibbaid, Janklow & Nesbit, 445 Park Avenue, New York, NY 10022. (Note: This is not an invitation for you to send her your manuscript or to solicit her to be your agent.)

If you want to know if I will be signing books in your city, please visit my website, www.stuartwoods.com, where the tour schedule will be published a month or so in advance. If you wish me to do a book signing in your locality, ask your favorite bookseller to contact his Penguin representative or the Penguin publicity department with the request.

If you find typographical or editorial errors in my book and feel an irresistible urge to tell someone, please write to Rachel Kahan at Penguin's address above. Do not e-mail your discoveries to me, as I will already have learned about them from others.

A list of my published works appears in the front of this book and on my website. All the novels are still in print in paperback and can be found at or ordered from any bookstore. If you wish to obtain hardcover copies of earlier novels or of the two nonfiction books, a good used-book store or one of the online bookstores can help you find them. Otherwise, you will have to go to a great many garage sales.